HOTHEAD

STELLA RHYS

HOTHEAD

Copyright © 2018 by Stella Rhys

Cover Design: Vivian Monir
Editing: Bex Harper

1

EVIE

Tequila or my phone – it was either one or the other, but I couldn't have both.

I wanted to, obviously, but there were too many risk factors involved tonight, starting with the fact that I was still a walking train wreck of a human being. I hadn't actually shed any tears today, but my eyes were still puffy and red from several weeks' worth of ugly crying at home, and I was still all weepy and heartbroken and steeped deep in this post-breakup fog where all I wanted was to just *talk* to him.

Five weeks.

It had only been five weeks since I'd gone from happy and engaged and all packed to move to the city with my fiancé, to single and bawling in a Starbucks while searching Craigslist for rentals I could afford alone.

The good news was that I'd found a cheap studio on Long Island.

The bad news was that until tonight, I hadn't left the place in about two weeks.

And while I *was* out for the first time in ages, I was pretty much at the bare minimum of presentable. For starters, the dress code tonight had called for cocktail attire and I'd trudged in wearing leggings and the grey raglan I'd gone to bed in. I *did* put on a bra, and I did bring makeup and a change of clothes in my purse, but I also got points knocked off for the fact that my purse was a reusable grocery bag from Trader Joe's.

I know.

My being-out-in-public skills had dulled significantly after spending thirteen days inside. Post-breakup, my existence had basically been a pants-less, bleary-eyed purgatory that involved me doing nothing but sitting on the couch, staring at the TV and trying to figure out just how broken up Mike and I were.

It wasn't the easiest task considering what he had said to me right before he left.

"We could get back together, Evie. I mean that's the plan. We're soul mates. But I need some time apart first."

Right. So...

Were we over? Were we not? Would we get back together in a month or a year? Or was that line just a fancy way of saying, "You're my safety in case I don't end up finding someone better?"

That was definitely the question of the day basically every day since the one he left, and it didn't help that last week, we spoke on the phone for over *three hours*. We'd poured out our feelings and even shared a few tearful laughs before the call ended with him saying, "God, I miss you so fucking much... but please don't call me again. I'll call once I've had enough time."

Fucking time.

It was the meanest word in the dictionary, as far as I was concerned, because it had me effectively trapped in a mental limbo – in this weird personal hell where I constantly jumped from depressed to confused to, most dangerous of all, *hopeful*.

Which was stupid.

I knew that.

But I just couldn't help myself. I'd known and loved Mike Stuart for most of my life. He was as much a part of me as any one of the limbs on my body. I mean we were Mike and Evie. Evie and Mike. For the past seventeen years, our names had rolled off everyone's tongues like one word, because we were a given. A team. Two best friends and lovebirds joined right at the hip.

At least we were.

Until now.

"You sure you won't change your mind about this, right?" the bartender asked, letting me slap my phone into his palm as he slid my second Paloma across the bar.

"I won't. Promise," I answered with as much confidence as I could muster. "Once the birthday girl arrives, she'll take my phone from you," I said, hoisting my ugly tote back onto my shoulder. "But till then, please keep it far away from me and give me zero access – no matter how hard I beg."

"No matter how hard you beg. Roger that," the bartender grinned at me. "And which one is the birthday girl?"

"You'll know. She's the adorable blonde who everyone's gonna yell 'surprise' at – if and when she decides to arrive," I grumbled, before sucking down a third of my drink in one sip.

That was the second reason I had to forfeit my phone.

It was Aly's big surprise party tonight. Her boyfriend Emmett had been planning it for ages, so I couldn't risk drunk texting her to have her convince me *not* to drunk dial Mike. She would undoubtedly ask me where and why I got so drunk, at which point I'd probably spill the beans about how I'd actually dragged my ass out of the house to be at her birthday. She was, after all, my best friend and the only person in the world whom I'd break my no-going-out streak for – especially when it required stepping foot in a place like this.

We were at Boulevardier on Ninth Avenue. It was one of those super trendy hot spots where even the staff was drop dead gorgeous, and aside from the fact that I was dressed for the gym and hadn't washed my hair in three days, I'd apparently also forgotten how to just *exist* in a crowded room. I'd been holed up in my apartment for so long that it felt as if I had no capacity to handle noise beyond the sound of The Office playing softly in the background of my day-to-day life.

So my solution was drinking.

Boozing, really. I was on pace to finishing my second cocktail in about thirty minutes, which was the opposite of pacing myself, but I reasoned that any tipsy mistakes I'd normally make had been taken off the table. For example: No phone? No drunk dialing. No heels? No falling. No Mike?

No desire to so much as *look* at another man, apparently.

It was nuts. The room was crawling with objectively handsome, well-groomed men wrapped in expensive custom suits. They were all friends of Emmett and they were all tall, built and beautiful – basically everything I'd fantasized about since the day I hit puberty. But they did absolutely nothing for me tonight because all I wanted was Mike, and after another hour passed without Aly's arrival, I found myself getting dangerously antsy.

Crap.

The tequila was feeding my restlessness, and my restlessness was feeding my brain. Suddenly, I had a million questions I was convinced I needed to ask Mike *now*, for example, what was to become of our joint bank account? There was no money in it, but still. Also, we agreed to cat sit for Hillary in August. Which one of us was going to do it? Also, which of our friends already knew about the breakup and which didn't, and should we hold off on telling the rest in case we got back together?

"Oh God, stop. Stop it now," I hissed to myself, recognizing well that I was spiraling fast into Crazy Town – population one drunk chick who was now staring thirstily at the bar, and not because she wanted a cocktail.

Ah-ah. You gave them your phone for a reason, so don't, I scolded myself. *Also, you are currently three tequilas deep, so anything you think you need to say tonight can actually wait till tomorrow when you're just a mess, and not a drunk, particularly emotional mess.*

Okay?

I knew my reasoning was sound but still, I could already feel myself breaking. I had so many questions, so little closure and such a desperate need to call Mike that I actually squished my body into a corner in hopes of keeping myself from heading for the bar.

Dear God, please, I groaned inwardly as I stared out the window overlooking Ninth Avenue.

Please, oh please. Either send me Aly or send me the world's biggest distraction.

2

DREW

"Hold up. You're not serious... are you?"

I squinted at Iain as we sat in the back of the SUV. He was holding out a pink leather pouch that belonged to his girlfriend, and I was waiting for him to tell me that he was kidding about wanting me to put on her makeup tonight. I hoped to God he was, but there was no telling for sure. From nine to six, Iain Thorn was strictly business, but six to nine were the grey hours when he slowly transitioned from being my no-nonsense agent to my some-nonsense friend.

And right now we were at 8:45, so I really wasn't sure if he was shitting me or not.

"It's just for your hand, asshole." Iain flicked his stare from the screen of his phone to my undeniably fucked-up knuckles. "And I'm not asking you to wear glitter. All I want is for you to cover up the bruising. Your bosses are going to be at this party tonight, and no one needs to be reminded of the fact that you decided to break your pitching hand on Cody Bryce's face last week."

My jaw clenched at the mention of Tuesday's game against L.A.

"One, I think the world would agree that he deserved it for bringing up Pattie, and two, I didn't actually break anything. Won't even miss a start."

"It doesn't matter. The team thought you injured yourself, and the false alarm was enough to revive the topic of what a high-risk investment you are. And since you don't want to exacerbate those concerns, you're going to unzip that bag and give your pitching hand the Sephora treatment tonight."

"Yeah, I don't know. Unless Sephora's a hot chick who wants to suck on my fingers, I'm gonna have to go ahead and pass."

"Funny," Iain remarked, looking somehow more annoyed with me than usual. "In that case, you can also go ahead and start house-hunting in Cleveland or Atlanta, because the Empires have been taking calls from other teams about you."

My eyes shot up at him.

"What?" I had to pause for a second, my pulse having jumped so suddenly that I needed time to recover. "Are you fucking with me right now or..." I trailed off. "Iain. What the hell are you talking about?" I demanded, frowning deeply as I studied his blank expression. Fuck me, I knew this look. It was very much a business hours look, and it meant that he wasn't joking about shit.

Adjusting the knot of his tie, Iain drew in a deep breath.

"I've been meaning to tell you this, but from what I understand, the altercation on Tuesday also revived the topic of trading you."

My heart slammed in my chest as I stared.

"I know I didn't finish college, but I'm pretty sure the word *revive* implies that they've had this conversation before," I said tightly. "And that's not possible considering you would have told me about it if you knew as far back as last year. Am I not right?"

I reevaluated my entire relationship with Iain as I waited for him to answer.

"Last season." He looked at me and gave another sigh. "They were thinking about trading you to Cleveland for Bautista, Gordon and Fields. The talks fell through because Cleveland took Bautista off the table."

My pulse jumped into my throat.

Jesus Christ. Apparently, the only reason I didn't wind up playing for Cleveland last year was because they wanted their rookie more than they wanted me. And I was grateful for that, obviously, but still. What a fucking blow to the nuts.

"So this has been an ongoing discussion for over a year," I muttered, keeping an even face despite feeling like my world had just flipped on its head.

Ten years in the league and I'd never heard the *trade* word once. Never worried about any team so much as thinking it. It didn't make sense in the same sentence as my name because I had been the country's most coveted prospect since I was thirteen, and I'd dominated the league from the day I came in. Rookie of the Year. Cy Young Award winner. Two-time ALCS MVP and ERA leader for the past five seasons running. I was the best pitcher in baseball. Ego aside, I had actual stats to back me up on that, so it didn't make sense that anyone would want to trade me.

Especially not the Empires.

"They signed me to the biggest contract in the history of their franchise," I argued, adding a bitter laugh since the car just so happened to be whipping past my Nike billboard on 34th Street. It had been there for so long that I'd driven by probably a thousand times without looking up. But tonight, I gave myself a glance.

It was a black and white billboard. I was wearing my Empires uniform and emblazoned across the huge thing were three bold words:

Earned.

Not Given.

They were the words that had followed me since I'd signed in New York three years ago, because good as I was, at least half the world doubted I was worth seven years at two hundred twenty-six million dollars.

"Also known as the biggest pitcher contract in the history of baseball. You're welcome for that seamless negotiation," Iain said with almost a smirk on his face. I blinked at him.

"Are you really laughing right now when I'm about to have a fucking heart attack?" I asked, annoyed that for once, our roles had reversed. Suddenly, Iain was the one at ease while I was so deathly serious that I was actually ready to skip Emmett's party and turn the car around so we could talk this out at the office.

"I'm not laughing," Iain clarified, which to be fair, was true. He smiled plenty but he never really laughed. "That said, if I were, it would be because for the first time in the ten years I've known you, I have your undivided attention – and presumably, your willingness to take my advice for once, instead of constantly needing to prove that only you can be right," he muttered, unzipping the makeup bag and tossing me a black tube that I thought was lipstick till I uncapped it and saw it was green.

"What the hell is this?"

"Color corrector. Keira says to neutralize the redness with it. 'Blend the NARS concealer on top if necessary,'" he finished by reading from his texts.

"Blend the NARS. Of course," I muttered, my sleeves hugging my biceps as I leaned onto my knees to study the weird lipstick thing. I stared at it for what felt like a full minute before breaking the silence. "And why the hell is it that the team wants to trade me?" I asked.

"Take a guess," Iain said dryly.

"I'm applying weird green shit to my knuckles for you. Just answer the question."

"Fair enough. They signed you hoping that your tendency toward trouble would cool over the years. I think we can both agree that it's only gotten worse."

"Yeah? *S.I* begs to differ."

The New Drew Maddox. That was the name of the article *Sports Illustrated* released for my cover issue last year. A "reformed man" was what they called me. I didn't buy it, obviously. I knew the truth. But at least it meant that I was faking my good behavior well enough for the world to believe.

Iain snorted.

"Yeah, the idea that you went from bad boy rebel to devout team captain is just a feel-good narrative that fans like to follow. It's also easy for them to believe because they and the rest of the league have had the luxury of witnessing your antics from afar. The Empires, however, have been dealing with your bullshit up close for awhile," he said as I dragged my palm across my jaw till I could tug on my lip – basically my go-to move to physically shut myself up.

Because there was nothing I could say to defend myself over this particular point.

That much I knew.

"This team has watched you tear apart the clubhouse after being tossed from a game. They were there both times that your wannabe girlfriend stormed the field during batting practice and harassed your teammates for your number. They're also well versed on the fact that these guys have been stalked to the doors of their hotel rooms by women who want to know where you are, and no, I'm not saying you're entirely to blame for these people's behavior. But your indulgent decision-making is generally what leads to these situations, and these situations – these 'persistent distractions' – are exactly what the Empires are thinking about when they entertain the idea of trading you."

My stomach lurched at the T word again.

"And here I thought I had something special with this team," I said wryly.

"If you think the Empires covered up your tracks all these years to give you a break from the media, let me give you a reality check. All that good PR they showered on you was solely to cover their own asses – so that if it came down to it, they could still trade you without other teams being too worried about that 'hothead reputation.'"

Well, damn. I managed to raise my eyebrows despite feeling halfway dead inside.

"That... definitely makes sense," I mumbled while rubbing both hands up and down my face. *Everyone in the world is out to protect themselves, and themselves only. Stop forgetting that,* I told myself while sucking in a deep breath. "Alright." I regrouped. I definitely hadn't expected this bombshell tonight, but I also wasn't the type to roll over and let it defeat me. "So, what now? How serious are they about trading me and what can I do to change their minds? Because this is my team. I'm not playing anywhere else."

"And why is that?" Iain asked.

"You know why."

It was because I'd sacrificed my life and everyone in it to baseball. It was the last thing I cared about in this world, and within the sport, the Empires were the only team that I wanted to play for. I'd been with some shitty organizations in the past and I knew that I had a good thing going on here. Aside from the fact that I actually respected management and ownership and got along with my teammates, I had the best chance of winning it all here. We'd lost the last two World Series to Chicago and St. Louis, which was fucking infuriating, but since acquiring some stellar relief pitching in December, we were favorites to win it all this year.

And considering that championship was the one thing I lived for, there was no way in hell I was going to miss out.

"I'd say your chances of being traded is at about fifty percent right now," Iain finally said, prompting me to let go of a long, whooshing breath. "But I don't think it's impossible for you to flip their decision. You just need to show them some drastic changes as soon as possible. Aside from keeping the temper in check, my suggestion would be to go cold turkey on the late nights and partying. It's May now and the trade deadline is July thirty-first. That means you have three months at most to convince the front office that you're a changed man, and that you've settled down."

"Great. And I'm guessing you want me to start tonight by drinking Shirley Temples and going home by midnight," I said as we pulled up to Boulevardier. Iain actually offered a laugh as he climbed out of the car.

"Before midnight would be ideal," he said as I followed him out. "If you can manage to do that *and* act like a civilized human being tonight, then we might very well be able to save your job in New York."

3

EVIE

Three cocktails and a Prosecco later, I found myself returning a bright smile to the bartender from across the room and giving a happy thumbs up after he mouthed, "You good?" I even mouthed back "thank you" for the firm no he gave me during my last visit, when I approached the bar and asked if I could please just check my text messages.

I couldn't be mad considering it was exactly what I'd asked for. I'd held this man to a promise, he was doing his job, and this whole thing would've been considered a perfectly pleasant and successful exchange if I weren't in fact a giant, conniving bullshitter who was on her way to the terrace so she could talk on a stranger's borrowed phone without Mr. Bartender ruining her fun.

And by fun, of course, I meant the opposite of that because the second I disappeared onto the terrace and out of the bartender's sight, I let my breezy gal act fade into oblivion and turned into a cheerless mess again. My bleary eyes scanned the deck for a quiet corner, my hands already sweaty and my heart beating out of my chest because I was really about to do it.

I was about to talk to Mike.

And not just talk to him – I was going to say everything I'd held in last time for the sake of sounding "okay" and "not too emotional." I was going to ask everything that was on my mind, and I was going to get all the answers I didn't get the day he left me and packed the moving truck *I* booked with only *his* stuff. I was going to do it, damn it – I was going to get my closure.

That was at least what I told myself until I got his voicemail.

"Fuck," I breathed just as I turned a corner to the empty, less scenic side of the terrace. I panicked as the automated voice began reciting his number then completely froze as I listened to that shrill beep and the deafening silence that followed.

Alright, go. *Come on. Say something – anything!*

"Um... hi."

Damn.

This was already off to a bad start. Somehow, I hadn't been as nervous for a live conversation with Mike. At least with that, I'd have his voice – someone to bounce my thoughts off of. But with this, it was like I'd just been thrust naked on a stage and asked to summarize my emotional turmoil in twenty seconds or less.

"Um."

Another 'um,' Evie? I took another half-second to mentally berate myself before getting my shit somewhat together.

"Okay. Hey," I restarted, clearing my throat. "So. I was calling tonight because I couldn't stop thinking about... things. And all these questions I wanted to ask you. I know it sounds stupid, but I was thinking about Hillary's cat that we were supposed to babysit in August," I said, floating toward the balcony. I kept my voice passably casual but my knuckles were turning white as I gripped the cold steel of the railing. "And I know August is forever away, but then I remembered that we both consulted on her restaurant, and we're supposed to go to her big opening next month," I said steadily. Then with a pause, I added, "Together."

And with that word, my voice cracked.

"Um..."

Oh, come on, *Evie.*

Thrusting a hand in my hair, I tried to collect myself. But as I gazed way down at the street below and spotted some pizzeria that merely *reminded* me of the place we had our first date, I lost my train of thought completely. My vision fogged, the tears came back, and boom.

I went off script.

"You know what, fuck it – my main thing right now is that I just miss you so much, Mike."

Yep, that was definitely not what I was supposed to say. I was supposed to tackle all these legitimate questions and concerns, but now I was talking a mile a minute about a bunch of sad, mushy bull-shit – like how I missed overhearing him call me *wifey* to his friends, and how I still leaned back in bed at night because I expected him to be there to hold me. I still put my monogrammed E mug next to his M mug so that it spelled the word "me" inside the cupboard, and by the way, did he want that mug back?

"I could mail it to the new apartment," I offered breathlessly, my eyes shifting as I bit down on my thumbnail and searched myself for more conversation. "How is it, by the way? The apartment?"

What the hell, why are you asking him questions like he's there?

"I mean I know it's great. I've seen it," I said hastily. I *chose* it. "I just wish I could see what you did with it," I added with a sheepish laugh, remembering that amazing wall of windows that overlooked the East River. "The amount of sunlight that place gets is amazing. Your basil plant's gonna get huge. I always thought it would be cool to put the dining table right by those big windows so we could just pick fresh basil off the stems during dinner," I said before suddenly catching myself and practically choking on my own spit. "I mean – not 'we' like we're still together 'we,' I just meant – " *Oh Lord, Evie.* I touched my fingers to my mouth for a second to collect myself, but I was quickly realizing there was nothing left to collect. "Okay, I don't know what I meant," I confessed hastily, my heart beating fast. "I mean you said you wanted to get back together eventually, and in case it isn't obvious, I want to get back together too, because... I honestly don't even recognize my life without you in it, Mike. I don't. I swear to God, it feels like when you're not here, I don't even know how to – "

"Fuck, woman. You gotta stop."

Blinking twice, I paused.

Excuse me?

I lowered my phone slowly, confused for all of a second before I processed that I was not in fact alone on this side of the terrace, and that a nearby stranger had just been eavesdropping on every second of my misery.

It was precisely then that my eyes lit on fire and transitioned from wistful tears to a death look worthy of Medusa. Right away, there were about a dozen profane versions of "mind your own business" warming up on my tongue, and I was beyond ready to launch every one of them at this random, remarkably *rude* and nosy asshole behind me. But as soon as I turned around and let my stare land on him, something inside me yelled *hold fire!*

And it was definitely not my brain.

Because wow.

Seriously. Wow. That was a whole lotta man standing in front of me.

Are you actually Thor? I was genuinely perplexed as my eyes traveled up the sheer length of this man's torso. *Jesus.* If any one person deserved to be the picture next to the Oxford definition of *masculinity*, it was definitely this prick right here. He was so big he cast a shadow over me. If I had to guess he stood at least six-foot-three with a negative percentage of body fat.

That said, I was heartbroken, not a fucking doormat, and there was no way in hell I was going to let him talk to me like that.

"I'm sorry, but who are you and *what* exactly is the problem here?" I demanded, my eyes still on fire as I watched the stranger exhale and dare to look fed up with *me. What in the actual fuck?* His enormous shoulders were slack and his head was tilted back just so. He had the gait of a man who was on his third hour of arguing with his wife, which made no sense at all because *he* was the one who'd come over to bother *me*. "Did you really show up just to interrupt my private conversation?" I asked incredulously.

"I'm pretty sure a conversation involves two parties." He looked down his nose at me. "Not one drunk girl rambling to the voicemail of a guy who's moved on with his life."

My jaw dropped at his nerve.

Okay, wow.

I paused to shift gears because clearly, the level of assholery I was dealing with was beyond what I'd originally expected. I was sure his words would've crushed me if I weren't so busy being completely appalled by how brash and mean he was. I guess it was appropriate that he looked like a frickin' Viking. His dark blonde hair was longer at the top than the sides and the scruff on his jaw screamed *man's man* like no other. Judging from that tan, he spent a very good amount of time outdoors, and while he wasn't flexing, every muscle on his body strained against his white button-down like they desperately wanted out.

I gave myself a second of eyeing the veins on his forearms before I squinted up at him.

"And remind me why my conversation is any of your business?" I questioned. He took no time responding.

"Because I found this nice, quiet spot to sit and think in, and then you came along and started crying everywhere and bumming me out."

"I'm bumming *you* out? Who *are* you?" I demanded just as the light shifted an inch and I realized exactly who the hell he was.

Oh.

Ohhh, I nodded to myself as I took in the asshole for a second time. *This guy.* I'd seen this guy before. Not just in tabloids and on TV, but also once at Aly's and my pop-up restaurant in East Hampton – the very place I'd quit working at for Mike.

But that was a whole other story.

Right. Got it. No wonder you look like that, I thought. I mean most of Emmett's friends were handsome and put-together but this guy was something else. The degree to which his body was built only made sense for world-class athletes, and that was exactly what he was.

An insanely famous, entitled and cocky star athlete.

"You know what – " I held a hand up. "You don't have to answer that because I actually know exactly who you are, and now I think I understand why you're so comfortable being this rude."

"Is that right. And who is it that you think I am?" he asked, amusement already curling his lips like he expected me to somehow get this wrong. I resisted the urge to roll my eyes.

"You're Drew Maddox," I said bluntly. "You play for the New York Empires. You're on the cover of everything. You're very, very famous, which is why you have very little empathy for normal people with normal problems."

"Ah." He raised his eyebrows and nodded in a way that was deliberately patronizing. "Very nice. You know my name, what I do and you can identify my face on a magazine. Beyond that though, I can promise you don't actually know anything about me. In fact," he paused for effect, "I know a lot more about you than you know about me."

I laughed right in his face.

"That's hard to believe considering you don't even know my name."

"Come on now." He broke into a grin that I would've found fucking irresistible if I didn't know he was seconds from roasting me. "I don't need to know your name to know that you're newly single, you hate it, and you really, really miss Mike. Looking at your matching coffee mugs makes you sad. You want to be called 'wifey' again. You can't sleep without him at night, you bought his bullshit line about getting back together, and right now, you're in desperate, desperate fucking need of a rebound," he said, looking pleased with himself as I stood there silent, fuming. A few seconds of silence passed as he arched an eyebrow and waited for my response. "So do I get a gold star now or what?"

All I could do was stare at him, so speechless and angry that I didn't even notice anyone coming up to us till I heard an almost comically sultry voice beside me.

"I'm sorry, but do either of you have a light?"

I turned and blushed immediately since I found myself staring straight into a pair of breasts – absolutely huge, barely covered breasts. They were stuffed into a painted-on dress worn by a statuesque blonde who was already tall without those six-inch heels.

"I, uh... don't have a light. Sorry," I said, forcing my eyes off of her cleavage and looking up to find her already eyeing Drew – assuming she was ever even looking at me.

"And you, Mr. Maddox?"

Only now did he turn from me to her, taking his time to reply.

"I don't smoke," he finally said, wearing a knowing look that said *I know why you're actually here.*

"Mmm, well." Her cleavage plunged as she gave a cutesy shrug. "You could have a lighter on you for other reasons, no?"

"Sorry. Not a pyromaniac either."

His voice was low and teasing, and it prompted the woman to giggle so sharply that I'm pretty sure the sound alone was what alerted the rest of the guests to our presence. Because suddenly, they were trickling over to our previously undiscovered side of the deck, and suddenly, I looked like an awkward, clingy, severely underdressed third wheel. Clearly, these two were flirting and clearly, our new audience was wondering what the hell kind of business the girl in the ratty leggings had standing between Drew Fucking Maddox and Miss Jaw-Dropping Cleavage.

"Excuse me," I said hastily, thanking God for the beat-up Nikes on my feet because they allowed me to practically fly away from that whole situation. Now, all I needed was to get off the deck to avoid all these other eyes watching me and, in all likelihood, wondering why I thought I could win the attention of Drew Maddox in the first place.

It's not what you think. I'm not a thirsty fangirl, and I wasn't trying to flirt, I wanted to explain to them, though I was quickly distracted by the sound of footsteps coming behind me.

"Hey. Wifey."

Seriously?

Without even hearing that low voice, I knew it was Drew because everyone's eyes had swiftly moved from me to something tall past my shoulder. I felt my cheeks heat up from all the unwanted attention as I spun around.

"What?" I hissed under my breath, further annoyed by the way Drew's smile broadened when he saw my pissed off face again. "What do you want? Why follow me when that woman is much more interested in talking to you than I am?"

"Because you and I were in the middle of a conversation and I don't leave things unfinished."

"Well, I know you're probably used to getting your way, but some things are meant to end before you're ready," I snapped before turning back around to head inside.

"Right. This coming from the girl who refuses to get over her ex."

I stopped in place, officially at my wits' end as I spun back around and shot daggers at Drew. I wanted so badly to fire back with some scathing remark, but in the past twenty minutes – between calling Mike and meeting Drew – I'd been on such a roller coaster of emotions that I was too mentally tired to get smart. I was just going to hit the bastard with the truth.

"Okay, you know what?"

My pulse spiked as I grabbed Drew's thick forearm to pull him out of earshot of the others. *Shit. Holy God. Hot damn.* I did my best to get past how absurdly hard he felt in my grip, and to ignore the look of sheer pleasure on his face as I led him to the wall next to the door.

"Fuck, baby. Get this part for me too," he groaned, wrapping his hand around mine and moving my grip on his forearm.

"What are you *doing?*" I hissed as he laughed.

"Sore from practice. I need a massage."

I tossed his arm away like a hot potato, my toes curling in my shoes as I fought to get rid of the heat that had just flooded my body. *Stop replaying the sound of his groan*, I begged myself while trying to regroup.

"Okay, just... *quiet* for a second, and listen." I caught my breath, forcing myself to look unflustered as I stared up at Drew. "I was with my ex for nine years. I met him when I was thirteen years old, and we were best friends for seven years before we even started dating. We grew up together, survived bullshit together, got strong together. We basically *made* each other, okay? Who I am now, everything he is today – that's all a credit to us being devoted to each other for the past sixteen years, because we weren't just boyfriend-girlfriend, we were a partnership for most of our lives, and yet you think it would be natural for me to just nod along with this sudden breakup and carry on without asking any questions?" I cocked my head at Drew, challenging him to say something. I was really banking on shutting him up with this, but I should have known he'd be much more of a challenge.

"You have all these questions because he didn't care to give you the explanations even I think you deserved, which makes him an asshole who doesn't deserve your groveling," Drew countered so matter-of-factly that my hands actually balled into fists. "You trusted someone. You shouldn't have. You learned your lesson, now move on."

Ugh. What the fuck? There was a chance he had a point, but also, why did he think things were that simple? I was flustered and angry and actually grateful that Drew Maddox was so fucking huge that he was blocking me from the view of the other guests, because there was no doubt in my mind that I looked like a red-faced, wild-eyed psycho right now.

"You know, I'm curious as to why in the world you're so invested in this," I said defensively.

"I don't know," Drew said with no hint of shame. "Probably because I just got my own reminder that you can't trust anyone for shit, and I was mulling that over when you suddenly showed up and forced me to listen to you pine for some asshole."

"You don't even know my ex."

"I don't need to, it's all the same. Whether they want to or not, everyone is going to wind up screwing you over at some point. It's just part of their survival instincts."

My face contorted as I squinted at his insane cynicism.

"Do you think we live in the wild or something? How do you even enjoy your life when you think like this?"

"I can assure you that I enjoy my life plenty."

I read that dirty look on his face and rolled my eyes.

"Of course. Because people are disposable to you, I'm sure, and all you have are one-night stands – right?"

"Yes. You should try it sometime." He nodded at our not-so-subtle audience on the deck. "Take your pick from any one of these guys. They're all staring anyway."

"At you," I corrected tightly. "And no thanks. I have nothing against one-night stands, but I really don't see them doing much for me now."

"No? Why not?"

"*Because*," I ground out before I'd fully formulated an answer. "Because I need… *history* and emotional context in order to feel good. I need to actually know the other person to get the full extent of pleasure," I said as Drew broke into the most condescending laugh known to man.

"You really think that because you don't know me personally, I wouldn't be able to give you the best orgasm of your life right here, right now?" He eyed my lips, visibly pleased with the way his question made them fall slightly open. "Baby girl, I could make you come so hard you'd forget his name."

Mike, Mike, Mike, Mike, I chanted in my head to fight the heat prickling across my thighs.

"Well, I'm happy you believe in yourself so much," I snarked, satisfied with even that brief look of irritation I got from Drew before he rubbed his bottom lip and smirked.

"I should let you know that I don't respond well to being challenged."

"Then it's a good thing I'm not going to let you fuck me on this terrace just to prove your point."

"Fine. Then give me those lips."

I froze.

What?

"You're joking, right? You want to kiss me just to win an argument?"

"Yes."

"Well, no thank you. I'm not really one to offer up body parts for arrogant strangers to pad their egos with."

"To be clear, I'd be interested whether or not we were having this stupid argument." His green eyes returned hungrily to my mouth. "But since we are, I should throw in the fact that my tongue alone could get you hotter than anything your ex could do, and the only reason you won't let me touch you is because you know I'm right." He brought his green eyes back to mine. "Again."

Reverse psychology. Don't fall for it.

"Fine."

Whoa, whoa, wrong direction!

"Go for it then."

Evie, what the fuck!

My brain screamed at me though my body took great pleasure in the second of surprise on Drew Maddox's cocky frickin' face. But before I knew it, the surprise was gone and I was backed up on the wall, his ridiculous torso towering over me as he caught my jaw, tipped my chin up and leaned in to hold his mouth an inch away from mine.

I closed my eyes.

Oh God. So hot.

My skin. His body. Everything. I couldn't even bear to look because I was quite genuinely convinced that if I did, I'd pass out. This was Drew I'm-Super-Famous Maddox we were talking about here, and on top of that, he was teasing me. He was *torturing* me with how close his mouth was to mine without touching. I could feel the warmth of his breath between my lips. On my tongue. He was giving me only the slightest taste of him and it was driving me mad.

"Kiss me, asshole," I finally hissed.

I heard his low, sexy chuckle.

Then I felt him tilt my face to the side and bury his face in my neck. *Oh my God.* The very first second of his rough tongue on my skin went straight to my pussy. My thighs pumped, my panties already slick as that tongue of his sucked and pulsed against me for a very, *very* good three seconds. Then it licked a slow, torrid line up to my jaw and finally returned to lingering an inch from my mouth. I opened my eyes, my chest heaving as I breathlessly waited for him to kiss me.

But instead, he caught my bottom lip in his mouth, raking it just hard enough between his teeth before sucking it like candy.

Then he pulled away from me, adjusting his dick in plain sight and looking thoroughly content as he soaked in my visibly dazed, frenzied pleasure.

Holy fuck.

I panted, unblinking as I stared at him in silence for what felt like ages. But finally, sliding his hands in his pockets and curving his lips, Drew spoke again.

"Seriously though," he murmured softly, his eyes moving all over my face. Then abruptly, his voice switched back to normal volume. "Do I get my gold star now or what?"

I blinked.

You bastard.

My body shook with irritation as my high crashed right back down to Earth. But I had brought this on myself so turning on my heel, I bit out, "Goodnight, Drew," before swinging open the door and marching swiftly back inside.

4

DREW

"No shit, they got Hi-Chews in here now?"

Ty's eyes lit up once he got into the clubhouse lounge. Most of the guys stuck with real cooked food from the kitchen, but every day, Ty Damon nourished his elite athlete's body with Fritos, Pop Tarts and candy from what Diaz dubbed the shit shelf.

"You ever wonder how he has any teeth left?" Diaz took a swig from his water bottle as we watched Ty dig into three different-flavored packs of Hi-Chews. I turned my backwards cap to the front.

"I try to think about Ty as little as possible."

"Yeah, that's fair."

"I can hear you assholes," Ty said with a full mouth, tossing us each a few Hi-Chews before we headed for our lockers.

It was 5PM at the clubhouse, which was usually everyone's downtime before the game. Most of the guys listened to music, played cards or squeezed in some more calories since dinner wasn't till probably about 11PM.

Contrary to what most others assumed, I was among those who preferred quiet before the game, even if I wasn't starting. It was for that reason that I was grateful to have a locker next to Diaz. He and I had a pretty rocky history, but things were solid now. Also, he meditated before every game, which gave me the silence I needed to balance out the singing and chanting Ty was generally prone to. Probably because of all the sugar.

"Hey. Turn that shit down, alright?" I called across the room at him while chucking back one of his Hi-Chews. "What did I buy you those headphones for last Christmas if you don't use them?"

"Fuck you. You bought those for everyone."

"And that makes me the asshole how?" I snorted as a text buzzed into my phone.

IAIN: I have something important to discuss with you. Got a minute?

I skimmed it while dodging the dry-fit shorts Ty chucked at me.

"If those were dirty, I'm gonna fuckin' whoop your ass," I informed him seriously before sending Iain a reply.

ME: Busy. Shagging flies.

I didn't feel like talking to him.

Since Emmett's party two nights ago, I'd been vaguely irritated with my agent, mostly because he hadn't told me about my risk of being traded last year, but there was also the fact that I had a hunch I knew who his source was on the trade intel. I'd asked him repeatedly about where he'd gotten it, and since he wouldn't say, I suspected it was Emmett. He was Iain's business partner, my good friend and the younger brother of the guy who owned this team. He was a good dude but I was clearly third in line of where his loyalties lie.

That much had become abundantly clear to me that night of the surprise party.

IAIN: I wasn't aware you took your phone with you on the field.

IAIN: Read: Don't bullshit me. I can hear you and Damon dicking around in the clubhouse.

I stared at the text then up at the closed entrance of the clubhouse.

Goddammit.

Muttering under my breath, I reluctantly got up and crossed the room to swing open the door. Standing in the hall plastered with portraits of past and present Empires – myself included – was Iain. He was in a suit, as usual, but he had the jacket draped over his arm, probably because it was ninety degrees outside.

I greeted him with an upward nod, raising my eyebrows when he didn't immediately tell me what was going on.

"What's up," I finally said, annoyed to have to be the one to break the silence.

"Did you read the papers today?" he asked.

"You told me to stop reading the papers."

I hadn't gone near them since my first year in New York. The Post had a particular affinity for shitting on me and as a result, I developed a reputation for mouthing off to their reporters during post-game interviews.

Iain nodded.

"True. Then I'll skip to my next question. Are you really willing to do anything to stay with this team?"

"Yes," I replied straightaway, despite feeling instantly wary and suspicious.

"Good. Because I have a proposal for you and I have to be back at the office at six, so I'm going to make it quick. We'll start with this."

He handed me his phone, which was already open to Page Six. My eyebrows pulled together as I read the bold headline up top.

DREW MADDOX PUBLICLY GROVELS WITH GIRLFRIEND.

I stared.

"What the fuck is this?" I looked up as Drew took his phone back.

"Walk with me," he said, nodding down the hall and away from the clubhouse. I was already anxious but thankfully, once we got far enough, he went straight into it. "That article assumes that you're dating the girl from Emmett's party the other night. Allegedly, you two had an obvious 'lovers quarrel' on the terrace, which resulted in your chasing her around and groveling till she forgave you. There's also mention of how other women were trying to steal your attention, but you only had eyes for your girlfriend," Iain summarized so fast my swirling thoughts could barely catch up. Looking at his phone again, he read from the article. "According to onlookers, Maddox referred to Miss Larsen as 'wifey' and even shared a deep and passionate kiss with her under the stars.'"

I blinked, completely floored.

"You gotta be fuckin' kidding me."

"I'm not," Iain deadpanned. "They think you did what you've never done before, which is show actual shame and remorse with another human being. Another important detail: they claimed this girl from the party was the 'mystery brunette' you were photographed 'wining and dining' at Mercer Street Kitchen five months ago."

"That was your girlfriend, and you were literally sitting at the table."

"I was in the bathroom when the picture was taken, but the point is the Post just threw you a bone, Maddox. They fabricated for you a relatively long-term relationship, which we both know you're thoroughly incapable of, and they portrayed a soft side of you that we've never seen. Granted it's a hundred percent bullshit, but still. If you play along with this and dedicate yourself to the story, you could change your image in the exact way you need to in order to keep your spot on this team."

I squinted at Iain, starting about ten different sentences that I never finished because I was still catching up on what the hell he was talking about.

"What exactly are you suggesting here? You want me to date this girl?" I finally asked.

"Actually, I want you to put a ring on her finger and move her into that famous bachelor pad of yours," Iain answered. "The media will jump all over it, and I can't think of a quicker, more efficient way to convince the Empires that you've settled down."

I took off my cap to get a better look at him. I had to stare in silence for a few seconds because I wasn't sure if I was losing my mind or if Iain was really asking me this shit.

"I'm confused by how casual you are about asking me to get engaged to a stranger and live with her," I finally said.

"It would be for show, Drew," Iain snorted. I exhaled. "Keep up the act till the trade deadline passes. That's a little less than three months. It's extremely doable."

I rubbed my chin as I stared at the floor. I was actually considering it.

"Well, I'm barely home anyway. And I definitely wouldn't mind hanging out with her again."

"Here's the hard part. I know when you say 'hang out' you mean you're interested in sleeping with her, but if you choose to do this, you agree not to sleep with her or anyone else."

I looked up and laughed in Iain's face.

"You want me to be celibate for three months? You're fucking with me."

"I couldn't be more serious, actually. You sleep with this girl and you'll undoubtedly hurt or upset her. Someway, somehow, you'll do it and the last thing we need is for her to run off and give the media a chance to write about how Drew Maddox's attempt at stability failed, and he's a lost cause," Iain said, looking so goddamned stoic and serious that I wanted to flick him in the face. "On the topic of the media, the reason you absolutely cannot pursue or sleep with other women is because that's the exact story they will be looking out for – Drew Maddox cheating on his sweet, innocent fiancée. You don't want to give the paparazzi even a chance to catch you with another woman."

When I started shaking my head, he held his hands out.

"What? You said you'd do anything to stay a New York Empire."

"And I meant it, but going three months without sex is crazy. I'm going to be wound up so tight I'll be throwing wild pitches every inning."

"Ever heard of jacking it?"

"It's not my preferred method of release."

"So it's settled. We're done trying to fix this trade situation, and I guess we've also found the one thing Drew Maddox can't do."

"There's nothing I can't do," I scoffed, despite the fact that I knew he was trying to appeal to my competitive side. "I just don't – "

"Want to?" Iain gave me the most unimpressed look I'd ever seen on his face, which was saying a lot. "And here I thought you wanted a championship more than anything in the world. I mean what's the point of all the shit that's happened to you if you don't give baseball everything you've got?"

I glared at him for daring to ask that question but at the same time, it sold me.

"Fine." I regretted it as I said it. "I'll do it."

"Atta boy." Iain socked my shoulder before checking the time on his phone. "Alright. I got a meeting, I gotta go."

"Hold on," I said, feeling the deepest frown creasing my brow. I was usually eager to get away from business mode Iain but I had about ten million questions right now, and the fact that he had to leave so abruptly was making me doubt this decision even more. "So I'm not supposed to party, I'm not supposed to go out. I can't go after other girls. What exactly am I supposed to do?"

"I don't know, Drew. Read a book. Start the Harry Potter series. Get creative. You never hesitate to wrack that brain of yours for new ways to torture opposing teams, so why not put it to use for something legitimately productive for once?"

"My ability to get under the other team's skin is legitimately productive. Even *The New York Times* backs me up on that one."

Iain ignored me as he started off down the hall.

"Pick up a hobby, Maddox." We started walking back toward the clubhouse. "If not, get to know that new girlfriend of yours – in ways that don't involve the removal of clothing. I believe in you," Iain said.

Then he took a call and headed off, disappearing into an elevator and leaving me alone in the hall, wondering what the fuck I'd just gotten myself into.

5

EVIE

M y no-motivation spell had definitely been broken, because
on Monday morning, I woke up early for the first time in
ages, showered, got dressed and then went straight to the restaurant
to have a boozy gossip and catch-up sesh with Aly.

I'd definitely missed them since becoming a zombie post breakup,
and I'd definitely missed co-managing with her at Stanton Family
Market – recently honored "Best Lobster Roll in East Hampton."

The place was basically Aly's and my baby. Since buying the
seafood wholesaler from her dad five years ago, we'd revamped the
brand to include this adorable summer pop-up that I loved to pieces.
Unfortunately, I'd quit my post as general manager there almost two
months ago, in preparation for moving to the city with Mike.

He had claimed the move would be beneficial to us as a couple,
and for the sake of my happiness, Aly had helped me justify it by
saying that living in the city would give me a chance to be an ambas-
sador for the Stanton Family brand. Since I did menu consultation
for so many restaurants there, I could take the owners I worked with
to our Stanton Family warehouse in Brooklyn, and better convince
them to source their seafood exclusively from our company.

It was the perfect plan.

Until the breakup, of course. Because now Mike was gone and I was still living on Long Island and that made me feel stupid for even quitting the restaurant in the first place.

"The worst part is I can't even come back to work here because I took all those consulting gigs in the city," I griped as I sat in the back office with Aly, both of us sipping on the restaurant's signature cocktail, the Hail Mary. It was a drink I had designed and was, as Aly called it, "a Bloody Mary on steroids" since it was garnished with not just the usual fixings, but also pickled asparagus, vodka-poached shrimp and a giant lobster claw.

"Are you just going to commute to the city every day for those meetings?" Aly frowned as she clicked about on the computer doing payroll.

"Yeah. That's another thing that'll kind of suck."

"Seriously. Fuck Mike for that shit. That frickin'... douchenozzle of an unredeemable asshole," Aly grumbled angrily as she worked.

I chewed my lip while saying nothing in reply.

I knew I was supposed to hate Mike. I mean he'd waited till the day we were supposed to move to Brooklyn together to tell me that he was dumping me. He knew I couldn't afford to rent our new apartment alone, so dibs went to him, even though I'd spent months apartment hunting without his help.

That said, he *did* pay for my stay at a not-horrible hotel while I looked for my own place, because he knew I was having money troubles of late. But still. He dumped me in a fairly classless way, and I knew Aly was particularly mad because even before the breakup, Mike and I had been having problems. He'd begun picking weird fights here and there and stopped letting me show any affection. Our sex life had been nonexistent for more than a year before he left, so on paper, it didn't really make sense that I was still pining to be near him.

But I personally knew what Mike still meant to me.

The reasons weren't things I discussed in detail with anyone – not even Aly – but I knew them in my heart, and that was all that really mattered.

"Yeah... I know, he sucks, but anyway – topic change," I declared, since I did have an actual order of business to tend to here. "As I told you before, I have a juicy story to tell you from the other night."

"Yes, yes! Hit me."

I wasted no time recounting everything I'd been dying to tell her for almost two days. I started with my voicemail to Mike and ended with the heat of the kiss Drew left on my neck. I also backed it up to include the detail of how he groaned when I squeezed his forearm, and how that deep, throaty, annoyingly *sexy* fucking sound had reawakened something inside me.

I said all that and when I finished, I dealt with five straight minutes of Aly literally shrieking in my face, squealing her ass off and kicking in her chair with a mixture of disbelief and delight.

"Oh my God, I can't breathe – that's amazing!" she gasped before getting swiftly angry. "Wait. You bitch! Why didn't you tell me the night it happened?"

"I wonder why, Aly. Could it be because you arrived completely shithoused and I was afraid you'd go and cause a scene with Drew if I told you that he was mean to me?"

It was a genuine concern that night because shortly after leaving Drew and his annoying skilled tongue on the terrace, Aly had finally arrived at the party. The reason she was so late, apparently, was because she'd gotten wasted with the staff here before going home to Emmett. She hadn't known about the surprise party, obviously, so she'd let the waitresses and kitchen guys talk her into doing an absurd amount of shots.

Emmett, bless his heart, had done his best to sober her up before hauling her into the city, but the effort was in vain. By the time they arrived at Boulevardier, Aly was still drunk and going to town so hard on a Philly cheesesteak that she didn't even look up at the first "surprise!" We had to say it twice for her to gasp, drop her sandwich, then drop to her knees and mourn the loss of her sandwich.

"Okay, fair. I was a complete shitshow that night," Aly relented with a sheepish giggle. "But clearly I got my punishment, because I'm *so mad* I didn't get to witness that ridiculous sexual tension between you two!"

"It wasn't – " My attempt to deny the heat of that night was dead on arrival. "Ugh, who am I kidding. It was one of the hottest moments of my life," I grumbled.

"And you sound so unhappy because...?"

"Because he was right and I was wrong, and I feel guilty for letting a complete stranger turn me on harder than I've been in recent or even distant memory," I confessed. But then I held my finger up. "*That said*, I maintain that he caught me during a special circumstance. I haven't been touched in a remotely sexual manner in more than a year, so my body was just particularly sensitive that night. But me and Mike in our prime? Like the days of our relationship when we weren't fighting all the time? We could have sex hotter than that kiss any day. Guaranteed."

"Mmm-hm," Aly said. I chucked a piece of shrimp at her. "Whoa, hey! Don't waste the garnish! What did I say?"

"You said 'mmm-hm' with an undertone of skepticism, which I think you made deliberately audible just for me."

"Did I?" Aly smirked. "Well, I do have to ask – *would* you ever want to be with Drew Maddox?"

I squinted at her.

"I mean he's not as intolerable as he seems."

"Nice. You really sold me there."

Aly laughed.

"I mean I'll always have a soft spot for him because he's the reason Emmett and I got together. But also, he's one of Emmett's closest friends, Evie. And double dates should be enough incentive as it is," Aly cracked as I shook my head adamantly.

"No. Absolutely not. I know he's your boyfriend's bestie, but he's also a famous athlete who's allergic to commitment of any kind, and I know you don't like to hear it, but I'm still..." My face contorted with guilt as I trailed off. "I'm still waiting to hear from Mike," I finally mumbled. "Even if it's just for closure purposes."

Aly chewed her lip as she nodded, which meant she was giving herself time to rephrase something in her head so that it didn't just blurt out and hurt my feelings. I braced myself for it.

"Speaking of Mike, did he ever text or call after the voicemail you left him?" she finally asked.

"Oh, no... I think maybe he didn't listen to it because it came from an unknown number," I said as she shot a dubious look.

Once upon a time, Aly tiptoed around Mike and my troubles because she didn't want to further stress me out about our already rocky relationship. But now that Mike was gone, those days were over.

"Yeah, no, I think he heard the voicemail but he's ignoring you because it's easiest for him. He's enjoying the single life right now, and he's not feeling remotely guilty about it – which means *you* should be doing the exact same thing."

"Well, damn, girl, I'm trying," I argued before realizing I totally wasn't. I caught a second of the *please* look on Aly's face before holding my hands up in surrender. "Okay, fine, I was totally not trying the past month or so. I was definitely wallowing and not doing anything with my days. But as of today, that stops."

"Good." Aly nodded. "Besides, if you *really* want to get back together with Mike, " she paused to eye me with a look that said *please don't,* "nothing's going to get him crawling back faster than knowing you've moved on."

"True," I conceded – because she was a hundred percent right.

I knew Mike well enough to know that the only reason he was comfortable ignoring me right now was because he knew well that I was still waiting around for him – pretty much on call to talk to him. It had always been like that when we argued. If I gave him the cold shoulder for long enough after a fight, he'd panic and agree that we needed to talk.

So, if I stopped being so available, and if I stopped calling and asking our mutual friends how he was doing these days?

I had a feeling he'd be much quicker to answer all my questions.

Taking in a deep breath, I let it out like it was a brand new day.

"Okay," I exhaled with a big smile as Aly gave my foot a playful kick.

"There's my Evie," she grinned. "So, what's the first order of business on your first official day of moving on?"

I thought about it. A sheepish look twitched on my lips.

"Well... I *did* always say that when I finally got a day off from here, I'd go read a book in the window of Poppy's Tea Room."

Aly snorted.

"Hey. Do you, girl," she shrugged with a giggle.

I couldn't blame her for the mild judgment. Poppy's Tea Room was an overpriced, heavily floral-decorated tea parlor that served flavorless finger sandwiches on three-tiered platters. It was all hype, but it spoke to the girliest part of my soul and I decided today was the day I was going to go.

So, grabbing my purse, I kissed Aly goodbye and headed straight home to change and pick a book to read. Then I drove fast to Poppy's to beat the lunch rush because that coveted window seat was mine. I was going to relax my ass off today. I'd already made that decision.

It was about to be the best, most tranquil and stress-free day of my life.

I could already feel it.

6

EVIE

Okay, so my best day ever was already off to a rocky start – but solely because of the ladies who lunch at the table next to me.

They wouldn't stop shooting dirty looks because I'd arrived a minute before them and was seated at the window table they of course wanted. After complaining in vain to the waitress *and* manager that they wanted my seat, their queen bee with the overdone lip fillers actually dared to approach me and say that I was affecting the enjoyment of *four* people, instead of just *one* by refusing to relinquish my spot.

I, of course, flashed my best *eat me* smile while politely saying, "I'm sorry, I'm not going to move."

And since then, it had been a silent war of dirty looks and under-the-breath muttering. To my credit, I only peered at them once when I heard one scoff that I was a "miserable person" and she "wasn't surprised" by my "lack of company." But since that remark, I'd been doing a pretty good job of keeping my nose buried in my book.

But shortly after my food arrived, I heard their hushed murmurs again. I paused, momentarily sure that they were now judging my choice of finger sandwiches, but then I heard the sound of shock and unfiltered lust in their voices.

"Oh my Lord, girls. I think it's our lucky day."

"Good God. Who gets dibs?"

"I say me because I'm the only one whose husband is out of town."

I bit back a giggle.

So they were ladies who lunched and also sometimes cheated on their husbands. I had to peek over at them, entirely too amused with how quickly they went from posh to vulgar. One of them was talking about her new sex swing now. *Okay. Wow.* I was so busy watching their purring, lip-smacking reactions to this random guy that I didn't care to look up till I tracked their gaping stares right back to my table.

They wore looks of pure indignity as their eyes flicked back and forth between me and their object of desire – who was clearly standing right in front of me.

Oh... God.

Slowly, I turned from them and looked up, up, up till I was staring straight at Drew Maddox — standing in the middle of the pinkest, frilliest tea parlor on the East Coast.

And looking like complete inked-up sex in a fitted white V-neck and jeans.

Holy fuck.

"What are you doing here?" I breathed.

"I hear they do some killer tea and crumpets," he deadpanned.

"Seriously. What are you doing here?"

"Can I sit?"

I eyed the ladies to my right, who didn't care to avert their big eyes when I caught their stares. I didn't want to give them the pleasure of overhearing whatever Drew was about to say, so with a reluctant pat next to me, I had him take the seat right beside mine.

"Good to know you have horrible taste in restaurants."

"How did you find me? I didn't even tell you my name let alone where I might be on this particular Monday."

"My agent told me your name, and your own best friend sold out your location. I went to find you at her restaurant – "

"Our restaurant."

"Sure. And she said you were on your way here," Drew said, prompting me to peek at my phone, which I'd put on silent. Twelve texts and two missed calls. Okay, yeah. This all checked out. Apparently, Aly hated Mike enough to aid Drew in completely breaching my privacy today.

> **ME:** WOMAN. haven't read any of your texts yet but I'm going to kill you very soon

I sent the message quickly before looking back up at Drew.

"Look, if you came here just to gloat then you have much less of a life than I'd imagine for a star athlete," I said.

"Gloat?" he smiled. "About what? Remind me."

Ugh.

Dammit. I ground my teeth as Drew played dumb. *Set yourself up for that one,* I told myself while trying to carefully word my response.

"You're under the impression that you won some bet about getting me hotter than Mike ever could. You *didn't,*" I insisted crisply. "But since your superstar ego is clearly as big as it is fragile, I'll let you go ahead and believe that."

"My superstar ego is backed by the dedicated stat keepers of Major League Baseball, so you're a hundred percent right about it being big. Fucking huge, in fact," he added, grinning as I rolled my eyes. "Fragile though? No. Not so much."

"Right. Then why did you travel all the way to Long Island just to gloat and give me a hard time?"

"I'm not here to do that. I was satisfied enough with how I got you looking that night."

"Which was like what?"

"Like you'd just been fucked for hours when all I did was kiss you."

I sucked on my teeth to refrain from retorting. I didn't have anything prepared and he was clearly fucking great at using my words against me. *Something tells me this dickhead's stellar at trash talking*, I thought, clenching my jaw and waiting out my seething irritation before I spoke again.

"Okay. Last chance, Drew," I said slowly between my teeth. "What are you doing here?"

"I'd prefer to talk somewhere private."

"*You* barged into my space to bother *me* – again – so I'm sorry, but you don't get that choice."

"Fine." I watched his bicep flex as he gripped my seat and swiftly pulled my chair over – so close to his that my legs were now crossed between his muscled, man-spreading thighs. *Holy shit.* "In that case, we're going to have to get a little closer." His smirk was inches from my lips as he cocked an eyebrow. "That alright with you? Or does it make you nervous?"

"You don't make me nervous," I lied, my heart beating damned near out of my chest as Drew braced himself with a thick forearm on the table, basically caging me in with his enormous body.

"Good." He eyed my lips. "Then I'll get right into it. I need to ask a favor of you."

"You're kidding. Why would I do any sort of favor for you when you've been nothing but a dick to me? *Don't* eat that," I hissed as he stole one of my sandwiches and popped it into his mouth. I anticipated the face he would make a second before he made it. "I told you not to eat it."

"What was that?"

"A cucumber sandwich."

"You like eating this shit?"

"No, but I did like the idea of spending an afternoon sitting in this pretty window and reading a book because I woke up feeling kind of good today, and it's one of my last days before work has me commuting *four hours* back and forth per day," I hissed just loud enough for him to hear. "I don't really have the money to eat at a place like this, but I told myself I'd splurge this once because I deserved to relax, which I can assure you, I am definitely not doing now that you're here."

For some idiotic reason, I actually thought I had a chance at making him feel a shred of remorse right there.

But nope.

"Well, then I have a solution for you," he said, a glimmer in his eye.

"I doubt you do, but for the sake of finishing this conversation, just tell me what it is you're here to talk about, and if you can do it in three sentences or less, I'll be really impressed."

My hot breaths were short and my chest heaved as I watched Drew smile and study my face for a few seconds. My lips, my cheeks, then back to my eyes.

"I need to show the Empires that I've settled down so they won't trade my crazy ass. After the other night, the New York Post claims you're my girlfriend of five months. I want us to pretend we're actually engaged for the next three so I can keep my job on this team." He cocked his head at the dazed look on my face. "Succinct enough for you?"

"I... what are you talking about?"

"What, you want more than three sentences now?"

"*Drew*," I hissed, so annoyed it felt like I might actually explode.

"Fine, I got you. Hold on."

I breathed easy – easier, at least – as he leaned back and away from me to slide his phone out of his pocket. Of course, I was back to wild-eyed and bewildered once I finished skimming the tabloid story he flashed me on his screen.

"What is this?" I breathed.

"That was my reaction too. I mean Drew Maddox doesn't grovel."

"And I don't date men who refer to themselves in third person."

"True. You date the Matts of the world."

"Mike."

"Whatever. The point is, this story is bullshit but we can use it to our advantage."

"No, *we* can use it to *your* advantage," I corrected as Drew leaned close again. But this time, I kept my cool. "You're the only one who stands to benefit from something as ridiculous as this. I mean, exactly what good does it do me to pretend to date *you*?"

"You just said it yourself. You have no money and you're about to commute four hours a day into the city. You took a job there, probably because you thought you were going to move there, but now you're living two hours from there all alone because Matt dumped you and took your new lease all for himself. Tell me I'm wrong."

"His name is Mike."

"Don't care. Am I wrong about the rest?"

I breathed hard through my nose.

No. Not at all, I conceded in my head. But my tongue refused to give Drew the pleasure.

"Yeah, I'll take your silence as a no," he went on briskly. "Anyway, on top of all the benefits I already listed, you'd be living at my penthouse in the city. We'll start you at a hotel while we adjust to each other, but move-in should happen within a week or so. Aside from the gifts and meals I'll be publicly buying you, you'll have a salary and per diem that you can discuss with my agent. I'm at the clubhouse nine hours a day, if I'm even home. Otherwise, I'm on the road, which means you're free to do your own thing ninety percent of the time. My driver can take you to and from your work meetings, or you can take the subway just to spite me – I don't care. As long as you act like you're in love with me while we're out together, I won't give two shits about what else you do with your time. Sound good to you or what?"

I simply stared. I was still going back and forth between being reactive and needing a second to even process all this.

"Also, speaking of your little shitstain ex, this would be a damned good way of getting back at him."

"How?" I squinted. "Being engaged to you would make him think less of me."

"No, being engaged to me would make him feel like he let go of the best thing he's ever had. Nothing gets a man's attention like his ex dating Drew Maddox."

"Do you do this a lot? Referring to yourself in third person?"

"It was fitting for that sentence. Want to keep deflecting from the point because you're realizing how tempted you are to say yes?"

I glowered.

"Don't you think Mike would see a ring on my finger and think, 'Well, damn. There goes my chance'?"

"No. I think he'd feel a sense of urgency and try to get you back. He's had you for longer, he's going to be naturally possessive, and he's also going to think that if Drew Maddox wants to wife it, then so should he."

"Can you not refer to me as 'it' or you as 'Drew Maddox' ever again?"

"Yes. But I need your answer on this already, because I can't sit here anymore. The Botox brigade is staring at me like they want to fucking eat me."

I chewed on my thumbnail as I stared out into space, listing all the pros and cons in my head just for shits and giggles.

You could live in the city. You could get out of that crappy apartment. You could be closer to work and save money on rent. You could get Mike's attention. He is obsessed with baseball. He hates the Empires. This would rile him up like no other, and there's no way in hell he won't call you asking for answers within the first week.

I chewed on my lip as I thought of the cons. *You have to play house with Drew Maddox.*

It was only one con but it was a big one. Drew growled with impatience.

"Look, whatever it takes to make it worth it for you, you can negotiate that with my agent. Money talks, and I'm sure you have a price."

Eyes narrowed, I crossed my arms.

"As charming as your insane cynicism is, you should know that I wouldn't actually accept the payment from you. I own a company and I have a job. Yes, money's tight but I don't want or need yours. Especially if I'll already be saving on rent by living in your apartment."

Drew raised his eyebrows, looking genuinely impressed.

"Unexpected," he remarked.

"Sorry to shake up your sexist view of the world, but not all women you encounter are gold diggers."

"Duly noted. Now let's get back on track. Are you in or are you out?"

I pursed my lips and dropped my gaze into my lap, trying to figure out at what point it was during this conversation that I'd begun to genuinely consider this.

Because I was, and I was only just realizing that now.

"Look, if the problem is that you don't trust how hot and bothered you get around me, then I understand."

I looked up to see Drew grinning that fucking grin, both of us knowing well that this was his stupid reverse psychology at work again. But just like the last time, despite the sane half of my brain screaming *no* on repeat, I tipped my nose up and put on my best game face. I pictured Mike's face when he saw me with Drew in the papers, and before I knew it, I said the words I told myself I wouldn't.

"Fine. Consider me in."

7

DREW

From: Iain Thorn <iainthorn@thornsae.com>

To: Evie, me

Just to fill you in, Drew – after meeting individually with Evie this afternoon, we came to the agreement that tomorrow would be a good start date since it's your only off day till next month.

We need to quickly convey in your first public outing that Evie is unlike any of the women you have been photographed with in the past, and since you've only been photographed with women at events, parties and nightclubs, we're going to lose the flash and go low-key/non-trendy for this outing

This will involve an 11AM lunch at a restaurant of Evie's choosing. Somewhere relatively unknown and outside of a trendy, hotspot neighborhood (SoHo, Meatpacking, LES) would be ideal. After your meal, you will accompany Evie while she completes errands around the city. The more mundane, the better.

Evie, once you send me your itinerary, I will arrange for photographers to be in each location you hit. These will be cell phone shots sold to the likes of TMZ so dress according to how you would like to be seen in the papers.

Thanks,
Iain

From: Evie Larsen <evieannelarsen@gmail.com>
To: Iain, me
Hi Iain,

I've chosen the following for our outing tomorrow:

Lunch: Louisa's in Cobble Hill (Brooklyn)
Errands: Groceries at Sahadi's followed by returns at Urban Outfitters. I will probably wind up dropping by Trader Joe's at some point since there's one in this area anyway.

Hope this works!
Evie

From: Drew Maddox <drew.maddox88@gmail.com>
To: Iain, Evie
I don't think I have the words to express how uninterested I am in all this.

From: Iain Thorn <iainthorn@thornsae.com>
To: Evie, me
That's fine. You're not supposed to be interested in errands. You're doing them because you're whipped by your girlfriend whom you love dearly. The world has never seen Drew Maddox do something unselfish. This is your chance to show them a change.

I have photographers arranged to be in both these general areas tomorrow. Keep me posted via text when you arrive at each location.

Thanks,

    Iain

From: Drew Maddox <<u>drew.maddox88@gmail.com</u>>

    To: Iain, Evie

    Did you have returns just sitting around your house for this moment Evie why didn't you do them earlier

From: Evie Larsen <evieannelarsen@gmail.com>

    To: Iain, me

    Because I bought this stuff online and there isn't an Urban near my part of Long Island. Also, Iain asked for mundane errands or I wouldn't be dragging you along on this. Trust me, I'd rather get this done without your inevitable commentary.

From: Iain Thorn <iainthorn@thornsae.com>

    To: Evie, me

    Right. I'm glad you two are already fighting over errands like a real couple but if you want to continue this argument please do so in a separate email thread.

~

D*ick*. I smirked at Iain's last email as I waited near the F Train stop Evie said she'd be getting out at.

I had no idea where I was. I went into Brooklyn often to get to the stadium, but I never ventured beyond that point. In my head, when I heard Brooklyn I saw either hipsters with handlebar mustaches or fat, loud guys who pronounced it "New Yawk." But clearly, Brooklyn wasn't just the stupid, stereotypical shit in my imagination because whatever this place was, it was nice. I liked it. It was busy but quiet. All the little streets were lined with trees and townhouses, and the main street I was standing on was full of small restaurants and colorful storefronts. I got a good amount of glances and a couple excited reactions –

mostly the wordless big smile-slash-point thing – but I went a full ten, twelve minutes out there before someone even asked for my autograph.

"Hi, Drew?"

My eyebrows went up as I looked down to see the tiniest, jet-haired kid standing in front of me.

"My mom said I could ask for your autograph if I was fast and I left you alone afterwards."

"Hey, man, it's all good," I laughed as the kid presented me with my latest ESPN cover and a new Sharpie. "Damn. You just had this on hand?" I grinned as I sank to a kneel.

"Huh?"

"You just had this magazine with you?"

"No, we bought it from the store when we saw you. We were getting bubble tea and then I saw you, and I told mom, and then we went to the newspaper store down over there to buy the magazine. And I think my mom had the Sharpie in her purse already. She has snacks in her purse too."

"Got it." I felt my eyes crinkling as I laughed. I loved when kids just rambled on about stupid shit you didn't really need to know. It was so honest. They didn't know how to censor themselves yet or present themselves as anything but what they were. And as annoying as kids generally were, only an asshole wouldn't get a kick out of that. "Alright, what's your name, boss?"

"Parker."

"Parker. Fuckin' solid name," I nodded. "Sorry. Don't curse."

"Okay." Parker flashed a toothless grin as I handed over his signed magazine. "Thank you." He looked down at it and up at me before covering a mischievous giggle. "Did you..." He paused as if to work up the nerve to ask his next question. "Did you really make Cody Bryce cry when you hit him?"

"Ah, shit, you saw that didn't you."

"Yeah." I hid my left hand in my pocket when I saw the kid glance at my knuckles. "Daddy let me stay up late, you're his favorite. And he said he saw Cody crying when he got kicked off the field. But my friend Braden said he wasn't. He likes L.A. But not me." Parker shook his head vehemently.

"Well, between you and me, I think I heard Cody kind of do one of these," I said, making a particularly bitchy sniffling noise that made the kid laugh like crazy. God, I was going to be the worst dad. "That said it's wrong to hit people. No matter what they say to try to provoke you. I mean that. Okay?"

"Okay."

"Alright. And do me a solid, don't tell your mom that we made fun of Cody," I said just as I saw a woman come up behind Parker.

My eyes landed first on her ankles strapped into heels then traveled slowly up those killer calves. *Fuck. And here it comes*, I thought, blood rushing to my cock as I made out that valley between her luscious thighs, all thanks to the sunlight beaming through the fabric of her peach-colored sundress.

Jesus Christ, this kid's mom was a smokeshow.

I knew I shouldn't be looking at a woman like this in front of her kid, but there was no stopping my sex drive when it kicked into gear, and goddamn did she hit all my weak spots. Those round hips, that little waist – they looked too damned good wrapped so nice and tight in that dress. I rose slowly to my feet, forcing myself to hold back a groan when my eyes made their way up to her full fucking tits. She was wearing a bra, but I could see that her nipples were hard under there and suddenly, all I wanted was to get this girl alone so I could rip that dress clean off her perfect body.

Maddox, you are one hell of a piece of shit, I thought just as I brought my gaze up to the bombshell's face – which greeted me with a wry smile.

"Hi," Evie said.

My eyes popped damned near out of my head when I realized it was her.

Wait. What? I blinked down, confused till I saw that the little kid had already run off and was waving his autograph in front of his smiling mom down the block. Evie turned her attention from him back to me.

"Well, that was annoyingly cute," she smirked. "Kind of pegged you for someone who despised children."

Her hair looked different today. A lot of things did. I couldn't tell what it was, but it had me at a loss for words for a good two seconds.

"All dressed up for the paparazzi today?" I asked.

"Certainly not for you."

The little grin on her pouty lips made me clench my jaw. *Smart little mouth.* There was nothing I wouldn't give to see it wrapped around my cock right now.

"Well, I'm surprised. You clean up nicely," I said, enjoying the eye roll I got from her. "I take it you brushed your hair today?"

"My hair was brushed the last time you saw me, too, so let's retire any future jokes about what I looked like the first night we met. That was clearly a fluke."

I gave her another once-over.

"Clearly," I muttered, getting caught on those tits again. She didn't have much cleavage showing, but it was apparently enough to keep my blood rushing.

Alright. At ease, I told my dick as Evie turned around and peered over her shoulder.

"Well, shall we? You're in for a very long, *very* boring day of errands. I really hope you're ready," she teased as I let her walk ahead so I could soak in the view of her ass in that dress.

Actually, I kind of *was* ready for this.

8

EVIE

Walking down the street with Drew Maddox was fascinating. Male or female, stares just flew to him. His height and physique commanded attention from well down the block, and he wasn't even the type who looked a little better from afar. He actually got mercilessly hotter as you got closer – I'd dealt with the experience myself coming out of the subway – and I could actually see some girls struggling to tear their eyes off of him.

Nah, I feel you, I thought as one girl flashed me a sheepish smile for instinctively checking him out.

"What?" Drew turned to me when he heard my giggle.

"Nothing. This girl was trying really hard to stop staring at you out of respect for me, and I thought it was polite and kind of sweet. Almost makes me want to tell her that this is all a sham and to check you out as hard as she wants."

Drew shot a look at me and stared for several seconds.

"You're insane."

"*Insane?* Geez. Kind of a strong choice of words, don't you think?"

"You just made friends with a complete stranger in your head."

"Uh, no, I *related* to her and we had a friendly, non-verbal exchange," I corrected.

"For two seconds. With a complete stranger," Drew reiterated. I squinted up at him.

"Look, I know that someone who doesn't even trust his own friends wouldn't get this, but it's not completely wild for girls who don't know each other to bond quickly over something. Do you know how many best friends I've made in the bathrooms of bars?" I asked, knowing well that I was losing him at this point. "No one holds your hair while you're puking in the bathroom of a bar like a girl you've never met before in your life. It's just part of the unspoken sisterhood among us women. Just because *you* don't know doesn't mean it hasn't been true for centuries."

Drew narrowed his eyes at me, looking confused to the point of irritation.

"You know, I thought this day might end up being tolerable but then again, maybe not."

I laughed, a bit too entertained by what big, bad Drew Maddox looked like completely weirded out by me. I couldn't out-muscle or out-snark him, but clearly I could out-sunshine him, so there was that.

Though admittedly, within minutes, I was out of sunshine myself.

"*Crap*," I cursed when we stopped in front of the "Closed for Renovation" sign hanging on the door of Louisa's.

Our lunch spot was closed, and Drew Maddox was hangry.

"Damn it. Dammit, dammit, dammit," I cursed again ten minutes later while waiting outside the deli where Drew was grabbing some "hold me over" food. Leaning against the window, I shot an apologetic text to Iain about the change of plans. He had seemed very nice and cordial when I met him in the city yesterday, and upon noticing my fidgety nerves, managed to make me laugh by assuring me that I'd have plenty of space to hide in Drew's triplex should Drew get too annoying. But he was also professional to the point of being intimidating, and I was afraid he was going to hate me for failing to pick a restaurant that was, at the very least, *open*.

"Oh my gosh... Evie?"

I had just sent the text when I heard the familiar, clear-as-a-bell voice in front of me. Blinking up in the sun, I gasped.

"Oh my God – Hillary. Hi!"

We laughed as we threw our arms around each other and went straight into talking about her new restaurant – the one with the menu *I* designed – and how the big opening was in just over a week.

"I can't believe it's finally happening!" Hillary laughed, pressing her manicured hands on her makeup-free face. Save for special occasions, Hillary never wore an ounce of it. Since college, she'd rocked that all-natural, girl-next-door, Chapstick-is-my-makeup beauty that I only wished I could pull off. "Evie, I am so excited for the masses to taste that amazing menu of yours. I literally haven't slept since last week! You're still coming to the friends and family opening, right?"

"Yes! Of course. How could I not?"

Her blue eyes were still bright though her smile somewhat faltered.

"Oh, because... I heard about you and Mike. And I'm so sorry. I know you were having a really rough time adjusting." She thrust a hand into her perfect hair. "God, what is even wrong with me? I'm just rambling on and on about my life when you just had your heart completely obliterated."

"Oh." Her blunt phrasing surprised me. "Oh... no, don't worry about it. I'm actually doing much better these days."

"Good! I mean, yeah, look at you! You're out of the house, you're looking great," she said enthusiastically, gesturing at my dress. "Where are you even off to?"

"I was on my way to lunch at Louisa's, but apparently it's closed for renovation," I laughed at myself as Hillary's bright eyes lit up further.

"Omigod, perfect! Come to my restaurant then! You'll have tons of privacy 'cause we're technically not open yet, obviously, but we're doing a menu tasting to train staff today, so you should totally come! I'm sure everyone would love to meet the mind behind the menu. *And* I really want to do something for you. Please." She took both my hands in hers. "You're being so incredibly brave about the breakup.

You deserve to have something nice," she said, giving my hands a squeeze just before her eyes flew up and behind me.

And... here we go. I knew that it was Drew who had just walked out even before I heard his annoyingly impatient question.

"Alright, woman. Where we going?"

I refrained from rolling my eyes, instead flashing Hillary my best smile.

"Hillary, um, this is my... this is Drew," I said, chickening out of dropping the B word. Hillary, poised as she normally was, took a good three seconds to find her words.

"Drew. Drew Maddox," she said for him as he extended his hand. There were visible stars in her eyes as she took it and broke into a grin. "Wow. I'm a huge fan," she said before stammering. "I mean – technically, I'm not an Empires fan since I'm from Baltimore, but I'm certainly an admirer of your game. And your career, in general. You're kind of a big deal," she said, blushing as she laughed at herself.

Drew gave an easy chuckle then nodded at me.

"Thank you. Well, maybe you can tell my girlfriend that. She's generally pretty unimpressed with me."

I raised my eyebrows. *Until now, Drew Maddox.* I had to grin up at him, giving a little wiggle of the brows to commend him for so smoothly dropping the G word.

"Yes, well, Evie's never been much of a sports fan, but I'm sure she's much more impressed with you than she lets on," Hillary laughed politely. "But anyway, hold the phone. I need to ask – how and when did you two even meet?" she asked, her voice a breathy mix of curiosity and excitement.

"Well, my friend Emmett has been dating Evie's friend Aly for a year and change now, and Evie and I met..." Drew squinted at me as he pretended to think. "When was the first time we met, babe? This stuff is your department," he grinned as he watched my face promptly fall with annoyance. Not only did his last sentence piss me off, he was suddenly forcing me to be the one to bullshit on my feet. *Goddamn you, Drew,* I willed him to hear my thoughts despite the sweet smile I flashed him.

"Umm..." I turned back to Hillary. "Actually, I'd seen Drew first at my restaurant in East Hampton. That was last year and I remember hiding behind a door and thinking wow, that's... a whole lotta man," I laughed, since that was actually true. Of course at the time, Drew didn't see me because yes, I was hiding behind a door, and of course, he had only shown up at the restaurant to meddle with Aly and Emmett's budding relationship. In the meanest way possible, too, but that was Drew. "Then I met him at one of Aly's parties a few months ago. He was just being... a *really* cocky asshole and I was actually super annoyed with him. But I guess he wound up feeling really bad, because he ended up reaching out to me pretty much right after the whole Mike thing. I think Emmett mentioned to him that I was single and Drew," I beamed up at him, "was just kind of pathetically desperate to see me again. I think to make up for what a dick he was the first time. So he begged and *begged* Aly for my number – for days, he did – and, well... here we are!" I finished brightly as Drew squinted.

"That's... not exactly how it happened."

"It is," I shut him down as Hillary gave me a playful smack.

"Oh, Evie, don't be smart – that's romantic!" she giggled as Drew circled an arm around my waist and pulled me tight into his side.

"Yeah, babe. Don't be smart." I looked up to find those wicked green eyes glinting at me. He dropped his gaze to my lips and his voice to a murmur. "You know what I like to do to that mouth when you get smart."

I swallowed hard, simply staring back at his look of mischief till Hillary broke the silence.

"Whew! Is it getting hot out here?" she teased, fanning herself. "Guys, I'm so sorry – I just realized I've been making my Lyft wait forever for me. I'm headed to the restaurant now. Tell me you're coming?" she asked me. Since I was hesitant, she appealed to Drew with a grin. "I'm sure you need tons of calories to nourish that body," she lilted. "And I'll have my kitchen make you anything."

"Sold," Drew said as Hillary squealed with excitement and squeezed my hand.

"Don't worry. Mike's been dropping by for PR stuff but he definitely won't be there today," she said before letting herself eye Drew as he went ahead of us to the car. "Not that you're even *thinking* about Mike anymore," she giggled, grabbing my hand and squeezing it tight as she dragged me to the car.

Well. That much she had right. Since the past couple of days, I'd definitely been thinking significantly less and less about my ex.

MERRYWEATHER WAS A BEAUTIFULLY BRIGHT, sunny restaurant located in the heart of Park Slope. Its main dining room was a creamy white color with white tables, wooden chairs and comfy booths topped with navy blue leather cushions. Prior to us walking in, the staff had been hanging around by the bar, huddled around an iPad to read a new press release about the restaurant.

It was actually one that Mike had put out, and it was about one of the dishes I designed, so oddly enough, it felt as though everyone were studying a keepsake of Mike and my famous teamwork. *Great.* I gulped, prepared to feel that dark spiral of emotion I fell into anytime I thought of the good I once had with Mike. Standing there, I waited and waited for it to hit.

But this time, it didn't come.

"Team!" Hillary's bell-like voice rang out. "This is my friend Evie Larsen who designed the majority of our menu, including our Truffled Lobster Pot Pie that all the blogs are talking about!" she gushed, gesturing toward me. But it was a lost cause. The whole staff was staring open-mouthed at Drew, and after an initial five seconds of dumbstruck silence, they ambushed him for pictures. "Guys! Hey, please – the man's here to eat!" Hillary protested but I brushed it off.

"Oh, don't worry. He loves it," I said just as I caught Drew's death look.

He hated this, I could tell, but I needed a breather from him. After filling my head with images of what he might do to my "smart mouth," Drew had sat next to me in the back of the Lyft, casually massaging the back of my neck while fielding Hillary's questions about everything from baseball to us to how he managed to see me on his tight baseball schedule.

"It's tough. The only way to see her every day is if she moves in, but she keeps resisting," he laughed with Hillary while I sat entirely too stunned to speak. "But I'll get her to cave eventually," he said, casually running his fingers up my neck and into my hair. My eyes went wide as he grabbed a handful and gave a firm tug. "I think she just likes to give me a hard time," he smirked as I felt a thousand hot tingles shoot fast up my thighs.

The bastard.

I didn't know what he was doing to me or why he was so good at acting like a boyfriend when he'd never been one in real life, but I needed time to catch my breath, so even after he got seated and Hillary had the kitchen send out food, I kept off to the side and caught up with her.

"But wait – how did this even happen so fast?" she asked in a hushed voice since we were within earshot of Drew's booth. "I feel like I liked a picture of you and Mike on your Instagram like, a month or two ago, and suddenly this? How?" she whispered excitedly while playing with a lock of her dark brown hair.

"I mean... the media thinks we've been together for longer but it's pretty much been since after the whole Mike thing," I improvised. "I didn't know what to do with myself, and I guess Drew did. He picked up the pieces of me, he put them back together and then... boom."

"Love," Hillary nodded.

"Yeah. I guess when you believe in it, it has a way of finding you," I said, making Hillary's face crumple with emotion just before one of the chefs in the kitchen called for her attention.

When I returned to the table, Drew was already laughing.

"Impressive crock of shit right there."

"I was acting," I said tartly, sliding into the other side of the booth since I wasn't sure I could handle sitting so close to him again just yet. "That said, I don't think it was a total crock."

"So if I believe in love, it'll find me?" Drew smirked.

"Yes. I think so," I huffed, taking a sip of my mimosa. "I think if you were more open to the idea of love and trust – platonic or not – you'd have more of it in your life."

Drew stared at me as he chewed for what felt like a full minute.

"I'll pass," he finally said.

"You don't love your parents?" I challenged.

"Not the way most people love their parents."

"What does that mean?"

"I have good memories of them. I text them back. I keep pictures of them in my house," Drew said, showcasing that long torso as he leaned back in his seat. "But I don't trust them. I would never rely on them for comfort. Or happiness."

I could feel my eyebrows rising higher and higher.

"That's... insane."

"Clearly, we have different definitions of that word."

"And were you always like this?"

"No. But I wasn't always a professional baseball player."

"Again, what does that mean?"

His lips hardened to a line as he eyed me with irritation.

"It means I appreciate my mom and I like my dad okay, but he treats me like an ATM and promises business loans on my behalf to people he barely knows, just because he wants to feel like the king of La Palma, Florida," Drew answered, drumming his long fingers on the table. "Before I even got drafted, he took out a million dollar line of credit in my name and maxed that shit out in three months. I said something he didn't like in an interview and he told my entire hometown I was on drugs. Tell me I should trust him."

The drumming stopped and he looked up at me with those intense green eyes. My mouth opened and shut.

"Okay. Yup. Definitely not someone I'd trust," I relented. "Sorry," I frowned, wondering why I of all people had the nerve to criticize his relationship with his family. "Really. I didn't mean to sound judgmental. I actually know all too well how that family stuff feels."

Drew's eyebrows pulled tight for a second and I thought he was going to ask me about myself.

But he didn't.

And for some reason, I let that hurt my feelings.

Jesus, Evie. Get it together, I scolded myself after several minutes of quiet. My first official date of this contract and I'd already let myself get hot and bothered over Drew's fake flirting, and irrationally upset by his lack of interest in my personal life. *Remember the whole part about this being entirely for show? Stop letting him fluster you*, I berated myself, taking one long, deep breath before mentally resetting.

Alright.

You got this. On with the show.

And for the rest of lunch, I was fine. Mostly fine. But somewhere toward the end of our meal – about three courses and two rounds of drinks later – I could tell from the way Hillary was peering at me and talking in a hushed but frantic voice on the phone that something was up.

"Hey. Hil." I caught her hand when she passed by our table. "Talk to me. Everything okay?"

She launched straight into her default cheery mode.

"Of course! Yes, everything's fine!" she said brightly, but when I gave her the look, her shoulders fell. "Okay, okay, Mike just called and said he was dropping off some stuff for the restaurant – *but* I totally saved it and now it's just his colleague coming! So don't worry, you're in the clear!" Hillary said breathlessly with a big smile. "Mostly in the clear." She winced. "Pretty sure in the clear."

I blinked, my heart stopping at just the thought of an unexpected run-in with Mike. While with Drew no less.

Really, Evie? You agreed to this. You wanted this, I reminded myself, though in my own defense, I had always imagined that Mike would find out about Drew and me from afar – probably in a tabloid, and definitely not in person. There was something a million times more nerve-wracking about debuting our coupledom to Mike in person. It gave me no wiggle room to act convincingly in love with Drew. I mean it was one thing to act passably couple-like in front of Hillary, but Mike? The one person in this world who knew me best?

It was a lot of pressure.

"Suck it up," Drew said the moment Hillary was gone. I flashed him a look.

"Excuse me?"

"You're pouting because you're afraid you can't convince Mike that you fell for someone else. But you're already in this, so suck it up and give it everything you've got."

"Are you recycling game day pep talks with me right now?"

"Yes. They work because ninety percent of all challenges are mental. If you believe in yourself, you can accomplish anything you want."

"That's something people say when they have multimillion dollar Nike contracts and zero percent body fat. That's basically as useless to me as 'believe in love' is to you."

"Well, the difference here is that you have no choice but to go with it, because you actually have to see Mike at some point."

"Of course. Whereas you never plan to fall in love because dying alone sounds so fun?"

Drew stared blankly at me. What little humor was left on his face disappeared, and suddenly I felt like I had crossed some line. I bit the inside of my lip, watching his broad shoulders stretch the seams of his shirt as he leaned slowly forward on the table.

"Listen." One gravelly word and he sent a chill up my spine. "If you want to talk about love, I can tell you honestly that the one and only thing I love in this world is baseball. I don't love people. I love this game. I love playing for this team. And right now, my career with them is on the line so if you don't think you can act like you belong a hundred percent to me, then you need to let me know right fucking now."

Jesus. I returned his stare, resentful of being spoken to like a child.

"Easy, okay? I can do it."

"Show me then."

"Show you what?"

"That you can play this role," he said. "Convincingly."

"What do you want me to do? Jump your bones right now? We're in the middle of a restaurant," I scoffed.

"Get creative."

I bristled at his completely humorless tone, but I also knew that between the two of us today, I was the one whose performance was slacking. And since I'd already vacated my tiny Long Island apartment and had zero intention of ever going back, I heaved a sigh, tossed back the last of my mimosa and slid out of the booth.

On with the show, I reminded myself, keeping my eyes locked on Drew as I rounded to his side and knelt facing him on the seat.

His stare was so unflinchingly serious that I wanted to roll my eyes.

Oh, I'll make you smile, asshole, I smirked as I put a hand on his muscled shoulder and leaned into his lips.

"Baby," I purred, managing to suppress my need to snort right in his face. A little thrill darted over my skin as I let my hand fall from his shoulder down to his chest. *Fuck, that's hard*, I noted as I leaned in close and bit my lip. "Please don't be mad." I rubbed his chest and took satisfaction in how I could feel him exhaling at my touch. "I promise I'm all yours, and if you don't believe me, I'll make it up to you when we get home tonight. Okay?" I finished softly, in the sweetest, breathiest voice I could muster.

Amusement gleamed in Drew's eyes. I could tell he was fighting it, but finally, the corners of his mouth curved up.

"And you'll wear the little maid costume with the garters, right?" he smirked.

I rolled my eyes.

"Totally. As long as you wear the male version of it and help me do my laundry."

"If you think this isn't getting me hard, you're wrong."

"Jesus," I snorted, pushing away from him.

Drew laughed as he caught my hand to pull me back but just as he did, I heard Hillary's gasp. I gasped myself, startled as I turned to find her standing at the other end of the room, staring at what I thought was us till I realized her gaze was going past my shoulder and out the window.

I looked over just in time to see someone turn away from our window.

He had clearly been looking in a second ago, but now he was storming toward the front door, and all I needed was a half-second glance at those brown curls and that red and blue polo to know exactly who he was.

It was Mike.

9

EVIE

I had to give Hillary credit for rushing outside and doing her best to convince him not to come in. She went as far as to tug on his arm and try to lead him across the street, but despite those efforts, it wasn't long before Mike was dragging her back to the front door of the restaurant, his neck and jaw so tight it looked like he might burst a capillary.

"Holy shit," I said, stunned and only vaguely aware of Drew's hands guiding me to sit next to him.

"Breathe." He was unfazed as he draped an arm over my shoulder. "We just did rehearsal and now it's showtime. I thought you were ready."

"I *am* ready," I insisted, close to believing it myself. I just hadn't expected this kind of wrath from Mike, and I was startled. It looked like I should be preparing myself for a war.

Of course, the Mike outside and the Mike that came in wound up being two totally different people.

I heard him hissing, "I'm fine. I'm *fine,*" to Hillary just as he came in. Then he jerked out of her grip and approached our table, wild-eyed and wearing a big, crazy smile I'd never seen on him before in my life.

What... on Earth.

He had tons of fake smiles in his arsenal after years of working PR, but this... this smile looked almost deranged in the way it twitched at the ends. Considering his completely unnatural expression, I was actually surprised that his voice came out sounding so passably cordial.

"Hi. Wow. Unless I'm mistaken, I do believe you're Drew Maddox," Mike said, holding out his hand and managing a chuckle, albeit a strained one in which he simply said the words "ha ha" without turning them into convincing laughter.

Oh God. This was already good.

"Hey man, nice to meet you." Lifting his muscled arm off my shoulder, Drew reached over my lap and shook Mike's hand. *Lord.* I felt an odd shriveling sensation when I noted how Mike's hand looked like that of a hairy child's in Drew's grip. "Sorry, I didn't catch your name."

"It's Michael. Michael Stuart," Mike said as I leaned in close to Drew. My heartbeat picked up as I caught Mike's eye while murmuring into Drew's ear.

"As in my ex, babe," I said, taking a sick pleasure in the way Mike flinched at the word "babe." "Hey," I offered Mike a polite smile while taking further pleasure in the way his wild, almost panicked eyes traveled in nervous ticks all over me. My face. My hair. My dress. His nostrils flared and most tellingly, The Vein made its appearance. It was notorious among our group of friends for coming out on Mike's broad forehead whenever he was worked up or pissed off, and today, it looked bigger than I'd ever seen it.

Still, he kept smiling that crazy smile.

"So. What's..." He trailed off, pointing at me then Drew with the clear intention of asking *what's going on here?* But instead, he cleared his throat and lamely asked, "You guys having lunch?"

I knew what was happening. If there was anything I knew about my ex, it was that he was prideful like none other. We didn't exactly come from a place known for manners or class, so growing up he overcompensated for it. In public and around others, he always carried himself with an almost WASP-y air – like we'd grown up boating and going to the country club on weekends, even though we definitely did not.

I saw his need for that image working double time now – especially as Drew smoothed his hand over my bare knee.

Oh God.

"Yeah, it's my one day off this month, and any time I can get off, I always spend with her," Drew said casually. I knew he was tracking Mike's gaze because the second Mike flicked his eyes down to his hand on my knee, he gave it such a dirty little squeeze that a burst of tingles shot up my thigh.

Holy fuck. I almost moaned on the spot.

"Right. Of course." Mike said tightly, visibly struggling to keep his eyes up as Drew began rubbing slow circles over my knee. My heart slammed in my chest. *God help me.* I did my best not to squirm. Meanwhile, Mike pulled at his collar. "One day off a month. I can't imagine living like that."

Drew chuckled. It was still smiles all around, but a palpable tension thickened the air.

"Yeah, but it's worth it to play for Major League Baseball. And ten years in the league – I'm used to it by now."

Yeah. Just another reminder that he's a pro athlete, Mike, and not a whiny little bitch baby.

"Well, I know Evie falls asleep at like, nine-thirty," Mike laughed, this time unable to hide his disparaging tone. "So I take it you two don't get to see much of each other."

"Oh, I stay up as late as I need to for him," I offered, my words coming out with much more of a sultry rasp than I intended. Drew cocked an eyebrow at me. *Oops.* Blame the impromptu leg massage he was giving me. It felt so damned good it made me feel almost drunk.

"That right?" Mike managed another chuckle, but I could tell from the way he fixed his unblinking stare on me that he was trying to ask me a million silent questions, all of them variations of *Evie, what the fuck is going on?* "Pretty sure I remember that when you sleep too late, you can't fall asleep at all."

"That used to be the case. But Drew's really, *really* good at tiring me out."

Fire lit Mike's eyes as Drew gave a low laugh of surprise.

"Easy, babe," he murmured as he straight up *rubbed my thigh* up and down. *God, oh God, oh my God.* I felt like I was about to combust just as Hillary glided over with a big, nervous smile.

"Guys! Gotta have dessert before you go!" she sang, catching my eye and mouthing *Oh my God, I'm so sorry* as she placed a Mont Blanc on the table. I mouthed back *don't worry* as she trilled, "I'll go get the check!"

Then she scurried off like a mouse, and it was insanely awkward as Mike just stood there and watched me take a bite.

"That's it?" he laughed at me. "Evie. Stop acting like you're not dying to inhale that. Mont Blancs are your favorite. I've seen you crush two in a sitting."

Good God. I could kill him.

"Yes, but I'm full," I said slowly, trying not to shoot him daggers so as to appear unfazed. But I was pretty sure I failed because the smuggest grin spread his lips, and he apparently found enough confidence to nudge Drew and laugh.

"Christ. You got her on an athlete's diet or what, Maddox?"

"Nah," Drew laughed, turning over to let his gaze drop down the front of my dress. "Definitely not. She knows that body's fuckin' perfect as is," he said in a low mutter before looking up at me.

Lord.

I did my best to return his eye contact without melting into the chair. With his hand still on my knee, it felt like an extremely real possibility. But luckily, Hillary soon returned, doing a silly dance and waving around a check that was just receipt paper on which she'd scrawled *on da house – thank you!*

"Hil!"

Drew and I spent a minute protesting against Hillary's staunch insistence, but the whole conversation wound up falling silent when Mike made a tacky joke about Drew being a millionaire who could afford to be charged double. After that thoroughly awkward moment, Drew tucked a wad of bills under his beer and we popped to our feet, hugging Hillary thank you and goodbye before waltzing outside to wait for the car.

"Wow. Okay. Breathe," I whispered to myself the second we got outside, still feeling the surging adrenaline rush for a job well done.

I did it.

I'd acted convincingly taken in front of Mike. I'd shown him that I'd moved on, *with Drew Maddox*, and I'd slipped away fast enough to leave him sputtering with questions that he'd be forced to mull over for a week before seeing me again at Hillary's family and friends dinner. Ideally, that week of confusion would give him some empathy for what he'd put *me* through after the out-of-nowhere breakup with no answers, and we'd wind up having a mature, productive chat about what the heck happened between us.

Despite Mike's surprise appearance, everything was still going according to plan, and it was perfect.

Until I realized I left something in the restaurant.

"Crap. I left my bag with all the returns in there," I blurted just as I was about to get into the car. My shoulders slumped as I turned around to look at the restaurant again. "Dammit. This totally ruins my grand exit."

Drew snorted.

"I'll go if you're scared."

"I'm not *scared*, I'm just – "

Ugh. I finished my sentence by simply marching back in, weaving quickly through the staff to reach my bag and then power-walking in my heels toward the door.

Of course, Mike caught me on my way out.

"Evie! Hey. Wait."

"Yes?" I turned around to find him stopping breathlessly in front of me, his eyes searching my face.

"Hey, what's... what's going on?" he asked. "What's this you and Drew situation? This is for real?"

I managed a confused smile.

"Yes? It's for real."

"Evie." Mike folded his arms and gave me a look. "It's me. Come on."

"Yes, I know you are, Mike. But what do you mean 'come on'?"

"You know what I mean."

"I don't. What is it?" I ground out, getting irritated. Mike threw his arms out incredulously and laughed big like I'd just made a great joke.

"Stop trying to fuck with me is what! Alright? Please. I know you're not with fuckin' *Drew Maddox*."

I squinted. "Then what do you think you just saw?"

"I don't know! You were just hanging out with Emmett and Aly and he just happened to come by. Right? 'Cause let's be real here, that man's a celebrity. He's famous. He's not the same as us."

"Us?" I repeated. I used to live for that word coming out of his mouth, but today I was sure I hated it. "And what exactly are we?" I asked carefully.

"I don't know," Mike sputtered defensively. Then he sneered. "But I can tell you what we're definitely not: *models*. And Drew Maddox could be dating models if he wanted to."

I stared at Mike, in awe of just how low he could go. It wasn't enough to dump your longtime girlfriend out of the blue, apparently. You also had to remind her, once she started dating again, that she wasn't a model.

"I mean am I lying?" he snorted.

"I'm leaving now," I said simply, letting just one more second pass before I reached for the door and marched the hell out.

Right away, I spotted Drew leaning leisurely against an SUV parked out front. The eyes of the street were staring at him as he stared at his phone. But the moment he heard the first angry clack of my heel on the pavement, he looked right up and frowned.

"Hey. You okay?"

"Yes. Just do me a favor." I was already breathless.

"What?" He stood up straight as I marched over to him.

"He's watching right now, so do something," I said hotly, heels clacking. "For him to see. Whatever you want, just do it now," I muttered fast.

Drew tilted his head warningly as if to ask if I was sure. But another second passed, and his gentleman window was gone. It was like a switch had flipped and suddenly his gaze was heavy, pinned to all the bouncing parts of my body as I stormed over to him in a fury.

The second I was close enough to grab his shirt he caught the nape of my neck and slammed his mouth over mine.

I squeezed the handful of cotton, pulling it away from his chest as his tongue collided against mine. Its roughness made my pussy instantly throb. When I felt his arm circle my waist, I let my knees go weak because his kiss was so instantly deep, hungry. Demanding. The way his tongue lashed and pulsed against me made it feel as if he'd been waiting forever to taste me, and I truly couldn't remember the last time my body felt this hot. And *wanted*.

"Touch me somewhere," I exhaled between kisses. "Put your hand on my – "

He cut me off with his palm flat on my ass, squeezing me so hard with those long fingers that I felt him spreading my pussy. *Oh my God.* Warmth pooled in my panties as he held his tight handful of me, refusing to let go as his shamelessly rough, greedy tongue stroked against mine.

Crap. This was going far beyond PDA. We'd surpassed three seconds at this point, but it felt too fucking good to stop.

"Trying to torture me?" Drew growled into my mouth, and only then did I realize that I was grinding my body against his – was it? Oh God, it was – his *enormous fucking erection*.

Holy shit.

I yanked away, forcibly removing myself from Drew's body. Once my brain caught up to my body and realized that he'd just had his swollen dick pressed up against my belly, I looked down and breathed out, "Fuck." There was no way to contain my shock because *good God*, it looked like a steel pipe was lying diagonally across his left thigh. My own thighs clenched at the sheer sight of his size, and I couldn't tear my eyes away till he grasped the front of my dress and jerked me back into his body.

"Drew!" I hissed as I felt every throbbing inch of him again. My mouth fell open when I tried pushing off and he tightened his grip, holding me right in place. "Are you really forcing me to rub up against your dick right now?" I whisper-yelled furiously.

He looked down his nose at me, lust mixed with irritation in that heavy-lidded gaze.

"No," he replied slowly, squeezing his handful of my dress. "I'm using you as a shield because I'm rock-hard in the middle of the street and half the sidewalk has their phones out. Which means if my dick winds up in the tabloids tomorrow, you owe me a fucking lap dance in that maid costume." He cocked his head with a smirk. "Deal?"

I blinked at him for several seconds. Despite my racing heart, I managed to give something of a laugh.

"Totally. Deal," I snorted, solely because this maid costume didn't actually exist. Of course that didn't stop me from fantasizing about it for the duration of the car ride, during which I sat in total silence while staring out the window because as much as I wanted to deny it, I was realizing something truly and severely annoying:

I kind of liked Drew Maddox.

He was an arrogant jock and everything I knew to avoid in a man, but I enjoyed his company. In fact, I was beyond attracted to him.

Which meant the next three months of resisting him were about to be chaos.

10

DREW

I woke up the next morning pissed at myself and the world –
mostly because I woke up harder than I'd ever been in my life,
and even in my dreams, I wasn't allowed to fuck Evie.

You idiot, Maddox. I really wasn't sure what I was thinking when I
agreed to this shit. I hadn't thought it through. I'd gone in blind and
banked on the fact that I wanted a championship more than anything
in the world. Anything pitted up against my need to win would lose.
No sex for three months? It wouldn't be easy but I could do it for sure.

At least that was what I had thought.

But that was before yesterday's "date" with Evie. It was before I
heard her breathy little fuck-me voice as she rubbed my chest and
called me baby. It was before I got to rub her naked thigh in front of
her idiot ex and feel every little twitch of her arousal right under my
palm. And it was definitely before I saw those perfect tits bounce
damned near out of her dress as she marched out of the restaurant,
all hot and breathless as she told me to do whatever I wanted to her.

Fuck, if she said those words to me now she'd be on my floor with
her ripped panties in my fist and my cock balls-deep in her pussy.

Do something. Whatever you want, just do it now.

I relived the exact words she murmured to me because it was

easily the hottest thing I'd ever heard in my life. And definitely a hell of a surprise.

I'd thought this whole thing was going to be a process. I was pretty damned sure that she was too hung up over that Matt asshole to get that into the act. But she proved me more than wrong, and now I was paying for it because this was morning wood like I'd never felt it before. It felt like a fucking weight on my abs once I freed it from my boxers, and it was so stiff I hardly had to touch it to feel sensation tingling from tip to root.

Fuck me.

If just the hard-ons Evie gave me felt this good then I needed to know what it was like to be inside her. I needed to feel her all wet and warm and stretched tight around my cock. I had already felt the heat of her pussy near my fingertips yesterday when I was squeezing her ass. That moment had been pure torture, so I didn't know why I was reliving it on repeat this morning. Though if it wasn't that, it was the cute little look on her face when she stared at my hard-on like she'd never seen a dick before in her life.

Long story short, I wanted to fuck her over every surface of my house, and I seriously couldn't imagine having to goddamned live with her soon. Just the thought of waking up this hard and knowing she was in some nightie down the hall made me want to quit this whole deal on the spot.

Of course, just thinking the word "quit" made the fucking Nike brain kick in and instantly hammer a million motivational quotes into my head. *Never quit. No pain, no gain. You are your own limit.*

So I jacked off.

I replayed the image of the sun beaming through her skirt and showing me the shape of her thighs. I remembered the softness of her skin as I was squeezing her knee. I pictured those perky tits bouncing in my face as she rode the hell out of my cock. I wound up coming faster than I probably ever had, but even after that, I was wound tight.

Still thinking of her.

You're a fucking madman.

I was convinced I'd be fine if she was just some knockout I met at a bar on the road. I could force myself to forget her. But I was stuck with Evie for the next three months, and it made me irrationally annoyed with her. I was legitimately bitter and pissed at her as I lay in bed fantasizing about what she looked like in her hotel room right now.

I imagined that tight body sleeping naked on a big bed. I imagined that tanned skin glowing against the white sheets she was probably tangled in.

The second I started fantasizing about that pussy again, I grabbed my phone.

> **ME:** Remind me why I can't sleep with her

I sent the text to Iain before thinking it through. I didn't have the ability to think anyway. The blood was taking its time to return to my head.

> **IAIN:** Aside from the fact that contracts are binding you promised me as both a client and a friend.
>
>   **ME:** We're friends?
>
>   **IAIN:** Ha.
>
>   **IAIN:** In case you forgot I was literally your only friend four years ago when you decided to wage a war against the whole league.

We were delving into subject matter I generally avoided or flat-out ignored when brought up, but I went for it today. At least it was making my dick go down.

> **ME:** To be fair the war was with just my team. I only wanted to see Los Angeles burn.
>
>   **IAIN:** Yeah well it doesn't look great for the league when you're trying to file a lawsuit against your own team. AFTER missing five weeks of your season with them because of the whole Lillard incident.

Fuck. I tossed my phone aside at the mention of Tim Lillard. There was my limit.

I couldn't think about Tim or any of the Lillards right now. It was a sore subject on a regular basis but my fight against L.A was still fresh in my mind, and it had started because of Cody Bryce taunting me about skipping Pattie's funeral.

Breathe, I told myself. Staring at the ceiling, I inhaled, exhaled and tried my best to remember all the shit Diaz said when he tried teaching me meditation.

It didn't work but on the bright side, I'd officially gone soft.

So there was that.

There was also the fact that I was three days from my next start. That meant that I had a bullpen session today with my pitching coach Lou Dickerson, and anytime I was on the mound, I wasn't thinking about anything but my delivery.

So I focused on that.

I got to the stadium and managed to clear my mind during stretches, which was followed by some good throwing in the bullpen, then shagging flies during BP. By the time the game started, I felt like myself again. I had some actual peace of mind, and it was a huge fucking relief.

Of course, that relief didn't last long because somewhere between the fifth and sixth innings, the sidewalk dick pics from yesterday's date hit the Internet.

I knew something was up when a couple of drunk girls sitting over the dugout got booted for yelling at me to fuck them with that big dick. Just minutes after that, Ty pointed at the curvy blonde along the first base line that all the guys had been staring at all game.

Apparently she had written a new message on the back of her sign. Originally, it had been "MARRY ME MADDOX." Now it was "WOW DREW!!! SHOW ME THAT BIG BAT!"

Since phones were banned in the dugout, the guys took turns disappearing into the clubhouse to look at the pictures and headlines about my giant fucking cock, because there was nothing homoerotic about that.

They thought they were being slick, but even if Ty didn't tell me, I'd have noticed. And since I did, I chose not to tune everyone out like I usually did during the game. As much as I knew I'd regret it, I listened to every fucking word the guys muttered under their breaths about Evie. I thought I'd find their stupid comments at least vaguely amusing. That was generally what I felt when they ranked and rated all my conquests like a bunch of middle school girls.

But as they talked about Evie, all I felt was my blood boiling in my veins.

"I say the tits are real. And she's gotta have a magic pussy to have Maddox carrying shopping bags."

"Magic mouth too. You saw those lips?"

"Yeah. Imagine what they look like after sucking dick for a good ten, fifteen – "

"Watch it," I barked, on my feet before I knew it. Diaz was in front of me in no time, wordlessly walking me back to my seat as I glared over his shoulder at Watt and Brewer. Watt held his hands up in surrender.

"Fuck. D, I didn't mean any disrespect. I'm sorry."

"Same. I didn't know you could hear."

"I can hear everything and if I hear my girl's name out of your dirty fucking mouth again I'm going to put you both on the DL."

Every head in the dugout was turned at this point, and annoyingly, I saw Diaz signal to our manager that everything was fine. Like he was my keeper or something.

It was a briefly heated moment, but dugout or clubhouse, they happened. Tempers flared but eventually, things got squashed and it was no different this time around. Watt and Brewer came by to apologize separately, normalcy was restored and I told myself I had just been putting on a damned good show just now.

And that was it.

Because once my blood simmered, the idea of getting that fired up over some girl I barely knew was disturbing, and I didn't want to believe that it happened. I needed to know that I could keep the focus I had every day at the stadium, especially during a game. Even when I wasn't starting, I was usually watching every at-bat and every delivery on every damned pitch. But today, I'd barely paid attention to shit and I was ready to give up, because the second I got my mind off Evie again, Diaz came around.

"You serious? You're seeing someone?" he asked. He could barely hide the fact that he was fucking glowing. I looked at him then back at the field. Technically not an answer but he still gave me a pat on the back. "Proud of you, brother. Can't let that L.A shit hang over you forever."

Then he left before I could respond, which I was grateful for because while I wasn't mad at Diaz, I really didn't need him mentioning L.A. I was already completely on edge and wound up tight over this Evie situation. I just needed a fucking break from my own brain.

It was for that reason that I was actually relieved when, an inning later, Ty came loping over with a big, dumb grin on his face. At least I knew he never had anything important to talk about.

"Yo." He plopped his ass down next to me. "I take it since you're finally wifed up, I can call dibs on your tittalicious blonde down the third base line," he said, nodding at the girl with the "show me your big bat" sign.

"Go nuts," I said.

"Nice. So you coming out tonight? Or is your crazy ass banned from nightlife now that you got a nice girl at home?"

I leaned my elbows on my knees as I stared out at the game. Ty was joking but I technically *was* banned from nightlife. Iain made me swear it off, save for "a few special occasions," and while he probably didn't count day two of the contract as a special occasion, I did because I suddenly felt the urgent need to blow off steam. I answered Ty the second he gave up on getting a response from me and started leaving.

"Yeah, I'm coming out," I said.

He spun right around.

"Yeah?" He pumped his fist. "*Hell* yes, dude. It's gonna be fuckin' tight. I can feel it in my *bones*, brother!"

He said that literally every time we went out, or any time we were about to eat at a new restaurant for that matter, but I prayed he was particularly right tonight. I sincerely hoped that wherever we went tonight and whatever we got into, it would be a deserving last hurrah for me.

Because if I was about to risk getting pictures taken of me doing all the shit the Empires didn't want me to do, then it had better be worth it.

~

AS IT TURNED OUT, it wasn't worth it.

I had stood barely a minute outside the club with Ty before finding myself mobbed by the girl with the "big bat" sign and all her screechy friends. From what I could tell, they were wasted and there were already cameras flashing as they basically rubbed up on me, posing on my body like I was a fucking stripper pole.

Goddammit. It was too early for this shit, and it was giving me nothing but anxiety so it wasn't long before I was peeling women off my body and ducking back into my car. Once I had the door shut, I texted Evie to come meet me. It took about five minutes but she eventually replied that she'd need "a minute" to get ready and find a dress.

I thought nothing of it because I thought a minute meant a minute. But apparently, it meant damned near an hour-and-a-half.

> **ME:** Jesus Evie
> **ME:** I don't understand. Are you making the damned dress?
> **EVIE:** Almost there I said!
> **ME:** You said that twice already
> **EVIE:** And I meant it twice!!

Any texts after that went ignored and I wound up sitting in the back of the car for another twenty minutes, killing time by checking scores around the league. But just as my patience ran up again and I whipped out my phone, she texted me first.

EVIE: I'm here

"Finally," I groaned, climbing out of the car. I stretched my shoulders and massaged the back of my neck as I stepped onto the sidewalk, and just as a large group passed in front of me, I spotted Evie.

She was turned around, talking to the bouncer and as my eyes took her in, I felt my jaw drop.

Fuck. Me.

My hand slid slowly off the back of my neck as I soaked in the sight of her wearing a black dress, a lace choker and a ponytail so high and bouncy I wanted to wrap it around my hand while I spanked her all night. She deserved it for the way she stood all cute – hip cocked and skirt stretched all tight over that gorgeous ass. *Christ. That ass.* There was no way in hell she was wearing panties under there. I'd bet anyone my entire fucking apartment that she wasn't.

Suddenly, I forgot about the hour-and-a-half wait it took to get to this point because the view in front of me now was something I could stare at all night. I was pretty sure it didn't get better than this.

But then she turned around.

11

EVIE

B*reathe, Evie. Lock those knees, girl.*
 I needed the reminder as I stared at Drew Maddox staring at me. He looked scary good in a crisp white button down with his hair still kind of wet. Did wet hair make me picture him in the shower? Sure did. Did I need that image in my head when I was already breathless from just the way he looked at me?

Nope.

But I'd asked for this.

Admittedly, I got dolled the fuck up for this impromptu hang, but who wouldn't? In all likelihood, I was going to be photographed by strangers and paparazzi all night. I'd already seen the way it happened yesterday morning, and I could only assume the cameras came out faster at clubs and bars where it was darker, and people were drunker, more brazen.

Also, today's tabloid pieces on yesterday's date had quickly piqued an interest in me, which meant tonight, some gossip hounds might actually recognize my face. And *that* meant I was going to be watched and scrutinized way more than I'd been just yesterday.

So why not dress up like crazy?

I don't know. Maybe to avoid moments where he looks at you like this and you wonder why not just fuck him for fun since the world already thinks you are?

Also a valid point.

Because while I'd been dealing with male attention for about fifteen years, nothing – and I mean nothing – in the world could prepare me for the way Drew was looking at me now.

He stood so still but that wolfish stare drank me in. His enormous body was completely unmoving as those green eyes traveled shamelessly up my legs then to my hips before getting caught on my breasts. I couldn't help but feel a thrill for the fact that I'd fully captivated something so big and powerful. It made me feel objectively sexy, which was far different than feeling normal sexy – and for all the confidence I had, it was definitely something I'd never felt before in my life.

"Hi," I said once I couldn't take the heat of his stare any longer. Drew looked up at me.

"Hi."

"So... are you going to take me inside or what?" I asked. I cocked my head when he just blinked, seeming to have forgotten that that was why I was here. When he finally shook his head and offered no further detail, I frowned. "What? Why not?"

"Because there's no way in hell I'm letting the guys go near you right now."

I bit my lip because I was sure there was a compliment in there. Somewhere.

"Well excuse me, but I didn't get this dressed up for nothing," I said.

"I know you didn't," Drew muttered, returning his eyes to my cleavage as I crossed my arms. I uncrossed them.

"And I definitely didn't get dressed up solely for your viewing pleasure, Mr. Maddox."

He groaned with irritation, finally sounding awake.

"Yes, thank you. I know that."

"So?"

He kept his stare fixed on me for two hard seconds. Then he nodded behind him.

"Just get in the car."

WHATEVER SEXPOT IMPRESSION I'd made on Drew outside the club before was swiftly annihilated once we arrived at our next location. But I didn't mind and I apologized for nothing.

We wound up going to The Roof on 5ᵗʰ, which was, unsurprisingly, a rooftop bar on Fifth Ave. I'd heard of it before and I was already excited to go, but when we actually rode the elevator all the way to the top, and the doors opened, I almost burst into tears.

"Omigod," I gasped because it was so unreal. Presented before me was the closest, most breathtaking view of the very top of the Empire State Building. It was like being an arm's reach from the moon. It was right next to this roof, and it glowed so magnificently close that I swore I could walk across the balcony, hold out my hand and actually touch it.

"What's going on? You alright?" Drew turned around.

"Yes. No. I don't know. I'm having a moment."

He stared for a second.

"Jesus," he said when he realized he wasn't going to get me to move.

But come on – this was surreal. I'd grown up looking at pictures of the New York skyline, obviously, and I still had a beloved, framed Polaroid I took of this building when I first came to see it in person.

I was fourteen years old. I'd just had the worst fight of my life with Kaylie, and Mom told me to sleep somewhere else for the night. When I arrived a sniveling mess at Mike's house, he announced that he was going to turn my worst day ever into the best, and took me on my first trip to Manhattan.

Our first stop had been the Empire State Building.

"Alright, enough." Drew got my attention when he took my hand in his. "If you're my girlfriend you need to act like I've taken you on a date before, because right now it looks like I kept you locked up for the past six months and just let you out for the first time tonight."

I laughed instead of retorting because I knew it was a hundred percent true.

"Geez. Sorry, okay? I just never thought I'd see the Empire State Building this up close and personal."

"Tourists and middle school field trips do it every day, so dream bigger."

"Eff you, dickhead."

"Also, cursing me off loses its edge when you say 'eff' instead of fuck."

"Fine. In that case *fuck*. You," I enunciated. Drew eyed me.

"Yeah. I wish."

The remark made my lashes flutter, but it was said in such passing that I really didn't have time to react before a hand shot out on our way to the table, viciously smacking Drew's side to get his attention. I startled for all of a second before I looked at who the arm belonged to and recognized that thick, dark hair and big, mischievous smile.

"Emmett!" I shrieked, bursting out of Drew's grasp to throw my arms around Emmett's neck. "Oh my God, dude, tell me Aly's here with you," I whispered desperately, though I could see he was sitting with a bunch of men in suits. Definitely clients. Who were all staring at me.

"She's not, I'm sorry," Emmett whispered back with a laugh. "How you holding up with the asshole though?"

"Um." I blinked, unsure if Emmett knew about the false nature of Drew and my romance. "He's... tolerable?"

"Alright." Drew cut in with two hands on my hips. Pulling me back against his chest, he whispered in my ear. "For fuck's sake, don't bend over like that. Your tits are falling out and those assholes are staring down your dress."

"Oh, and you've decided that you're the controlling type who dictates what I wear and how I act?" I hissed.

"Trust me, I'm pretty fucking pleased with what you're wearing, but there's a difference between showing you off and letting guys eye-bang you right in front of me," Drew muttered hotly. My eyes narrowed at him.

"Fair," I bit out.

"Thank you," he grumbled.

"Alright, you two," Emmett chuckled, still turned around in his chair. He cocked an eyebrow at Drew. "So you been dodging my calls or what, Maddox? If we're fighting, you never gave me official word."

"I don't have time to fight with you, Emmett, I'm just a busier man than even you are."

"Clearly. Ty just texted that you were at Godsend with him ten minutes ago then disappeared. Should I tell him that you're here?"

"Only if you want me to throw you off this roof."

"I don't think you should risk straining the pitching arm. I noticed your velocity was down your last start."

"Good to know you were watching so closely. Should we let Aly know about your creepy obsession with me?"

"Fuck off," Emmett grinned. "I'll meet up with you two after I wrap up with these guys."

"Please don't," Drew said before sliding a hand onto my back and whisking me off. I stared up at him.

"Jesus, what's up with dude friends? Why do you guys love talking to each other like you hate each other?"

"Maybe we do."

"What? Are you mad at my best friend's boyfriend?" I asked defensively. "Because on behalf of my best friend, I take offense to that."

"I'm not mad at him. Aly's one of your best friends. Emmett's one of mine," Drew said without a hint of emotion, giving the canned answer like I was some reporter he didn't want to do an interview with.

I kept my eyes narrowed on him as we followed a hostess across the roof and up a small flight of steps to a VIP area. Ivy-covered partitions provided us a decent amount of privacy, but that didn't stop people from passing by our section with their phones stealthily positioned to snap quick photos. I noticed two people do that before we even sat down next to each other.

"So you and Emmett are cool?" I asked once the hostess left – though obviously not without a last lip-biting peek at Drew. Couldn't blame her. He looked sexy as sin tonight and as screwed up as it was, he was particularly hot when he was angry.

"Emmett and I are cool," Drew said, measuring his words. "He knew I was at risk of being traded as far back as last year and told just Iain instead of me, but aside from that, we're cool."

"Oh. So what, now you don't trust him either?"

"I never trusted him or anyone in the first place, so nothing has changed. We're good."

Jesus. I blinked with surprise as I watched Drew's hard eyes study the menu.

"Well... his brother owns the team you play for so I'm sure he wanted to tell you, but there was just a conflict of interest," I offered.

"Of course. Family first," Drew said in a sardonic tone that reminded me of the fact that 'family first' didn't ring true with him. After all, he'd mentioned that his family treated him like an ATM.

Damn. I chewed my lip through the silence that followed, hoping that Drew had at least *someone* in this world that he trusted fully. I mean I didn't trust my own family, and I obviously didn't trust Mike anymore, but at least I had Aly. She would stick by me through anything. I knew that, and I quietly cherished her as I studied Drew.

"Oh, wait, this is the food menu," I finally said to break the silence.

"Perfect. Let's exchange."

"Didn't you just eat dinner?" I laughed as he eagerly swapped menus with me.

"Yeah, but that was over an hour ago."

"Oh my God. You and your food."

"Yeah, me and my need to nourish my body to stay alive. So crazy," he muttered though he peered up with amusement when I giggled. "What?"

"Nothing. I'm more so laughing at myself."

"Why?"

"Just remembering something from when I was a kid."

"What is it?"

I looked up from my menu to find Drew's undivided attention on me.

"You really want to hear a story from my childhood?" I asked dubiously.

"I thought that was implied when I said 'what is it.'"

"Okay, relax, smart ass, and it's not a good story, it's just that when I was younger..." I trailed off, chewing my lip when I realized I didn't actually want to say this aloud. It was probably only funny in my head. "Actually, I forget what I was saying. I'm all drunk."

"You didn't drink yet."

"Maybe I drank at home."

Drew caught my jaw and pulled my face to his. My heart stopped in my chest as he tilted my mouth up, holding my lips an inch from his.

"No." His thumb stroked my jaw as he breathed me in. "You didn't." He lifted his gaze from my lips to my eyes and held it there for one painfully hot second. But in a flash, he released me and returned to being blunt. "Now tell me the story."

Just like that, his attention returned to the menu – as if he hadn't just done something ridiculously freakin' intimate that required time for me to catch my breath.

Or maybe that wasn't super intimate and you're just overthinking things? I thought before promptly catching myself. *Okay, stop. It's way too early in the night to get this deep in your head.*

"Um... yeah, anyway. Where was I again?" I mumbled to myself, pretending to casually scan my menu though I was honestly too flustered to read shit. "Oh right. Long story short, when my sister Kaylie and I were kids, we thought that once you were an adult and you stopped growing, that meant you didn't have to eat anymore. We literally thought that eating just ceased to be a necessity once you turned like, twenty-five."

Drew looked up again, eyeing me with feigned seriousness.

"So you guys were held back a few grades, huh."

"Shut up!" He grinned big when I burst out laughing. "Asshole. If you must know, we were like four and eight when we thought this and it was only because my mom would make us grilled cheeses every day and just wait around to eat our crusts. And when we asked why she didn't make one for herself, she said she only wanted a snack and adults don't need to eat like little kids do," I said, my smile slowly faltering as I finished the story. *Okay, yeah. Definitely less funny said aloud,* I nodded awkwardly as I peered up at Drew. I could see the humor in his eye flickering away as he looked at me and put two and two together.

Yep.

I grew up dirt poor and my mom was definitely hungry. She just couldn't afford to eat and feed her kids too.

Well, hello, buzzkill, I scolded myself as I blurted, "Anyway," and tried to think of a topic change. *Come on, come on, hurry up,* I desperately begged myself while coming up painfully empty.

Drew surprised me with a reassuring hand on my knee.

"So tell me about the Empire State Building. What's up with your weird little obsession?" he said, returning his casual gaze back to the menu.

I blinked for a second of confusion, but then a little smile wiggled onto my lips. I knew Drew couldn't care less about this story – he was just giving me an out from the last subject we'd touched on, since it clearly had me so flushed and embarrassed. It was a tiny gesture, but still a lot more than I'd ever expected from him.

"It's also a boring story," I warned.

"Tell me."

"Well, this was just the number one stop on our first ever visit to New York. We got off an Amtrak at Penn Station, walked to the Empire State and took about a dozen Polaroids from different angles – which was a huge deal because Polaroid film was *not* cheap."

"And by 'we' you mean you and Matt."

"Mike."

"Sure. Where are you from originally?"

"Belfield, Massachusetts. Don't Google it."

"Why not?" Drew snorted.

"Because it sucks. We called it Hellfield."

"That's just how every kid feels about their hometown."

"No, trust me. My hometown is depressing enough to be featured in like, two different documentaries on Netflix."

Drew looked up with genuine interest. "Really. About what?"

"Uhh." My voice was higher pitched than usual as I paused and realized I'd wound up on another topic I liked to avoid. "Opioids," I finally said.

Drew's eyebrows went up and stayed there.

"Oh."

Another silence. *God.* I let it stay quiet for all of two-and-a-half seconds before clapping my hands together.

"Anyway! My turn to ask a question," I declared, grinning at the instant wariness on Drew's face. "I want to know why the heck the Empires are even looking to trade the best pitcher in baseball."

"It's complicated."

"That's not a real answer."

"Well, it's the only answer you're getting."

"Fine. I'll just Google you."

Drew looked up with surprise. "You haven't done that yet?"

"No. I said yes to this whole thing so quickly that I didn't get a chance to, and after, I was kind of too scared to do it and see exactly what the heck I'd gotten myself into," I admitted, making Drew's eyes crinkle as he laughed. Ugh. So cute.

"Good choice. There are things that are true, but there's also a ton of bullshit out there," he said just as the waitress came to take our orders.

I ordered a cocktail before I realized Drew was ordering an entire bottle of champagne, but oh well. Not the worst problem to have. If anything, the bigger dilemma was how to deal with the fact that as he started ordering and chatting with the waitress, his hand began unconsciously rubbing my knee.

And considering I had no panties on under this dress, I was pretty much dying.

Thank God my skirt, albeit tight as hell, stretched down to just above my knee. Also, once the drinks arrived, I was able to calm my nerves. Conversation flowed for a good twenty minutes after but then we reached a point where Drew's eyes drifted off as I was talking about something, and suddenly he said, "Hey. No Googling me. Alright?"

I blinked. "Why?"

"Because it's not fair. I can't Google you back. It's not a level playing field."

"I wouldn't care if you Googled me."

"Because none of your personal information is out there. It's all work-related."

"Fine. Then you can ask me three personal questions right now and I promise that I'll Google you as seldom as possible," I said. Drew smirked.

"Five questions and you Google me once while I'm present."

I thought about it for a second.

"Okay. Deal." I knocked back the rest of my cocktail. "And there's your insurance that I'll be completely truthful."

"Great, then I'll start with a hardball. How the hell did Mike end up with a girl who looks like you?"

I blinked, surprised by the question and actually, kind of insulted.

"I realize you're somewhat complimenting me here, and I promise I feel no need to defend Mike right now, but considering I was dating him for nine years, digs at him are also digs at *my* taste and life choices," I pointed out.

"Yes. I'm aware of that."

Dick.

"Of course you are," I snorted as I gave myself a tall pour of champagne. "Okay, well now that we've established how comfortable you are with insulting me, here's my answer: I'm from a place that's listed as one of the most white trash towns in Massachusetts. Every woman in

my family had a baby by the time she was eighteen, and when my eigh-
teenth birthday came and went, my mom and grandma literally threw
me a 'no baby shower' with decorations from the Dollar General. If
you're thirty years old from Belfield and you have a job at the 7-11 a few
towns over, you're considered a pretty huge success. And I'm pretty sure
I would've been that hugely successful 7-11 clerk if it weren't for the fact
that Mike told me we were allowed to dream bigger."

I took a break from my ramble to take a gulp of the champagne I
would've never dreamed of even holding in my hands when I was
younger.

"So he got you out of there is what you're saying," Drew said as he
watched me knock back most of my champagne in one big slug.
"Easy," he said, taking my glass and holding it away from me. "We
don't have to talk about this if it upsets you."

"It doesn't. I'm over it," I said, and with all this bubbly in my
system, I actually believed it. "I'm fine talking about it. Maybe in that
sense, I'm bigger and badder than you are."

"I think you're just drunker than I am."

"Yeah, well. You probably don't even get drunk. You're like... ten
feet tall and three hundred pounds of muscle," I mumbled as Drew
smirked.

"Six-three, two-twenty, but yeah. Ninety-eight percent muscle as
of the last physical."

"Jesus, really?"

"Yes."

Ugh, of course, I thought, letting my eyes dip down his front as he
leaned back in his seat. God, those huge shoulders. Those abs. What
did they look like under there? I was dying to know.

"Stop."

"What?"

I didn't even realize I was biting my nail till Drew removed my
hand from my mouth and placed it in my lap.

"You look like you want to get fucked when you do that and I'm
entirely too willing, so you need to stop while I still have enough
blood in my brain to think straight."

Oh... kay.

Wow.

His words shot straight between my legs and I wound up staring speechlessly as his eyes devoured everything from my squirming thighs to the stunned look on my face. I felt enough like his prey without even hearing his next question.

"When was the last time Mike even fucked you?"

Shit.

My cheeks burned at both the question and the answer, which was four months ago. And before that one time, it had been six. He caved to my crying over his lack of affection, humped me for about ten minutes and then rolled over without either of us coming. The worst part was that he faked his orgasm and when I asked if he really came, he said, "No. Can't we just go to sleep though?"

Oh God.

I covered my face. "Skip," I said.

"What?"

"That question."

"That's not allowed."

"Four months ago. Next."

I avoided his stare of pure disbelief. But just because I wasn't looking at it didn't mean I couldn't feel its heat on my skin.

"When was the last time you came more than once in a night?"

"Are you really asking me that right now?"

"Yes."

"You're an asshole."

"We've established this."

I glared for several seconds.

"If you must know, I literally can't even think of my answer."

"Too long ago to recall?"

"Yes! Maybe! Who cares? Why do you need to know?" I demanded.

"Because the idea of you not being properly fucked is driving me crazy right now."

His answer had me speechless again but this time, the intensity of his stare also had me breathless like I'd just run a five-minute mile.

He's a player, an asshole and you'll regret it, I answered myself before I could ask why I shouldn't just fuck him. But even knowing that, it was hard to ignore the tension heating up the air between us, making it feel almost too thick to breathe in.

"It's been awhile," I finally said, trying to sound unaffected as he dragged his heavy stare up my legs. "And you have two questions left."

"I know."

"I think you should save them for another night."

"No thanks. Hottest unfulfilled fantasy?"

I rolled my eyes at him.

"Getting a five-figure tax return."

He returned my eye-roll.

"Sexual," he clarified.

"Pass, because I know what happens when I answer this," I said, pinning my stare on him. "Whatever I say I want, you're just going to imply that you could do that for me right here, right now because you love making me nervous, so let's just bypass that whole self-indulgent process and say yes, I've been sexually frustrated before and yes, you could probably make me come very, very hard. Much harder than Mike ever did," I said hotly, wondering when the hell Drew's lips had made it so close to mine. His arm was draped over the back of my seat as he hovered over my body, heat smoldering in his green eyes as he stared at me.

I didn't even know what I was feeling.

Kiss me. Or don't. Fuck you, I thought, my brain a mess of confusion as I heard a stampede of footsteps come clamoring our way. I frowned, watching the heat in Drew's stare become fire as he slid his eyes over my shoulder. Suddenly, he was shaking his head at something.

"The fuck, Ty," he growled just as a voice boomed behind me.

"Found ya! Hope we didn't interrupt anything."

You did, but thank God for that, I thought.

And when I turned around, it was his whole damned team.

12

DREW

Thanks to Emmett's tip that I was here with Evie, Ty had not only come but had brought half the team. It was chaos, the staff was quickly overwhelmed and it wasn't long before Emmett suggested we take the party to some lounge at one of his new hotels.

I had zero plans of going but Evie was apparently eager to get the hell away from me. Much to my irritation, she did two shots with Ty before following the group without hesitation, and because I wasn't leaving her alone with any one of those animals, I wound up with them on the nineteenth floor of some new, overly swanky and pretentious hotel in the Meatpacking District. The massive lounge or bar – or whatever it was we were at – had six rooms, all of which I lost Evie in at least once.

Then again, I was pretty sure she was actively ducking me.

"You're playing the role of dedicated partner much better than I thought you would," Emmett said when he found me scanning the crowd for her in one of the bigger rooms.

"When I picture Watt or Brewer so much as touching her shoulder, it makes me want to slam someone's head in a wall," I explained before my brain did a playback of his words. *Playing the role of dedicated partner*. I shot Emmett a weird look. "By the way, I don't recall telling you that this whole deal was fake. And Iain said he had no plans to, either."

"Aly told me, fucknut. She doesn't keep secrets from me."

"Adorable. I'm sure I'll be hearing wedding bells soon."

"In a year, probably. I'm proposing to her next month."

I snapped my head over to him. He already had his phone out to show me a picture of the giant fucking ring.

"Christ. That's nice." I had to give it to him. "You're serious then."

"Yeah. Which means you're in for a lifetime of stink-eye from my wife."

"What? Why? Aly loves me."

"She won't after this shit between you and her best friend blows up in all our faces."

"What the hell are you talking about?" I had no clue but I was preemptively pissed.

"Both of you are already deeper in this than you're supposed to be. That much was made clear by the cute little whisper fight you had after my clients checked her out."

"Yeah, nice clients by the way. Literally saw one guy tilt his head to get a better look down her dress."

"I'm sorry. Trust me, I'm not a huge fan of those guys either, but you don't make money by doing business with just the people you like."

"Sounds like something your brother would say."

"It is. Speaking of Julian – "

"Let's not."

" – I know you're pissed because you think I heard about the trade thing from him and decided to just gossip about that shit with Iain instead of telling you. But the reality is that I spent the past year sweating my ass off for you and doing everything in my power to either buy time or change Julian's mind."

"I'm honored. And thanks for the visual of your swamp ass."

"You're welcome. Also, I didn't tell you because I thought I could fix things before you found out and fucking killed someone over it."

"Got it. Thanks for the vote of confidence, by the way."

"What? I never know what's going to make you black out and damned near put someone in a coma, so I played it safe," Emmett said, looser-lipped than usual thanks to whatever the hell he was drinking. I knew he was making a rare reference to the Tim Lillard incident, and the fact that I never told him why it went down. The only people who knew about that shit were Iain and Tim himself. And I guess Pattie before she died.

"Man, you really know how to brighten my mood," I muttered just as my eyes spotted something well across the room – the bounce of that honey-colored ponytail. Jesus. Apparently, just the swing of her hair from twenty yards away could make my dick twitch in my jeans.

"Well, if it makes you feel any better I want you over Julian for my best man."

My head whipped over to Emmett.

"Fuck off," I blurted. "Now he's really gonna trade me."

He laughed.

"Nah, he's all lost in Dad-land right now. He's so wrapped around Luna's finger he'll barely notice that I passed him up," Emmett said. "So what do you say? Are you in or what?"

I didn't have to think twice.

"Of course I am, fucknut," I grinned, before pushing off the bar to rush toward Evie. She'd been on the phone since I spotted her a minute ago, but I could tell from the expression on her face that the conversation was taking a bad turn.

And that had me suspecting that she was talking to Mike.

"Who is it? Give me the phone," I muttered to her as she hastily wiped the corner of her eye, mouthing *hold on* before walking away from me.

I followed, catching up with her just as she hissed, "And you don't think *you* made me feel hurt and embarrassed?"

That was all I needed to hear.

"Drew!" Evie gasped as I grabbed the phone from her and held it to my ear.

"What's up, Mike, do me a favor – unless it's to apologize for all the shit you pulled on her, don't call my girlfriend again. And while we're at it, keep my name out of your mouth. Sound good?" I let him stammer a string of non-words before cutting him off. "Cool. 'Night."

"*Drew!*" Evie hissed the moment I hung up. She jumped in an attempt to grab her phone but I held it over her head. "What the hell, Drew!"

"What did he say to you?"

"Nothing! Give my phone back!"

"Look, we've both had more than a few drinks tonight, and the last person you need to be talking to is this asshole who's going to get you so riled up you might say the wrong thing in front of him."

"You think I'm going to spill to him about our whole deal? I'm not *wasted*, Drew, and I don't need you to fight my battles!"

"I'm not trying to fight your battles. I just want to know what he said to get you this upset. You were crying – I can see that," I said heatedly, my observation instantly stopping Evie mid-reach for her phone. She crossed her arms and puckered her lips with defiance.

"I wasn't crying," she lied with such insistence that I actually saw her tears dry up on the spot. *Damn.* Impressive.

"Fine then, you weren't. But tell me what he said." I waited two seconds and when she didn't answer, I waded through all the noise in my head, which was mostly thoughts about how goddamned sexy she looked all mad at me. It took awhile, but I finally remembered what I heard her saying on the phone before I grabbed it. "He said I would hurt and embarrass you?" I asked, feeling my blood heat up again.

She chewed the corner of her mouth, making that plump bottom lip look even plumper.

"Yes."

"Alright. What else?"

"That being with you would degrade me."

"*Degrade* you?" Jesus. "What else?"

Evie heaved a sigh.

"That you don't care about me. And you don't know how to make me laugh."

"Yeah? Well, fuck this guy," I said, turning around.

"What are you doing?"

"I'm calling him."

"No you're not," she snorted. But as I started dialing and walked away, her tone changed. "Wait. Drew? No you're not!"

She dashed after me into the next room, which had a dimly lit dance floor and an empty table in the corner.

"Drew!" Evie hissed, reaching for her phone in every direction that I held it. Frustration pinched her eyebrows tight but once I did some behind-the-back knockoff NBA move, she burst out laughing. "Drew, stop! You look so stupid right now, I'm just trying to save you here."

"Oh, really."

"Really," she snorted as she reached around my body to grab her phone from behind. She fell onto me as I sat down on the chair, and her mouth fell open when I suddenly held two empty hands up. "Drew Maddox! If you're sitting on my phone, I swear to God..."

"You swear to God what, tough girl?"

"If you break it, you're gonna pay for it," she said threateningly.

"Well, that could be a problem. I don't think I can afford that."

Evie narrowed her eyes at me for a few seconds. I expected an eye roll from her but what I got instead was a sexy smirk and a breathy little laugh that went straight to my cock.

My jaw tightened. Somehow, it took till that moment for me to realize she was straddling me. I knew it had only just hit her too because we fell suddenly quiet as we eyed each other, and she bit her grin, shaking her head when I caved to my temptation and peered down between our bodies.

Goddamn. Her thighs were parted wide over my lap and stretching the limits of that tight skirt. I was in a trance as I watched the fabric roll up slowly, slowly, treating me to more and more of that smooth, soft skin. I gripped the edges of my seat in an effort to keep from ripping her clothes clean off her body, and I was painfully turned on as it was without even remembering my observation from earlier tonight.

That she wasn't wearing any panties.

Fuck.

I actually held in a groan as I processed the fact that Evie was sitting in my lap wearing a thin, rolled-up skirt and no fucking panties underneath.

"Get off," I said suddenly.

She blinked.

"Oh." Her voice was startled, borderline hurt as she moved to get off me. "Okay," she said defensively.

But the second I felt her weight lift off me, I growled and slammed her back down by the hips. She gasped but let me capture her mouth with mine.

And from there, we lost all control.

As my tongue swept ferociously through her mouth, Evie rubbed her hot pussy against me, grinding so hard in my lap that I had to hold her skirt in place. It had shot up like a rubber band on her perfect thighs, and I'd yanked it down fast before anyone could see a thing.

And since "anyone" included me, that right there was torture like I'd never felt it before.

I wanted Evie naked and yet I was covering her up. The irony would've amused me if my blood weren't pumping with such merciless force to my cock that I thought I might explode. That bouncing ass. That chokered neck. That swinging goddamned ponytail. There were a million places my hands would rather be than stationed at the edge of her skirt, but I kept them there because that was the responsible thing to do, and apparently I was a responsible fucking person now.

"You're so hard," she breathed, rubbing harder against my dick.

"I wonder why," I growled as she whimpered something inaudible.

I didn't ask her to repeat it because as much as I wanted to hear it, I really didn't, and I was already on my last ounce of self-control. But as she stroked my clothed cock with her barely clothed pussy, she whispered it again.

"I want to feel it, Drew."

"Don't fucking say that."

"I really want to."

"You're drunk," I hissed.

"I'm not, you prick, I'm just wet," she hissed back, squeezing handfuls of my shirt as she kissed me hard. I was lightheaded when she pulled away. "You tortured me all night by making me talk about sex, so put your money where your mouth is, Drew, and fuck me. Make me come."

Christ.

Make me come.

I heard those words and apparently blacked the hell out, because the next thing I knew, I was a madman stalking Evie out the front doors of the hotel. My car was already waiting and ready to take us back to my place. I already knew which couch I wanted to bend her over before I buried every inch of me inside her.

But all I needed was to see her slightly trip on the sidewalk before she got in the car, and suddenly, I stopped in my tracks.

Fuck.

Stop.

My pulse hammered in my ears as I froze in the middle of the sidewalk and stared at Evie waiting for me in the backseat, writhing for me in that painted-on dress and looking desperately at me with those big doe eyes. I clenched my jaw tight. My chest heaved as I breathed out hard and realized what I was hoping I wouldn't till tomorrow:

That this was a bad idea.

And it couldn't happen.

Whether or not she was drunk, I couldn't do this to her. We had three months of contract left and I couldn't promise myself that I wouldn't be a piece of shit after we fucked. That I wouldn't be cold as stone to her the second I came. There were a lot of lies out there about me, but my being an asshole wasn't one of them. In fact, it was a well-practiced skill. I was as good at maintaining a distance as I was at throwing an unhittable pitch. Like baseball, callousness was something I'd perfected over the years. It gave me a sense of comfort. Stability.

That was just how I was, and there was a reason Iain said not to fuck her.

Approaching the car, I stuck my head in the backseat.

"Gary. She's going to the Adelaide Hotel."

"You got it," Gary said as Evie blinked at me. She knew exactly what was happening – her cheeks were already flushed pink with embarrassment – but I could see her trying to give me the benefit of the doubt with her confusion.

"What's going on, Drew?" she asked, failing to hide the tinge of hurt in her voice.

"Gary's going to take you back to your hotel," I said, watching her process my change of mind. She paused. Then her lips formed into a wobbly little pout for all of a second before she switched gears and narrowed her eyes at me.

"What's your problem, Drew?" she seethed.

"Just go home. Get some sleep," I said. I was being a condescending prick, but I needed to do what I had to do to get her out of my sight fast.

"You promised to help me with something," she enunciated, as if I'd forgotten that I'd agreed to and still desperately wanted to make her come all over my cock. Every muscle in my body was fucking aching to like never before, but that was all the more reason to push the big red button and let the trusty walls go up.

"You can do it yourself," I said, catching the fire in her eyes before I stepped back to close the door.

The right move at that point was to just close it, and on any other day I could've done it without hesitation. But Evie's sudden calm piqued my interest.

And it just about spiked when she leaned back and said, "You're right, asshole. I can."

Then she started touching herself over her dress.

My adrenaline stalled and my gaze grew heavy as I watched her part her legs, sliding her hand between her thighs.

"Don't do that."

"You told me to. Now close the door."

"Gary, give us a minute," I snarled, fully aware that I was taking the L here. I didn't enjoy being called on my bluff – especially when I wasn't bluffing to start with – but fuck it. Evie had me.

Once my driver was out, I let her pull me in by my shirt. I growled into her neck and before I knew it, my hand had replaced hers, my fingers rubbing over her dress, between the lips of her pussy. I could feel her warmth and her wetness through the fabric and I wanted nothing but to reach under that skirt and feel her skin-to-skin, with no barrier between us.

But I was going to hold up one part of the promise I'd made to myself tonight.

I would make her come. But I wasn't going to fuck her.

My ego convinced me my logic was sound. If we weren't having sex, then I was in the clear. If I was touching her over her clothes, it was the same as what we were doing upstairs. If anything, I was just proving to her how loud I could make her moan without getting my dick involved.

And so far, I was doing a fucking stellar job.

"Does that feel good?" I murmured as I sat beside her, one hand gripping the base of her ponytail as the other stroked furiously between her thighs. The way her body responded to every bit of my touch drove me wild. I was ruining her dress and the fact that she loved every second of it was making me crazy.

"Don't stop," she exhaled, clamping her hand over mine and grinding against me. "Faster," she pleaded.

I happily obliged, giving longer, faster strokes that made her tits bounce nonstop under her dress. God, I wanted to rip it right off. I wanted to see her spill out and I wanted to suck on her nipples while she came all over my hand. But none of that was going to happen without me fucking her senseless, so I refrained, convincing myself that I was in control here.

I kept telling myself that, even as I looked down and saw the damp fabric of Evie's dress clinging to her pussy, molding over those luscious lips and turning me into an animal.

"Fuck, Evie," I growled, my eyes drinking her in from head to toe when she came, squeezing my shirt tight and letting out a moan so ragged and sexy I almost whipped my cock out and fucked her on the spot.

I could've basked forever in the scent of her pleasure that lingered thick in the air.

But once her satisfied body went fully limp in my arms, I released her and pushed open the door. Her heavy, dazed stare followed me but she said nothing as she sat there with tousled hair and flushed cheeks, still catching her breath as I got out and finally closed the damned door.

I made eye contact with Gary and watched him climb back in the driver's seat, and the second I heard the engine start, I turned on my heel and headed back into the building. I walked into the first restroom I could find, kicked open a stall and furiously jerked off inside, reliving the shape of Evie's pussy in that dress as I came faster than I ever had in my life.

13

EVIE

I had zero – and I mean zero – contact with Drew in the *six* days that followed the absolute chaos of that night.

In all fairness, this was all pre-planned and exactly according to the itinerary Iain had sent.

Drew had two road series against Boston and Tampa, so he was out of town and wouldn't be back in New York till his start against Baltimore Monday night. When we first did the schedule, Iain had in fact asked me to attend one or two road games in Boston, or even Tampa if I could swing it, because traveling was just a part of being a "baseball wife."

But the days conflicted with my consultation meetings and new client tours at the warehouse, so the mini road trip plan was nixed.

Which meant we weren't *supposed* to see each other. There were no dates on the schedule, and that was technically fine. We'd gone hard staging photo ops for the first few days of our contract so this, according to Iain, would just be our "breather" before move-in day.

So really, I shouldn't be over-thinking a thing.

But still.

The fact that Drew didn't so much as text did kind of bother me.

As a matter of fact, he didn't even shoot a snarky one-liner in reply to Iain's latest email in our shared email thread. It was radio silence from him since he closed the car door behind me that night, and as much as I wanted to believe I was easy, breezy and completely unaffected, I definitely was not.

Because I couldn't stop thinking about everything that went down.

How could anyone expect me to? Drew and I had gone completely off script. Hot as it was, our kiss outside Merryweather had clearly been for show, but the filth we got into the other night was behind closed doors. No one had seen it but us. Every word Drew spoke, every bit of heat in his touch had been entirely for me.

And only me.

"Geez, woman. What got into you that night and can I buy some off of you?" Aly asked as I sat with her in the back office of our restaurant. After finishing my meetings on Thursday, I'd gone ahead and hopped on the Hampton Jitney. It was late at night, but this was an emergency. I'd had an extremely hot night with my extremely fake boyfriend, I was still thinking about it, and I needed to talk it all out before I did something stupid like text him even a "hey what's up."

So I went to see Aly.

"Alright, so remind me who started it?" Aly asked, trying to get to the top of all my breathless rambling. "Who kissed who first?"

I blinked. My toes curled in my flats as I remembered Drew telling me to get off his lap before yanking me right back.

"I have no idea who started the kissing, but he definitely started the precursor to the kissing."

"This is confusing."

"You're telling me."

"But *you* asked to go home with him, right?" Aly clarified.

"Yes," I answered, chewing my lip. "And before you ask, I wasn't drunk."

"I didn't assume that," she laughed. "I know what Drew looks like. He's like, top one percent good-looking, so I'm pretty sure any woman sitting on his lap would have trouble keeping her clothes on."

"Did I mention that I was commando? And he was hard? And huge?"

"Several times, yes."

I buried my face in my hands.

"Sorry, it was just so hot. But then he was such a *dick* afterwards, my God. Who gets someone all hot and bothered and then just snatches sex away last minute?"

"Drew Maddox," Aly answered. "To be fair, he did still finish the job for you," she smirked. "*And* it's probably a good thing that you guys didn't have sex. 'Cause imagine if this week of silence happened after, you know, *actual* penetrative action."

"You say that as if what he did to me in that car wasn't already the hottest thing that's ever happened in my life."

"Trust me, I'm not underestimating how hot it was. I legit read the text you sent me that night and woke Emmett up so I could jump his bones. Which reminds me, he asked me to thank you," she giggled before holding her hands out and giving a shrug. "All I'm saying is it would've been even more complicated if you actually went home with him, had mind-blowing sex and then spent the night before being hit with this no-contact situation. Am I right?"

"You are," I groaned toward the ceiling. "I'm just... all over the place right now. I'm not supposed to care about Drew not talking to me. In fact, I'm supposed to care about that ex of mine who I legit called Matt in my head this morning."

"Really?" Aly's eyes lit up. "Evie. I'm so proud of you. Does this mean you'll skip going to that whole restaurant opening? Who needs to see him after all the vile shit he said to you?"

I took a second to remember what vile shit Aly was referring to.

Oh. Right.

He could be dating models if he wanted to. Ew. The memory of Mike's words made me actually stick my tongue out of my mouth.

"I'm still going," I sighed. "But only for our friend Hillary. She's texted me a variation of sorry every day since Drew and I ate at her restaurant, and I don't want her to think I'm mad at her because Mike randomly showed up that day. I should actually tell her that seeing him act like such an immature dickhead has significantly lowered my need to talk to him."

"I think it's that combined with all that Drew Maddox dick."

"That I'm not actually getting, Alyson Stanton, because this isn't *actually* real," I grumbled, dragging my palms down my face. "And yet here I am acting all paranoid and crazy and wondering why he's not giving me live updates of every thought that's passing through his brain. Am I legitimately nuts?" I asked Aly seriously.

"Evie, no," she burst out laughing. "It's just been awhile since you've had butterflies over someone. And no one's going to blame you for having butterflies over Drew. People have butterflies just looking at him on TV. *You're* dealing with him in person."

"Exactly. So how am I supposed to survive this? I'm moving into his house *tomorrow*."

"Umm." Aly tapped her pen on her lip. "Well, when I was trying to stave off sexual tension while living with Emmett, you told me to call him 'dude' as much as possible. Something about how it desexualizes the person."

"That only works if I'm trying to convince *him* that I'm not deathly attracted to him, and right now, I'm trying to convince myself," I protested.

"Then stop doing things that involve touching his penis!" Aly sputtered, laughing. "You can hold hands in public, you can even kiss in public. But slow down the other funny business. Especially behind closed doors. It's clearly driving you crazy, and as much as I like the idea of you and Drew being together for real, I know from Emmett what he's like in the woman department, and I... I don't know."

"What? What were you going to say?" I frowned.

"I don't know, Evie." Aly wrinkled her nose, taking a second to carefully choose her words. "I don't blame you for how things escalated the other night, but I personally don't think it's a good idea to sleep with him this early on. Like you've seen yourself, Drew can get... difficult sometimes. Emmett says he can just 'flip a switch' and ice people out like they never even mattered. I mean, he was trying to do it to Emmett over the whole trade rumor thing, but you know my man," she smirked. "He's persistent."

"That he is," I nodded, remembering the particular craziness of their courtship. "So what now? Strictly acting and friendship with him from here on out?"

"Just get to know him for now," Aly said. "You're both attracted to each other, obviously, but slow it down. Exercise self-control. You're going to be stuck living with him for awhile, and he can be unpredictable, so do your best to keep things simple. You don't want to risk making things awkward at home. Right?"

"Right," I echoed, finally processing the severity of the situation.

It was all fun and games when I could go home to a hotel and be physically separated from Drew. But as of Monday, that would no longer be the case.

"So it's settled," Aly gave a clap of her hands. "You're going to be fine living with him as long as you stick to your new rule. Which is?" she quizzed me.

"No more touching his body of any kind?"

"No, it's not *that* extreme," she snorted. "Just stop making contact with his penis, for God's sake. You haven't known him for that long, so if it's already a necessity that you touch his dick every time you're near him, you might actually be in love with him already."

"Um, excuse you, and never," I said indignantly.

"Atta girl." She wheeled her chair over and ruffled my hair. "You got this. I believe in you," she added, but she said it with such a funny, tight-lipped smile on her face that I knew she didn't mean it completely.

And honest to God, I couldn't blame her.

14

DREW

I eked out a win in Boston, but barely.

It came two days after my night in the backseat of the car with Evie, and it took every ounce of my focus to refrain from thinking about her. I had a precise physical regimen in the four days leading up to a start, and that wasn't hard to follow.

But the mental game this week was a different story.

It was harder, more work to keep my mind on task, and I blamed it on the ritual. There were a ton of official rules in baseball, but a million more if you factored in all our pre-game rituals and superstitions. Some made more sense than others, but there was no questioning anyone's routine.

We all had our rules, which meant we respected everyone else's.

For instance, Ty took the same route to work every day, even if it meant traffic up the ass. Watt had to have exactly twelve broccoli florets in his daily pregame meal. Brewer listened to the same Kendrick song at the same volume at the same time before every game, and Diaz tapped his heart twice with his right hand before every at-bat.

Everyone had their one rule and I was no different. In fact, I shared the same one as most pitchers on the team, and that was no sex on game day.

No jerking off either.

And while the no sex part was clearly no issue of late, the lack of the latter had me hurting today. I'd relied heavily on that relief the past few days. I needed it to get her off my mind. I hadn't talked to her since that night in the back of my car, but that sure as shit didn't mean I wasn't thinking of her.

I was. Constantly.

And it wasn't just the fact that I got to watch her come, it was the fact that she tested me. She tried my patience, got the better of me and she looked good doing it. I didn't know if I loved it or hated it. All I knew was that it brought me right back to the cycle of doubting the contract, fighting the Nike brain, and reminding myself why I was doing this in the first place.

The game, this team, and a championship – my first one in a ten-year career.

I managed to get her out of my head the second my cleats hit the mound, and though I only pitched six innings, I got the win. So what little focus I had still managed to work.

But the case would definitely change once we touched down in Florida.

CONTRARY TO WHAT a few of my teammates liked to think, not every female baseball fan was a groupie. But the ones who hung in the lobby of our hotel after our games, when it was close to midnight?

Definitely groupies.

They had their tits pushed most of the way out of their kid sized Empires shirts, which were always cut down the middle, damned near to the navel, and on a regular basis, they didn't tempt me. Aside from the fact that they were the type to prick holes in condoms, they had about a minute to make an impression on any one of us as we made our ways to the elevators, and the frantic desperation wasn't exactly a turn-on.

It was usually the rookies who succumbed to their temptation. Even Ty didn't go for these girls.

But just looking at that amount of skin had me feeling tight as I rode up to my room, and it only got worse when I got in and checked my texts.

IAIN: Good sign. Paps are following her while she's not even with you.

A link from some gossip site followed. I texted him back in a heat before even clicking.

ME: This just means she's getting stalked by those fucking animals while she's walking around by herself. How is that a good sign?

IAIN: If they're taking individual interest in Evie, that means you've piqued a very good amount of interest as a couple. Take comfort in the fact that these are NY paps. If this was LA it would be a different story.

ME: Fine

I left the conversation at that and clicked on the link.

And shortly after, I was on my bed, dick out of my sweats and jerking off to the pictures of Evie walking around Manhattan in a black V-neck T-shirt and ripped denim shorts.

There was a particularly scummy shot of her through the window of a store, innocently bending over in those shorts to pick up a shopping bag. It made my blood fucking boil and at the same goddamned time, I was jacking my cock even harder because just the slightest glimpse of her denim-covered pussy was enough to send me reeling back to that car. It brought me right back to my fingers rubbing over her clit. My cock twitching at all those sexy, breathy moans escaping her lips.

And I fucking hated myself for it.

Not because I was getting off to the sight of Evie, but because I was using paparazzi photos to do it. Considering what cocksuckers they were to me, I hated supporting them in any way. For four straight years now, I'd avoided all sports and entertainment media. Instagram was the plague. Twitter was straight up ebola. I didn't read headlines let alone articles about myself, and I never Googled my own name. I used to read the New York Times sports section every morning, but now I didn't do even that.

I was staunchly against media consumption of any kind because all the lies and misconceptions I saw out there generally made me feel fucking homicidal. Though of course, I contributed to a ton of these mistruths. I didn't clear up certain controversial aspects of my past because I didn't even fucking want to touch it. I didn't want to open up my personal life to even more scrutiny and questions, so I kept my mouth shut, let them write their bullshit and pretty much avoided the Internet.

I was on a four-year streak of that.

But I broke it in Tampa by Googling Evie's name for the rest of the trip, just to see if new pictures came up. When none did, I Googled both her name and mine. I wasn't sure if I was trying to see just how close the paparazzi dared to get to her, or if I just wanted more material to jerk to. I told myself it wasn't the latter but it didn't matter either way – this was a risky game for me, and it really wasn't surprising when I eventually stumbled over the exact kind of headline I lived to avoid.

EVEN AFTER FALLOUT, LILLARDS STILL CHEER FOR THEIR HOMETOWN KID.

Fucking hell.

I didn't have to click to know what that article was about.

Tim and his family still cheered for me. I knew that much. He decked his son out in Maddox gear just to watch the game at home. He'd dared to send me pictures once before I deleted my old email address and made a new one.

Long story short, I'd fucked myself for my start against Baltimore tonight.

A day later, I was still thinking of the headline, and I was pissed at myself – at my lack of self-control during that Googling spree. I was focused more on how much I'd already fucked up than how I could fix it, and I had a feeling that was why I was paying so much attention to stupid shit like the sound of Watt's teeth hitting his fork with every damned bite of his food, or the smell of Brewer's stupid fucking chicken.

It reminded me of the Lillard house.

Specifically, it reminded me of the day Mom found out about Dad and the neighbor, Carly. Or Carrie. I remembered her perfume, but not her name. Mom found out, left the house, but didn't tell me – she was just a no-show to pick me up from practice.

That particular day, I remembered staying awhile at the ballpark and talking to the older kid who worked the snack bar. He was nice, and I wanted to wait till after dinner to call the Lillards. The last time Mom didn't pick me up, I called them and they drove back to get me in the middle of dinner. Up and left everything. I remembered going back to their house and watching Tim and his little sister bring an extra chair over while Pattie fixed me a plate of that amazing butter-milk fried chicken she was famous for – that Tim had been going on and on about even before the game.

It was his favorite and I felt like shit when I excitedly bit in and it was cold. It was a big day in the Lillard house when Pattie made the chicken. It wasn't the same reheated, and I was the reason it went cold.

The worst part was how Tim and Pattie just smiled and talked about my great game while eating their cold chicken. They didn't try to make me feel bad, and that made me feel worse.

So I waited till after dinner to call and when the Lillards brought me back to their house, Pattie reheated some leftovers while I played Nintendo with Tim in the den. Like she would so many more times in the future, she dragged the extra twin mattress up from the basement and made it up all nice with fresh sheets and a memory foam pillow from her own bed. "Don't worry, I have two nice pillows and only one head!" she reassured me.

Neither she nor Tim ever acted like I was a pain or a burden, and it was such a stark difference from Dad, who never let me forget how much Little League fees were. I memorized all the lower range prices for bats, gloves and cleats by the time I was nine.

So the Lillards were a breath of fresh air. They were my only sense of comfort.

I wound up staying with them a lot over the years. Definitely that week that my mom moved out, and any other time she threatened to move out for good. I bounced back and forth between the Lillards and my house so much it was confusing, and by the time I was in high school, I just lived there some weeks, whether Mom was home or not.

Baseball was becoming a bigger responsibility in my life – I was getting enough serious attention now that Dad came to all my games and bragged about the cars he'd buy with my first paycheck – and I needed a break from the craziness. Dad could get intense about my career, even when I was just trying to relax at home, and I needed a quiet place I liked being at with people I enjoyed being around when I wasn't playing or practicing.

And that was the Lillard house with its fresh buttermilk fried chicken every Thursday.

"Hey. You good?" Diaz frowned when I got up abruptly to leave the room. I gave him a thumbs on my way to the lounge, where I could hopefully get away from the smell of Brewer's food. I did, but at this point, I couldn't get out of my head.

Something had tipped the scale, and I'd gone from focused to overwhelmed in just a matter of seconds. I was thinking about things I didn't normally think about. I had a constant barrier up to keep these particular memories out, but now they were seeping through, and the idea that there were actual cracks in my mental game drove me fucking nuts.

I wasn't myself right now, and I blamed it all on Evie.

Irrational, probably, but oh well. I needed to blame someone and she made it easy, especially with the text she'd just sent after successfully leaving me alone for almost a full week.

EVIE: Hey welcome home.

EVIE: So I just wanted to say that you were right to send me home alone the other night. It's probably best if we keep the show simple from here on out. Hand holding and pecks while we're out in public. Nothing behind closed doors. We're both bound to this contract for awhile so we might as well be responsible and keep our boundaries clear.

I clenched my jaw as I read it then tossed my phone aside.

Jesus.

This was becoming much more of an effort than I'd imagined, and if I had my choice, I would've already gotten rid of Evie by now. She was too much of a distraction. But I couldn't just ghost her. She was throwing me off my game, yet she was apparently necessary for my career.

She was both my problem and my solution, and I was pretty sure I hated her for it.

I was also sure that I was either going to pitch a great game today or a fucking disaster – I wasn't sure which. All I knew was that no matter what happened, I'd be going home livid because I could already feel that I needed to be alone tonight.

But tonight was the night she was moving in.

15

S o, move-in was a total disaster.

And he wasn't even home yet.

But within the first two hours of arriving, I'd broken the fridge, tripped up the alarm and failed to tell the alarm company the right password when they called, so the police wound up coming. They took one look at me in my panicked state, wearing twelve-dollar bottled kale juice from the fridge that I'd spilled down my shirt when the alarm sounded, and laughed their asses off for a solid minute.

And for some reason, as they laughed, I thought it an appropriate time to ask whether they knew what the heck I'd just done to the refrigerator, and why was it beeping like that? Was it broken?

"I've never seen a fridge like that, that looks like a time machine," the lady said.

"You might want to fix it before Mr. Maddox gets home," her partner chuckled. "I don't think he needs anything else to deal with after tonight's game."

Shit.

"Why? What happened?" I asked before they basically laughed some more, reminded me to get the password for the alarm company, and left.

A quick search of "Empires score" on my laptop showed me that they lost tonight, 17-4. Holy God. I didn't know much about baseball, but I knew that was bad. *MADDOX STUMBLES IN DISASTROUS FIFTH INNING* was the only headline I saw before clicking the hell out.

Of course, clicking out brought me to my open Facebook tab, and a reminder that I should probably unfriend Mike.

He rarely posted anything unrelated to work, but twenty minutes ago he'd posted a status that read: *Baltimore SPANKED NY tonight! There goes your big win streak Empires #sorrynotsorry #someoneisoverpaid #damyoureallyblewit*

"Seriously?" I hissed at my screen because one, he wasn't even a Baltimore fan and two, his stupid passive aggressive hashtags were clearly directed at Drew and three, he spelled the word "damn" wrong.

What an ass.

I was still frazzled and wearing kale juice when I typed a dirty, bitchy, completely inappropriate reply to him that I really, really wished I had the nerve to actually post.

Just do it. He deserves it. Hit enter, the devil on my shoulder urged me wickedly as Iain finally texted me back.

"Thank God," I exhaled, but then I read his text.

> **IAIN:** Unfortunately I don't know the answers to any of these questions but I'm sure the fridge is fine and the alarm company will understand. Just breathe and remember the password in case there's a next time. I let Drew know to come home early to address any further issues you might have.

"No! No, no, no, no!" I yelled at my phone, typing back a dozen different replies and settling on none to actually send because it was probably inappropriate to ask Iain what he was thinking texting Drew when I texted him specifically to *avoid* talking to Drew. I already felt dumb for caving and texting him about our new rule today, and even dumber since he didn't respond, so the last thing I needed was for him to be informed that I "needed" him home.

Ugh.

I wasn't even unpacked yet.

Dragging my feet upstairs, I went into the guest room where I'd left my bags and pulled out something clean to change into. I was in the middle of yanking my top on when I heard the elevator humming up to the entrance of the penthouse downstairs.

Drew was home.

I ran out of my room eagerly before realizing that I wasn't sure if I was even eager to see him. We hadn't spoken since that bizarre and incredibly hot night that almost felt like a dream at this point, and he was no doubt in a crappy mood over tonight's epic loss.

On top of that, Iain had texted him something about me and all the stupid issues I'd been having in his home, which I now realized were pretty trivial, and the last thing Drew needed to deal with. So I felt kind of bad about that.

And I felt even worse when midway down the steps, the elevator doors opened and Drew's eyes were pinned immediately on me.

"Hi," I breathed out, freezing in place as I took in the sight of him looking hard, steely and hotter than I was comfortable with in a white crew neck and grey sweats.

God, that body.

He said nothing to me, instead striding silently into the kitchen and tossing his wallet onto the counter. He eyed the still-beeping fridge and conveyed the utter lack of emergency it presented by taking a swig from his water bottle and returning a few texts before walking over to it. Then with a look at me, he hit some button that I swore I'd hit ten times to try and shut it up, and the damned thing stopped beeping.

At that point, I pretty much wanted to turn on my heel and go back upstairs, but I forced myself to at least attempt to break our three-day silence before going to bed. He was clearly a seasoned pro at intimidating others, but if I was going to be living under the same roof as Drew Maddox, I refused to be scared of him.

I watched him pay attention to everything but me as I joined him in the kitchen. I thought about what Aly had said the other day, what I'd texted him today, and nodded silently to myself.

Yeah. Definitely. No fucking this moody prick. Now, soon or ever, I resolved as I drew in a deep, inaudible breath and worked up the nerve to break the silence.

"So. Have you eaten yet?"

It was all I had in my arsenal since "how was the game" was out of the question. Plus, it had always been my daily greeting to Mike after I got home from work. It helped me figure out whether I needed to take care of him or whether or not I could go shower and do my own thing.

I rested my palms on the countertop to convey casual calm, but my toes were tapping away in my slippers as I waited for Drew to respond to my question. He took his sweet time, opening the door of the freezer and taking out what looked like an ice pack before finally speaking.

"Password for the alarm is Christopher," he said coldly. "Memorize it."

Okay. I see how it is.

This was probably how he started the ice-out Aly was talking about, but I wasn't having it.

"Who's Christopher?" I dared to ask, earning myself a look from Drew as he made his way over to the living room.

"No one you'll ever meet, so don't worry about it."

God.

I rolled my head back and shared a *can you believe this guy look* with the ceiling, because I had no one else to gripe to. Still, I wasn't letting him break me. I was going to remain unflappably civil and find a way for us to leave off on a decent note before going upstairs. This was where I was sleeping for the next three months, and I wasn't about to let it become a toxic environment. I was too old for that shit.

"Look, Drew, I know you had a rough night," I started as I trailed him to the living room. "But I just wanted to say that before all the fridge and alarm drama happened, when I first walked in here, I realized just how grateful I was to be out of that apartment and living in this city," I said, stopping him in front of the couch. "And since I still have energy and you're probably wiped right now, I'd be happy to do something for you to make your night easier. I can cook something, I can run to the store. I saw a twenty-four hour place around the corner. If you need something, you can let me know."

Drew hit me with another look.

"I'm not your ex, Evie. I don't need to be coddled."

"I wasn't implying that, Drew," I said, trying to be patient. "I was just trying to do something nice for you."

"Why?"

"Because we're living together now. We can't just ignore each other. We have to try to strike a balance together."

"Strike a balance?" He was about to sit down but apparently something I said piqued his interest. "You mean between being strangers and people who fuck in the back of cars?"

I swallowed the instant knot in my throat. This was his first mention of what happened the other night since it happened, and it took a second for me to gather myself.

"Yes," I finally said. "Although..." I had to work up the nerve to go on. "I think we both know we didn't... *fuck*. And that we definitely shouldn't. We should keep it simple between us from now on. Civil to friendly at home. Romantic in public. No sexual touching of any kind. Right?"

It seemed like a perfectly reasonable thing to say considering it was exactly what was stated in our contract, but when I looked up at Drew, there was a hint of a sneer on his lips.

"Right," he said, though with a mocking undertone.

"I mean if we've known each other for two weeks, Drew, I think it's possible for us to dial things back to a happy medium," I said in a positive tone, despite my absolutely pounding heart. "If not, we're just giving up on the contract, and I know neither of us wants to do that now. Right?"

"Right." His eyes burned into mine, his lips barely moving as he said it.

Relax. Breathe. Be positive.

"Okay. So," I exhaled, trying to reset. "Is there anything I can do for you now before I go upstairs?"

"Yeah," Drew muttered.

Then without warning, he reached up behind his head, gripped his back collar and peeled his shirt clean off his torso.

Whaaat.

The. Fuck.

Is happening.

I didn't even try to avoid staring. I straight up let him watch as I checked out his unbelievably wide, hard pecs and those perfectly chiseled abs. And those *tattoos.* God. They were hot enough peeking out from under the sleeves of his shirt but with him completely undressed, they were that much sexier. They punctuated the raw masculinity that was his ripped, hard body, and it was physically impossible not to imagine what that body was capable of beyond athletics.

Ah-ah, Evie. No more touching his penis, no more touching his penis, no more touching his penis, I reminded myself of Aly's rule as I unstuck my tongue from the roof of my mouth, taking a second to find my words again.

"Is... there a reason you're stripping?" I finally asked, watching the lines of his six-pack deepen as he leaned forward to grab the ice pack off the table.

"You asked what you could do for me," Drew started tersely, forcing my eyes on his biceps as he reached across his chest and pressed the ice pack to the back of his shoulder. "And what you can do is rewind this night back a few hours so I'm still at the stadium instead of skipping my post-game massage to tend to your ridiculous non-emergencies."

I clenched my jaw, annoyed with my own lack of a response for that. I wanted to blame Iain, but that was immature so I simply held my tongue as I watched Drew sink into his seat on the couch, stretching his neck and wincing with pain as he took care of his soreness.

Still holding an ice pack to his shoulder, he used his free hand to work the muscles on his legs, digging the heel of his palm down his hamstrings, along his calves. I eyed his hand. Bruised knuckles. Taped fingers. He was basically hurting all over.

Geez.

"Look, I can do that for you," I blurted without thinking.

The out-of-the-blue weirdness of my offer was confirmed by the odd look Drew gave me.

He kept his eyes on me for several seconds, still massaging himself before asking, "What?"

"Massage you," I said, my cheeks burning because it sounded so damned sensual even when I didn't mean it that way. "Not in a weird way or anything," I added, making the situation a hundred times more awkward. *Come on, Evie. You already said it. Just own it.* "It's just I'm known among my group of friends as the go-to girl for this. I got good at massage therapy growing up because my sister... had these aches," I said hastily, trying to skip over the mention of Kaylie. "So anyway, I know how to handle muscle pain. It's just an offer, Drew."

He stared up at me, his lips curling into a sneer.

"Could've sworn you just made a new rule about how we touch each other behind closed doors."

"Massages don't have to be sexual. I just told you I gave massages to my sister, for God's sake, and you get rubbed down every day by presumably a dude you're not sexually attracted to, so." I shrugged, smiling a bit because the huff of air he let out sounded something like laughter. "I don't know, Drew, I'm just trying to be nice. I'm trying to help."

"Fine. Then do it."

I blinked in surprise.

"Fine," I said, just to disguise my own uneasiness.

Really though, Evie. What were you thinking?

It seemed like an obvious thing to me at the time. He was hurting. I was good at this. I wanted to make up for the mess that was tonight.

But I could feel my heart beating out of control as I prepared to kneel in front of Drew's wide-parted legs. There was no smile on his face but I read the look of amusement in his eyes as I stood over him, trying to figure out if there was a less sexual position I could do this in.

Of course, the answer was no.

So after about twelve seconds of hesitation, I got on my knees. Before I could even let myself process how much it looked like I was about to blow him, I held his ankle with one hand. With my other hand, I cupped the back of his calf, applying pressure as I pushed my thumb up the line of where his bone and muscle came together.

He groaned in such pain I snapped my hands back.

"That hurt?" I asked apologetically. He blew out a long breath.

"Yes, but it felt good."

I bit my lip, taking a second to shake off the throaty breathlessness of his voice.

"I should keep going?"

"Yes."

So I did, keeping track of his every twitch and groan to get a better understanding of what felt good or not. I put all my focus on those powerfully muscled legs, looking at nothing else but my own hands because I knew Drew was watching me.

His attention was rapt on me, and it felt like he was trying to figure me out. I wasn't just good at massages – I was fucking stellar. A "miracle worker" according to Aly, Mike, Hillary and a dozen other friends who'd experienced my back rubs.

No one would expect this kind of strength from my slender hands. I knew that, and I knew Drew was getting reluctantly curious about me. I could feel him wanting to know where this skill came from without having to ask, but after another few minutes of silence, he caved.

"Why are you so good at this?" It was slightly more accusation than compliment.

"I told you. My sister."

"Why did she have aches?"

"I don't know. She just had... bad legs."

"Was she elderly, this sister of yours?"

I looked up at him and narrowed my eyes.

"She was sick," I said curtly. "Also, I know you love giving me a hard time, but people have real feelings and real sore spots, and maybe you should just read the room sometimes and recognize when you shouldn't ask any more questions. You're not the only one who doesn't want to talk about certain topics."

I didn't look up to see his reaction, and it was silent for another few minutes.

"I'm sorry," he said.

"It's okay," I replied, though only because the mention of my sister took my attention off my nerves. I wasn't normally happy to talk about her. Just her name raised my blood pressure. But apparently, massaging a shirtless Drew Maddox raised my blood pressure even more, so somehow, the topic of Kaylie tonight was almost like a vacation.

"What was she sick with?"

I looked up at him, wanting to give him shit for his persistent curiosity. But I didn't.

"She was a heroin addict," I said, focusing on the pressure I was applying to his muscles. "Whenever she tried quitting, the withdrawal symptoms included muscle aches. Leg cramps in particular for her."

"You were the younger one?"

"Yes. By four years."

"How old were you when you started helping her with the cramps?"

"Exactly twelve."

"Exactly twelve?" Drew repeated. "How do you remember that?"

"Because her first overdose was on my twelfth birthday."

I remembered because Mom had hyped me up for a big surprise the whole day before, but on the morning of my birthday, I woke up to an empty house that remained empty all day.

I wouldn't find out till Mom got home at night that she'd taken Kaylie to the ER first thing in the morning, for her first overdose in a year of using. Mom had stayed a few hours at the hospital before getting in her car and driving furiously to the middle of nowhere, screaming and crying the whole way, and eventually stranding herself with no gas or phone. She was so tired by the time she got back that she couldn't handle all my questions and tears. She just closed her bedroom door on me and went to sleep.

"She quit after that?" Drew asked.

I looked up at him, still so suspicious of him when he asked questions about me. I really couldn't imagine that he actually cared about anyone's story. My theory now was that he was using the grim topic of Kaylie the same way I was – to distract from the overly sexual nature of what we were doing.

"That was her first try. There would be many others. In fact, she's in the midst of another try right now."

"How often do you speak to her?"

"Never. I moved out when I was seventeen and I've been no-contact with her since," I replied, trying to sound cold and casual, as if I didn't carry guilt with me every day.

I knew I succeeded because without even looking at Drew, I could see his eyebrows lifting up high. I was sure he was judging me. I felt like I deserved to be judged.

But when he spoke, he reminded me of his own relationship with his family.

"You didn't do anything wrong," he said, his words kind but his tone harsh. "People act like blood means more than your own sanity. But it doesn't."

I didn't look at him as I moved my hands up to his thigh, right above his kneecap.

"I know. And I tried to help for a long time," I defended myself, because I always felt like I had to. "She stole from me, hit me, spit on me, and I'd take it because she was sick. She didn't 'mean it.' But even after she broke my arm, my mom defended her."

"How the fuck did she defend that? And how the fuck did she break your arm?"

The genuine anger in Drew's voice made me look up in surprise, but it was nothing compared to the fiery blaze of his stare. Okay, so it wasn't so much sympathy for me as rage for the world.

"Well." I looked back down, using both hands to work the seemingly impenetrable muscle of his lower thigh. "My mom kept saying she couldn't help it, and to remember when Kaylie and I were best friends. But after six years of this and being thrown down a fucking flight of stairs one day when I wouldn't give Kaylie any more money, I said I was done. I wasn't going to keep waiting for the day she went back to who she was. As much as I loved her, as much as I still miss her, she's not there anymore. It's not her. And I can't let her bad decisions dictate my life anymore."

"Of course," Drew said, his voice almost gentle. By his standards at least. I looked up at him. "You have to take care of yourself before you can take care of anyone else," he muttered, wincing and groaning in between words as I worked up to the middle of his thigh.

I couldn't help but smirk a little.

"You'll hate knowing this, but those were the exact words Mike said to me when he convinced me to cut them out of my life."

"You're right, I do hate knowing that," Drew shot back fast. But then he relaxed again, rolling his head back and sucking in a long, deep breath between his teeth as I pushed the heel of my palm along his hamstring. "God, Evie, that feels so fucking good."

The gravel in his voice shot straight between my thighs. Suddenly, I recognized the sheer proximity of my hands to his cock, and it made me bite my lip. Clearing my throat, I tried distracting myself with an unpleasant subject.

"Well, just because Mike gave me good advice before doesn't mean he's got a lifetime pass. He's still an asshole who – oh *shit!*"

My sharp gasp jolted Drew, and I caught a half second of his confusion before scrambling to my laptop and trying to remember if I'd actually hit enter.

Before Drew came home, I had been seething over Mike's Facebook post. I'd written that dirty, snappy comment just to blow off steam and make myself laugh, but I hadn't actually hit enter.

Right? I would never, I told myself just as I hit the space bar, woke up my laptop and stared at a good thirty-six notifications staring at me at the top of the page.

"Oh God," I breathed as I realized that *I would never* did not actually apply, because apparently, I very much would. My eyes were wild as I reread his post – *Baltimore SPANKED NY tonight! There goes your big win streak Empires #sorrynotsorry #someoneisoverpaid #damyoureallyblewit* – followed by my reply:

Guess that means someone else is getting spanked tonight. Not that I mind ;) #loveit #heshotwhenhesmad

Oh.

My God, Evie.

I had no other words for myself as I knelt in front of my screen, hands clasped over my mouth while taking in all the likes, loves, shocked emojis and sassy GIF replies under my insane comment – some of them from Mike's own coworkers.

Omigodomigodomigod.

"What?"

The second I heard Drew's voice, I slammed my laptop shut.

"Nothing!" I said, though when I turned around, Drew was sitting forward, as if he'd just been reading over my shoulder. I squinted at him. I knew he'd looked, but I couldn't tell if he'd read everything on my screen, so I kept my narrowed eyes pinned to his vague smirk as I returned to massaging his legs. And after ten seconds of quiet, I concluded that he hadn't seen a thing.

But just to be safe, I kept his mouth shut by throwing myself into massaging the hell out of him, using all the strength in my body to push, rub and knead his thighs till I was breathless and he was growling from the pain.

"Trying to hurt me, little girl?" he snarled.

"I thought you said it hurt but felt good."

"Kind of like being spanked?"

Oh God. My heart slammed in my chest. *Okay, so he did see the comment,* I breathed, trying to play it off and gather myself. But when it was clear that I wouldn't, I looked up at him, cheeks burning.

"That was clearly for show. Just to shut him up," I said as amusement danced in his eyes.

"So you have no interest in getting spanked."

"That clearly breaks our no-touching rule. I think we both know that."

"I could use a paddle to avoid actual contact."

"So... do you *want* me to finish this massage or do you want me to go to my room and ignore you till the end of time?"

"Finish me off," he smirked, breaking into a full grin when I whispered *ass* under my breath and returned to the massage.

But at this point, it was impossible for me to rub my hands all over his body without wanting to combust into flames. Drew's gaze was fixed tight on me as I avoided looking up, still breathless, my chest still heaving from using all my strength on him. Both physically and mentally, I was faltering, getting weak, and all I could do was remind myself that he'd get cold and frigid if we caved and had sex.

Don't do it, don't do it, don't do it, I chanted on repeat. *Don't even look at him.*

But just as I thought the words, Drew reached into his sweats and grabbed his cock.

16

DREW

There were a lot of things on my mind when I came home tonight.

There was the fact that I lost my first start of the season. And I didn't just lose. I gave up eight runs in one inning. I couldn't get out of the fifth inning. I wound up getting pulled early, and my teammates avoided looking at me for fear of catching the yips.

I had to grit my teeth and bear the media crowding around me directly after the game, the ones who particularly hated me almost grinning as they asked me what happened to cause such an "epic disaster."

I had to sit there, staying outwardly calm as I gave them the usual canned replies.

Bad games happen.

It was a bad performance.

No excuses. Next time.

Those were the answers I stuck to, because I couldn't say anything resembling the truth. Not that I wanted to confess that a woman – a damned near stranger – had weaseled her way into my head and for once, I couldn't manage to get her out. I couldn't say that I spent the game hating the fact that I had to go home to her, because she was finally moving in with me tonight.

It was bad enough without a reporter asking me about the Lillards.

"Do you think you're finally feeling the effects of losing the mother figure in your life? My condolences by the way."

Yeah.

Your condolences my ass.

There was a lot to be pissed about when I got home today, and that wasn't even counting Iain's texts to rush home to Evie's bullshit. It wasn't counting the soreness in my muscles. The aching in my bones. The bruise on my shoulder from getting hit by a line drive.

I was in bad shape, both physically and mentally, and I was convinced tonight would be the night that I quit on this contract by kicking her ass out.

But now I sensed I'd be breaking this contract in a different way, because while I prided myself on having no limits, I'd apparently found my first one.

Resisting this damned woman.

"Drew, what..."

The shocked words barely made it out of those lips. Those pouty fucking lips. They were pink and swollen, frozen in a little "o" as Evie watched me reach under my sweats, gripping the hard base of my dick. Her mouth fell open as I flipped my erection onto my abs, tucking the pulsing tip under the waistband of my boxers.

I knew she'd been seconds from blowing up at me, but once she realized I was just adjusting my hard-on, she somewhat relaxed.

Key word: somewhat.

"Figured you didn't want a tent pitched in your face."

"No, yeah." Her lashes fluttered as she spoke fast. "You're right. I wouldn't."

"You should probably stop that now," I muttered since her hands were still pressed flat on my thighs, not far from where my cock was swelling fully hard. It was begging for attention by now. Thanks to the game, I'd neglected it all day. And now that I was sitting here, hard as a rock with Evie kneeling at my feet, I couldn't wait a second longer.

My jaw tightened when she finally dropped her hands from my thighs.

"You should probably go upstairs now, too," I said, unapologetic as I stroked my cock over my sweats. I wet my lips as her gaze dropped like a brick.

Goddamn. Her eyes glimmered as they traced every inch of my erection, and I swear I watched those pink lips get even pinker and plumper, like they were just waiting to wrap themselves around the swollen tip.

Come on, baby girl. Suck on it.

Give it a little lick.

I wanted to let every filthy thought in my head roll off my tongue, but I controlled myself because she looked pitifully tormented right now – hot, bothered and going through a mental crisis.

"You're torturing me, Drew," she whispered finally.

"Trust me, I know how that feels."

"You're not the one who hasn't had sex in five months."

"I haven't jerked off in twenty-four hours, and considering the sounds you made when you came the other night, that's starting to feel a lot like five months," I muttered.

"Please don't talk about that night."

"Why?" I growled. "Because it makes your pussy wet?"

"*Yes*, Drew," she hissed. "And considering how weird things got after that, we definitely cannot have sex. We can't."

"Are you telling me, or you telling yourself?"

"I'm telling us both," she glared, sitting back on her feet with resolve. "No sexual touching."

"Right." I stared back at her for a second. "In that case, I'm going to jerk off. And since that requires taking my dick out, I'm going to need you to be a good girl and go up to your room."

She shot me a look for the deliberately condescending tone. But she didn't leave, and I wasn't going to stop on her behalf.

With my eyes pinned on Evie, I pushed my sweats down, letting my erection spring free right before her.

"Fuck," she breathed out, her lips parting and her wide eyes getting wider as I cradled my heavy shaft in my palm, rubbing my thumb slowly against the ridge of my head. I was already rock-hard, but I felt myself get harder as Evie stayed put, hypnotized by the sight of pre-cum beading at the tip.

"Are you going to watch me, baby?" I rasped as I began stroking my dick right in front of her. She answered by eyeing me for a second before letting her gaze fall once again. "What, this doesn't break the rule?" I muttered, my thighs flexed because the sensation was already unreal.

"I'm not touching you," Evie murmured in a daze, unconsciously licking her lips as she watched me pump my cock faster now, my head rolling back every once in awhile.

But I could never take my gaze off of her for long. I had to enjoy my incredible view. Fully soak it in as much as I could, because for fuck's sake, I was relaxed on my couch, cock out and jerking off right in front of Evie's gorgeous face. She looked so cute, so transfixed as I started jacking it hard like I did when I was home alone. She squirmed in her kneeling position, playing nervously with the hem of her shirt. *Yeah. Keep doing that,* I urged, watching her twist her top harder and harder as I pumped my dick faster and faster. She was stretching her neckline down so far on her full tits that I was one twist away from watching them spring free.

"Not wearing a bra?" I panted.

"I am."

"Then why can I see your nipples so clearly?"

"Because they're hard."

"Show me."

She startled out of her state, looking up with surprise at my demand. But it lasted barely a second before she turned the tables on me, grasping her neckline and giving one hard yank so her tits popped out.

"*Fuck*, baby." My fist was a blur on my cock as I devoured my view.

"Jesus fucking Christ, Evie," I growled as I watched her push those perfect things together, rolling those tight, rosy nipples between her fingers. "I need to touch them."

"You can't."

"Let me suck on them."

"No."

"Then bounce them for me."

"That I'll do," she smirked. I growled as sensation tingled from every corner of my body, the pressure building so hard in my cock that I was sure I could blow my load that second. But with a long groan, I slowed down, knowing well that the second I was done the show would be over. I shook my head, blowing out a harsh breath of air as I watched Evie gaze at my cock while playing with herself.

"You weren't kidding about doing something nice for me, were you?"

"Trust me, this is as much for me as it is for you."

"Then take your panties off and touch your pussy."

"My pussy is staying strictly clothed."

I would've laughed if I weren't so busy staving off my orgasm.

"And why do you draw the line there?"

"Because I don't trust you to see my naked pussy without burying your dick inside it."

"Baby, you're saying all the right things to get your ass spanked right now."

"Too bad you can't. No touching." The wicked look glimmering in her eyes made me feel warm all over. "Don't tell me I have more will power than the famous Drew Maddox."

"If I didn't have will power, you'd already be wearing my cum all over your tits."

Evie bit her lip.

"You're close?" she asked softly.

"I've been," I snarled, feeling the buildup of pressure reach a breaking point. My cock was engorged, begging for release. I felt numb all over, all my senses flooding to one focal point. And since I was seconds from liftoff, I ran my eyes all over Evie, soaking all of her in – her big eyes, her pink lips, those perfect, bare tits. I pictured myself fucking her senseless on the ground, then like a gunshot, the pressure exploded.

My head hit the back of the couch as a jagged groan dispelled from my lungs. I felt the jets of heat fall over my stomach as I closed my eyes, every last thought from the day rushing out of my brain and dissolving into sheer ecstasy.

I barely knew what was happening by the time I heard Evie's footsteps padding back to me from wherever she'd gone. I could barely move. All I could do was sit there, blissfully drained as I watched Evie – tits still out – clean me off with a warm, wet towel.

Holy fucking shit.

Maybe she'd killed me, because this had to be heaven. Her eyes were hazel. I noted that for the first time as she kept her soft gaze on me, biting back a little smile as she wiped the cum off of me.

"Doesn't count if there's a towel between us," she grinned, referring to our no-touching rule. "Loopholes."

"Watching me touch myself was a loophole. This is breaking the rule."

"Well, as long as we're not having sex, I can live with it," she smirked, letting me watch her tits bounce between her arms as she finished cleaning me off. And once she was done, she said goodnight, going up to her room and leaving me completely fucking stunned on the couch.

17

EVIE

I'd fallen asleep at some point – specifically after touching myself under the sheets, coming with an uncontrolled moan and then passing out. But somewhere around 3AM, I woke up with a hangover. Not from drinking, since I hadn't, but from being drunk off Drew Maddox.

A shiver rippled up my spine as I relived the image of his clenching abs as he came.

Holy shit. That happened, I thought, sitting groggily up in the dark of my room for a few seconds before getting up and going out in the hall. I peered over the railing to check if Drew was still downstairs where I left him, but when I saw the couch empty, I turned to look down the hall.

His bedroom door was closed, but the light was on in his room, and I had to physically stop myself from going down the hall. I literally held onto my doorknob, anchoring myself down in case I floated off like a balloon to Drew's room.

I wanted to see him. I wanted to know what he was doing or thinking right this moment.

But I was also scared to find out so, rather than cave to that need, I went back in my room, closed the door and climbed into bed. I closed my eyes, praying to fall asleep before I got sober enough to analyze what the fuck I'd just done tonight, and why the hell it was physically impossible for me to resist Drew Maddox.

But when I heard him rustling in his room, my eyes shot open.

I stared into the darkness as I lay on my side, holding my breath as I heard his bedroom door creak open, his bare footsteps coming down the hall. I was barely breathing by the time I heard him pass the stairs because all that was left past that point was my room.

There was no knock before he opened the door, and the second he did our eyes quietly found each other.

Our gaze stayed locked as his stride continued into my room without a moment's hesitation. I caught the fact that he was still shirtless in those grey sweats before he closed the door, and it was pitch black again.

I couldn't see even the faintest bit of his silhouette as I heard him step toward the bed. Then I felt the sheets rip off my body.

"Drew!" I gasped as he climbed on top of me and flipped me swiftly onto my stomach. My heart pounded against the mattress as I felt him wedge a hand between my thighs and part my legs. "What are you *do*ing?" I exhaled, already short of breath. My pussy throbbed out of control as I felt him pull down my panties. "Drew!"

I could practically hear the smile curl his lips as he savored a few more seconds of my writhing breathlessness before answering.

"I don't do double standards. If you get to break the rule then so do I," he said, holding my legs open by my ankles.

My mouth hung wide open as I hugged my pillow tight. It was dark, I was on my stomach, and I couldn't see a thing. All I knew was that my naked pussy was bared to Drew, and I had no idea what he was going to do with it.

But whatever it was, I was already aching for it.

I stared into the black of the room, my senses on high alert as I waited to feel something. A rolling shudder moved up my body as Drew pushed his hands up my calves and my thighs. There was no doubt in my mind that he was hard, but I wasn't sure if his cock was out. I wasn't sure if I was seconds from feeling it plunge inside me. I waited to hear maybe the crinkle of a condom wrapper but all I heard was my own heartbeat and the sharpness of my choppy breaths.

The hairs on the back of my neck stood up as I felt Drew's weight shift on the mattress.

Then suddenly, I felt the warm flick of his tongue on my pussy.

"Oh God." I dug my fingers into my pillow and squirmed, but he pinned me down by the backs of my thighs, holding me perfectly still so his tongue could part my folds and lick up my wet pussy.

Oh... fuck. Yes. Fuck yes.

My thighs tensed but barely a squeak escaped my mouth, the shock and pleasure of it all paralyzing me completely stiff. I was at the mercy of Drew's mouth as he continued his gentle assault on my nerves, rolling his tongue against me, pulsing it skillfully, till I could hear my own wetness smacking against his mouth. He let out a low, leisurely groan as if I were his favorite meal, and as I relaxed enough to feel my grogginess again, I wondered if I was dreaming.

Is this even happening?

Maybe it wasn't. Maybe I'd gone back to bed, fallen asleep and dreamt of Drew silently entering my bedroom to strip me of my panties and bury his mouth between my legs.

Because this felt too good to be real. It felt too *right* to be real. I was shocked, nervous for all of a second but now I was starting to calm. Eyes closed, I hugged my pillow to my breasts as Drew rubbed his hand all over my ass, laving against me, easing my juices onto his tongue with his every wet stroke.

"That's it, baby," he muttered as I arched my back, presenting him more of my pussy to lick. I felt delirious as he lapped at me for what felt like five minutes straight, sending full-body shudders rippling from head to toe before finally forcing me to wake up a little bit.

"Drew," I breathed in surprise. His sweats were still on but I could feel his cock falling between my calves, dragging heavily up my legs as he kissed up the curve of my bottom, then up my back.

It wasn't long before he buried his mouth against the curve of my neck, kissing me furiously as his fingers pumped in and out of my pussy.

"Fucking knew you'd be this tight," he growled low in my ear as I gasped for breath, digging my nails into my pillow.

"Oh my God, Drew. That feels too good."

"Do you want to come on my hand or my mouth?"

Jesus. Was that a serious question? Was "both" a reasonable answer?

"I don't care, just make me come," I whispered just before he withdrew his fingers and flipped me onto my back. I couldn't see what was happening, but I knew he went down on me fast because in a second flat, I felt his warm tongue on my clit. I cried out hard, one hand clawing the sheets and the other tugging his hair as he gripped the tops of my thighs. Pulling me tight to his mouth, he held me still, licking the wet length of my pussy before sucking my clit till I came. The moan I let out stretched longer as Drew let out a rumbling *mmm* that buzzed so pleasurably against me it felt like I was coming again.

Oh God. Oh my God.

Holy shit.

I felt Drew's weight lower on top of me as I caught my breath on my back. I closed my eyes as I felt his mouth return to his favorite place on my neck, and I reveled in lying with him for a little, his teeth skimming my jaw as his fingertips stroked the sopping wetness between my legs.

No yeah, that was a dream, I decided.

Especially when I felt Drew get up and leave, closing the door behind him and leaving me to listen to his footsteps return down the hall.

18

EVIE

It was 11AM by the time I made it down the stairs the next morning. I'd woken up barely ten minutes ago, which was nuts. That meant I slept like a rock.

I was nervous when I heard Drew in the kitchen because I had no idea how he'd be this morning. I mean last night was crazy. It was crazy *twice*. It all felt like a dream quite honestly, and the only reason I knew it wasn't was because I woke up to find the top right corner of my fitted sheet ripped off the bed.

And I remembered being the person who did that.

"Morning, babe."

My eyes fluttered first, and then my heart followed suit when I heard Drew's voice ring out from the kitchen. *Whoa. Babe? Really?* I was instantly as relieved as I was confused by the unwavering affection in his greeting. *Okay, so I guess we know exactly where his head is at?* I thought to myself, my heart pitter-pattering.

But then I got downstairs and realized the truth.

We had company.

"Oh. Hello," I smiled politely at the older man standing beside the kitchen counter, wearing a blue Empires cap and a polo with the

Empires logo on the breast. He gave a big, jolly wave before extending his hand as I walked over to him.

"Lou Dickerson. I'm your fella's pitching coach. Nice to meet you."

"Oh, so nice to meet you! I'm Evie," I smiled bigger now that I knew who he was – or maybe it was because Drew placed his hand on the small of my back, wearing a convincingly proud smile on his face as he looked from Lou over to me.

"Lou's just here to meet me so we can head to the stadium early and watch some tape from yesterday," Drew said. The look of surprise I gave him was real.

"Wow. That's super early." Three hours earlier than usual. I had hoped to have even a minute of time alone with Drew before he left today. If anything, I just needed to see where his head was at. But apparently that wasn't happening thanks to Lou.

I couldn't be mad at this Lou guy though. He was just so nice and happy and he had the voice of a radio guy from the 1950's.

"Evie, I wish I didn't have to cut into your morning together, but when you see something that needs fixing, you gotta fix it!" he said.

"*Ohhh* right, the game." The catastrophic 17-4 loss, to be specific. I didn't even realize that Lou was talking about that until now. "Wow. I completely forgot that was last night."

"Well, then it must've been you with the good influence," Lou marveled. "I tell you, Evie, I came here prepared to talk Drew off a ledge this morning, but when I arrived the man was whistlin' a tune in the kitchen!"

"What can I say, Lou? She's good at helping me forget," Drew said with such uncharacteristic wholesomeness that I had to suppress a laugh.

But then I chewed my lip over the fact that he was being so obviously fake with that line. *Does that mean I did* not *in fact help him forget anything? Is he just happy he got to break the no touching rule and shove something in my face? Oh God, this is it, isn't it? This is the start of the ice-out.*

And... here it was.

The paranoia.

As I carried on with the typical small talk with Lou – Drew's hand on my back the entire time – I wondered what the hell was next. When would I get alone time with Drew next? Tonight after the game? That meant I'd have to endure a whole day of being in my head about last night, overanalyzing everything and trying not to text Drew before he finally got in. God, that sounded like torture.

Especially since I was half-convinced that this was it for us.

We'd proved last night that, new rules or not, we couldn't control ourselves around each other, so this was it for our contract. Tonight, Drew would come home and tell me that in the end, the fauxmance wasn't worth his blue balls. *Or* he would try to get me to sleep with him, I staunchly would not, and then he'd just kick my ass out, invite some girls over and deal with Iain in the morning.

That sounded like such a Drew Maddox thing to do that my stomach preemptively twisted.

"Shoot, look at the time!" Lou suddenly looked at his watch. "We gotta split. Grab those waters, will ya, Drew?"

"Got it." Drew slid his hand off my back and went over to the fridge, taking out two water bottles and setting them on the counter. "Car's downstairs, so we're all set."

"Perfect. Just gotta use that restroom again. You know me."

"No problem," Drew said.

And as Lou crossed the living room to get to the bathroom, I simply stood there, watching Drew close the fridge and just waiting for his attention.

The second I heard the bathroom door shut he lifted his eyes to me. My pulse picked up as he let them linger for a second before coming over. The look on his gorgeous face was so blank and unreadable I swore I was seconds from breaking into a sweat.

Here it comes, I told myself, even though I had no idea what was coming. My head tilted up slowly as he came closer, closer till he was standing with his toes nearly touching mine.

Then just as my heart jumped into my throat, Drew raked his fingers into my hair and crushed his lips to mine.

Despite the shock, I melted right into his body, sliding my hand up from his hard chest to his shoulders, hanging on for dear life as his tongue swept voraciously against mine. For a full ten seconds, he kissed my every question away, letting me practically climb up his chest as our tongues collided.

By the time we pulled away, I found myself perched on the edge of the counter, my arms wrapped around his neck. My lashes fluttered.

"How... did I get here?"

"I've been asking myself the same question all morning," Drew smirked.

I looked at him, unsure of how to interpret that. But with one word, Drew quickly quelled my concerns.

"Morning," he murmured, repeating his greeting from before. But this time, it was just for me.

"Morning," I returned his crooked little smile. I was outwardly at ease, relaxed, but electricity shot all through my body as Drew casually rubbed his hands up and down my thighs. He eyed the clock over the oven then grinned at me.

"I take it you slept well?"

"Amazingly. You?"

"Yeah. You heard Lou," Drew laughed. "Slept so good I was 'whistlin' a tune' this morning."

"Right," I grinned, feeling actual butterflies when I realized that whole whistling in the kitchen thing was real, and that it might've had to do with me. Feeling fully awake now, and not completely riddled with nerves, I let myself flash back to last night.

Biting my lip, eyeing the living room couch over Drew's shoulder, I remembered everything in sordid, vivid detail.

For God's sake, I had knelt at Drew's feet as he took his dick out and jerked off in front of me. I had flashed him my breasts and watched him release thick jets of cum all over his abs before grabbing a towel and feeling the steel of his cock in my palms as I cleaned him off.

That was hot enough without him coming into my room at night and going down on me in the dark.

"What's that face?" Drew asked.

"I'm just... thinking about last night."

"Yeah, I've been doing a little of that too." Drew cupped the back of my calves now as he looked at me. The look on his face was back to unreadable so I had no idea what he was about to say. But then he gave my calves a little squeeze. "Say the word and I'll eat that pussy again on this counter."

A shiver ran up my legs.

"Sounds like a great breakfast, but I don't think you have the time," I laughed as I heard a flush from the bathroom. "What, um... what time will you be home tonight?" I asked hesitantly, scared of sounding too much like an actual girlfriend.

Because technically, I still had no idea what was going on here. All I knew was that there was no radio silence. We were talking, we were *touching* and despite pushing limits last night, we were good. At least for now.

And I was too relieved with that to question anything.

"I think I'll be home before midnight. Depends on whether or not Lou has more tape he wants me to watch," Drew said as Lou came out of the bathroom. He gave a salute when Drew peered over his shoulder before looking back at me. "So, what's your day look like, babe?"

Babe. I guess that was our equivalent to saying *lights, camera, action!*

"Umm, I have a meeting in the Gramercy area and uptown. And I should probably get on Facebook to do some damage control after the comment from last night," I said with a sheepish grin.

"Uh-oh. Facebook fights. My wife gets into those," Lou said by the door. Drew laughed.

"Yeah, she was defending my honor last night. It got a little heated," he said, squeezing my knee. When he turned to me, the slightest frown pinched his brows. "That reminds me."

"What?" I whispered.

"I still need to spank your ass over that couch," Drew smirked, dropping my jaw just as Lou called out.

"Alright! Let's boogie!"

"Coming," Drew said before turning back to me and catching my chin to give me a peck on the lips. "See you tonight, baby?"

"Yeah. See you," I managed when he pulled away, leaving me breathless, dizzy, and already analyzing the possible difference between the use of the words "babe" and "baby."

Great, Evie. I shook my head at myself, still perched on that counter for a good five minutes after Drew left.

Just great.

19

EVIE

Even after a busy day of meetings all over the city, followed by cooking myself dinner, followed by dealing with the aftermath on Facebook, which included a long, private message from Mike that included the line "I won't stoop to public immaturity and hope you'll join me in acting like an adult the next time we see each other" – ugh, *retch* – I was still very much focused on one thing, and one thing only.

And that, of course, was Drew.

I found myself actually tuning into the Empires game while eating dinner, even though Drew wasn't starting, and I didn't know what was happening anyway. I was just waiting for the occasional shots of Drew leaning against the dugout railing with Ty, his green eyes looking so deliciously intense as he scrutinized the game from under the bill of his cap.

Just a two-second flash of him on the big screen made my heart thump.

That, Evie, I kept telling myself. *That beautiful hunk of man was in your bed last night. Putting his mouth in places where a mouth hadn't been in years. That man – that insanely hot man in that ridiculously sexy uniform – blew your fucking mind last night.*

It was hard to process.

At one point, when the commentators mentioned Drew's name, I had to do my best not to squeal.

What the fuck? Easy, woman. He's not really yours, I scolded myself, though I almost did it again when the screen flashed a graphic of the league's ERA leaders, and I saw Drew's name at number two.

Crap.

I could feel it. I was getting a little crazy. And ahead of myself. I was slowly starting to sip the Drew Maddox Kool-Aid despite the fact that, just a few weeks ago, I was convinced he was a typical athlete playboy who would never in his life care about anything but himself.

So before I knew it, I was grabbing my laptop and Googling him to help myself pump the brakes on the butterflies.

I went straight to searching "Drew Maddox womanizer," and while I did get tons of pictures of Drew stumbling out of clubs with insanely leggy, short-skirted women, I didn't see anything *that* scandalous. There was a story about one of his flings storming the field during Spring Training because he gave her a fake number, but that was more funny than anything.

"Okay," I said aloud, opting next for the keywords "Drew Maddox infamy." *Alright,* I nodded at the tons of results for that search, clicking through as many as I could.

There was a story about him trying to sue his own team when he played in Los Angeles. There were stories about him butting heads with teammates. Cursing off reporters. Smashing a paparazzo's camera. There were *multiple* articles about bench-clearing brawls that broke out during games because of him.

There was also, for some reason, a video in the results labeled *"THE INFAMOUS INTERVIEW."*

I clicked on it immediately, prepared to see another video of a shirtless Drew in the clubhouse, looking insanely hot while sounding deeply uninterested in all the post-game interview questions he was being hit with.

But instead, it was an actual sit-down interview from seven years ago.

"Oh my God," I murmured, biting the slow grin that drifted onto my lips, because the Drew I was watching was happy, bright-eyed and only twenty-three years old. His dark blond hair was cropped short and his face was completely clean-shaven. He was still beautiful as ever, but his look was far less rugged, and both his voice and his smile were boyish in a way that I had never thought possible.

In the video, he was absolutely glowing about the mother of his best friend, a woman named Pattie Lillard.

Yeah, because this will really help you not fall completely in love with him, I thought as young Drew raved on about how Pattie had raised him for chunks of his life, and how her son Tim was like a brother to him. He had served as best man at Tim's wedding, was at the hospital for the birth of Tim's son, and called the Lillards "the most important people" in his life.

"Yeah, this is really not helping," I muttered aloud to myself.

Because somehow, knowing that Drew was human at some point in his life simply fanned the fire of my infatuation. It made my heart soften for him, and it made me wonder where Pattie and Tim Lillard were today.

"Oh. Fuck," I mumbled as the interview took a turn, and Drew began talking about his efforts to raise money for treatment after the return of Pattie's cancer.

Right away, I paused the interview and Googled the name Pattie Lillard, and my heart instantly dropped at the first headline I saw.

PATTIE LILLARD LOSES BATTLE WITH CANCER AT AGE 58.

The headline was from two years ago.

"Geez," I breathed, holding a hand to my cheek as I clicked back to the interview of young Drew, tormenting myself by hitting play again and listening to him talk hopefully about all the fundraisers he was putting up for Pattie's treatment.

"She's going to make it. She means too much to too many people. I know she'll beat it."

God.

No wonder Drew was cold and hard now. He'd gone on national television, poured his heart out and still watched Pattie die a few years later. It made my heart ache for him. It made me wish I could just be near him right now and wrap my arms around him.

Basically, it was the exact opposite of what I had hoped to accomplish with this Googling session.

As the video ended with old photos of Drew, Tim and Pattie, I stupidly scrolled into the comments.

"What the fuck is wrong with people?" I whispered to myself as I skimmed the section. Considering the vulnerability and the outpouring of emotion I just saw, it was not at all what I expected.

DREW MADDOX IS A HYPOCRITE.

This dude is a fucking sociopath!!!

Can't believe he'd do that to his best friend whose mother RAISED him. SMH.

"What the..."

Without thinking, I clicked on the link that was posted with the last comment and suddenly I was on a YouTube video labeled "*TIM LILLARD KNOCKED OUT – ORIGINAL.*"

I watched about two seconds before slamming my laptop shut.

No.

No, no, no, no.

I already knew I didn't need to watch that. First of all, Drew wasn't in the video and all I could see was a shaky, blurry image as the cameraperson ran to a body lying bloodied at the foot of a suburban driveway.

It could be fake.

It could be real.

You don't know the whole story. Just don't.

The last thing I needed was more questions, especially at a time when Drew didn't necessarily owe me the answers. So walking my laptop upstairs, I placed it on my desk in my room, leaving it there before going back down to wait for Drew on the couch.

I still felt a weirdness hanging over me as I lay there, dozing in and out of sleep. It prickled over my skin and kept jolting me awake.

But at some point, I remembered seeing Drew's face on the screen again – still leaning on that dugout railing, still standing next to Ty. They were laughing big about something or another, and just the sight of that smile was enough to curve the ends of my lips before I drifted off to sleep.

20

DREW

By the time I got up in the morning, Evie's bedroom door was already open and she was already gone for whatever work meeting she had. Apparently I was disappointed because I found myself standing in her doorway for a second, staring at her empty bed.

After last night's game, I'd watched more tape with Lou and wound up getting home past 1AM, which meant Evie was already passed out hard on the couch. I'd said her name a few times as I emptied my pockets on the kitchen counter and laughed to myself when she didn't stir at all.

The TV was on and wrapping up post-game coverage of the night's win, which meant she'd been watching the game by herself.

Unexpected.

Also unexpected was the little black thing she slept in. It was short and silky, and I was forced to watch it flutter up her thighs as I carried her up the stairs to her room. It was like walking a tight rope as I made my way up the steps while sliding my eyes all over her body.

By the time I got to the stadium, I was still thinking about the way she exhaled as I put her in bed. She didn't wake up at all but when her body hit the mattress, she rolled onto her side and immediately curled up to her pillow.

Then she let out that breath and smiled. Like she was in a fucking Ambien commercial. She was peaceful in a way I didn't think was real, and I was still switching between laughing at the memory and agonizing over it when I got a text from an unknown number.

Hi Drew. Sorry about texting and please don't tell Tim but I'm just so proud today and I couldn't have done this without you. Wish you could've been here.

P.S Christopher says hi. He still loves his Uncle Drew.

My eyes darted over the words just before the picture came in.

When I processed the faces in it, the whirlwind of emotion was instantaneous, and I knew I'd failed to suppress the first second because Diaz peered over at me from his locker. But he said nothing and I thanked God for that because I needed a second.

I needed a fucking second to digest that Abby Lillard had graduated from Temple University today.

Holy fuck. I wanted to smile but I couldn't, because as innocent as she probably was in the whole mess with her brother, it wasn't like I could look at her without thinking of him. I couldn't even be happy about the fact that I'd put her through college. I'd sent her check for tuition exactly a week before my shit with Tim went down, and I still remembered her refusing to cash it for awhile and being scared that if she did, it meant she was on my side and not her brother's.

"Jesus," I muttered when another picture came in – this time of her holding Christopher.

I smiled. Kind of. It was a tense, conflicted one, but it was a smile nonetheless because this was my favorite kid in the world.

Christopher Drew Lillard. Tim's son. I took him on his first trip to Disney, I was there the day he was born, he was named after me, and aside from Pattie he had to be the one Lillard I missed most.

As quickly as it came, my smile disappeared.

Fucking hell.

Four years later and I was still haunted by this family. I was still hounded by the press to give quotes on Pattie's death. On the incident with Tim. I still had opposing teams' fans use their names to heckle me when I was in the dugout or on the mound. I tuned most of it out but it was impossible to completely ignore, and I fucking hated the days when I had to wonder if I'd ever actually move on from them.

Sitting in front of my locker, my elbows on my knees, I stared at my jersey. I stared at the number twenty-one I'd been wearing since my rookie year, tapping my left foot and trying to shift the dark thoughts in my brain to something else before the game started.

But a few minutes passed and it didn't work.

I stared into space for a little longer. Then picking up my phone, I sent a text.

ME: What are you up to

I watched the ellipses blink for a bit. It took awhile before her reply came in. I shook my head as I kept watching it go in and out. What the fuck was she doing?

EVIE: Hey. Sorry typing slow I'm walking and texting. What's up? Did I forget we had something today?

ME: I would have opened with that if you did.

EVIE: Oh. Excuse me then.

EVIE: In that case to answer your question I'm just shopping for something to wear to the thing tonight.

ME: What thing?

EVIE: Hillary's restaurant opening. Merryweather where we went for lunch

My eyebrows pulled tight. I wasn't sure what I was even frowning about so I tried to jog my memory on what I knew of that restaurant. It came up surprisingly quickly. *Right*

Both Evie and her ex had done work for that place.

ME: Mike going to be there?

EVIE: Yes. Yay for you getting his name right. I owe you a gold star.

ME: You owe me several gold stars. What time is the thing

EVIE: Starts at 8 and goes on till forever bc there'll probably be an after party. But I'm only making an appearance for Hillary then I'm dipping

EVIE: Why do you ask?

ME: Go there late. I'll meet up with you at 10:30

No idea why I said that. Aside from the fact that I had a day game tomorrow, tonight's game was bound to end at or past 10PM, which meant I'd have to book it to get to the restaurant from the stadium in time. But considering Evie slept at grandma hours, I knew I'd have to throw out the earliest time possible.

EVIE: If you're offering to come with because you think I need protection from Mike you are sorely mistaken

ME: I'm not worried about that. I've seen his scrawny ass and your naked one. I'm pretty sure you could squat him.

EVIE: Except it was pitch black when you decided to steal my panties off me so technically you haven't actually seen my naked ass

ME: I haven't but I've felt every inch of it. If I described it to a sketch artist he would draw it to a tee

EVIE: Omg

EVIE: What on earth did my ass do to warrant a police sketch?

EVIE: Something something being wanted for a spanking?

"What's going on with you? You're laughing now?" Diaz asked as he looked at me.

"Leave me alone," I said, a leftover grin on my lips as I replied to Evie.

ME: You get the gold star for that one. Now stop texting while you're walking. See you at 10:30 tonight.

21

DREW

It was closer to 11PM by the time I got to the restaurant, which definitely felt different than the last time I'd seen it.

The last time I was here it was quiet, sunny and mostly empty, but tonight there were candles on every table, indie folk on the sound system, and a good fifty to sixty buzzed to drunk people standing around dirty, plate-littered tables, engaged in animated conversation.

Definitely not the type of nightlife I was used to. If I was out and drinking at 11PM, The Lumineers weren't exactly my soundtrack of choice, but to each their own. I wasn't here to party anyway. I was here for Evie.

The usual eyes flew to me as I angled through the crowd, but the setting was intimate enough that no one yelled my name or mobbed me for pictures. They just kept watching as I made my way to the group of women Evie was talking to.

My eyebrows lifted when I got closer.

She was wearing red lipstick tonight. And she looked fucking stunning. The first thing I saw was her big smile as she burst out laughing over something that was apparently funny enough for her to be the last of the group to notice me.

"Um, Evie..." The redhead to her left kept her unblinking eyes on me while smiling nervously and tapping Evie. "Sweetie, I think some-one's here to see you."

"Drew! Thank God you're here!" She surprised me by bursting over and throwing her arms around my neck. When my hand touched nothing but skin, I realized her dress was completely back-less. *Whoa, whoa.*

"Hold on a second. Let me see this," I muttered. Evie's friends giggled and nudged each other as I held her hand up for a moment to step back and get a full look.

I wasn't doing it for show. I genuinely needed a second to process that body in that coffee-colored dress. She was completely covered in the front but when I turned her around, her naked back was on full display. If it weren't for the bow tied around her neck, I would've thought she was walking around topless with just a skirt on.

I shook my head before facing her front once again.

"God, you look fucking beautiful," I said, getting to enjoy about a second of her smile before her friends burst into a loud chorus of "*awww.*"

Jesus.

"Thank you. I didn't think you'd get here till late," Evie said breathily before introducing me to all her friends. I forgot all their names on the spot. "And you know, um... you know Hillary," Evie said, suddenly fumbling and eyeing her redheaded friend as she gestured toward Hillary. Hillary didn't seem to notice because she smiled brightly.

"Hey again! So happy you could come, Drew."

"Thank you for having me," I smiled back just as another familiar face came damned near shoving through the crowd behind her.

Mike.

"Drew! My man. Happy you made it," he said with a broad smile, offering a hand over Hillary's shoulder.

"Thanks. Good to see you," I lied as Evie leaned her gorgeous back into my chest. Despite her outward calm, her body was trem-bling a bit. I frowned. I could tell from the way she grabbed my hand

and squeezed it twice that she was trying to tell me something. I had no idea what it was thus far, but I was on alert.

"Drew. Buddy. What happened the other night?" Mike frowned, leaning on Hillary with an arm tossed over her shoulder. I didn't have to fake the smile that quirked my mouth as I ran my hands down to Evie's waist.

"You're going to have to be more specific, because a lot of things happened the other night."

It was supposed to be just a joke for Evie but she blushed so hard the girls read the situation fast and gave a scandalous "*oooooh*." Mike bristled.

"I'm talking about that crazy loss. That had to be the worst outing of your career, right?"

"It was. Thankfully, it was my first loss this season."

"Well. It's a long season."

"It is. I've been playing awhile in this league so I know firsthand," I laughed while sliding my hands down to Evie's hips. "Luckily, I have this secret weapon right here."

There was another "*awww*" from the girls as Mike sneered.

"Well, I know firsthand that Evie doesn't know a football from a baseball, so I don't know how she comes in any way handy."

"She's more of a lifesaver in the sore muscle department," I said, rubbing Evie's hips to calm her down. I could feel her breathing deep, shaking a little less now.

"Oh, her *massages*, right?" the redhead gasped. "They're so frickin' good. And that's so perfect for you as an athlete! Oh, oh, you should get her a job at the stadium!"

"Jesus, no." I grimaced so hard the girls burst out laughing. "Trust me, my teammates would love that but she's strictly mine."

"Well, we'll see how long that lasts," Mike chuckled as the circle fell promptly quiet. The girls' eyes were wide, and Hillary visibly cringed. Despite the palpable awkwardness, he went right on. "I mean, Maddox, I think anyone who's been on the Internet knows you're not exactly a one-woman kind of guy."

Evie stiffened in my arms. The girls were covering their faces at this point but I gave the prick an easy laugh.

"Believe it or not, tabloids are sometimes bullshit. Some people just get brave with what they say when they're hiding behind a computer screen."

"I don't know about that," Mike scoffed.

"Come on. I'm sure you've said things on the Internet that you'd never have the balls to say in person. You could be standing right in front of the person and still be too scared to say shit."

Based on the redhead's giant snort, I assumed she'd seen his post about me on Facebook. I wore a placid smile as I cocked an eyebrow at Mike. I was challenging the little shit to prove me wrong and call me overpaid to my face, but all he did was grunt, clear his throat and look away.

Then it was silent for a bit, Evie and the redhead exchanging looks I couldn't read.

"Anyway, I could never be a professional masseuse," Evie finally said to break the awkward silence. "I only bust out my A game for my man."

"Yeah, I remember that," Mike said.

This motherfucker.

Hillary up and left as Evie hugged my arms tight around her waist. She gave my forearms a quick but firm squeeze, and this time I read what she was saying. *I got this one.*

"Trust me, it takes a *whole* other level of strength to rub this one down," she laughed good-naturedly, beaming up at me before returning her eyes to Mike. "I mean Drew's all muscle. So it's literally night and day between you two."

Jesus.

Savaged.

Mike went red as Evie's friends failed at suppressing their fits of laughter.

"I'm gonna find Hillary," he muttered, that forehead vein beating with a life of its own as he turned around and left.

I was pretty sure Evie could be nothing but pleased with herself after that, but once we excused ourselves from her girlfriends, she took my hand and tugged me into the kitchen. By now, it was only the dishwasher in there and he gave barely a look in our direction before going back to his own thing while nodding to the music on his headphones.

"Evie. What?" I frowned when I saw her hands trembling as she rubbed them over her face. "Jesus, baby. What happened?"

She took a few seconds to answer, and I didn't realize I'd turned to hunt down Mike till she grasped a handful of my shirt and pulled me away from the door.

"Hillary might be living with him," she blurted. I stared at her.

"What?"

"My friend Kate with the red hair. She's the manager here and before you came, she told me something. And I've just been trying to hold everything in and act normal, but – "

"What? What did she tell you?"

"She said she saw the address on some of Hillary's mail. It's my address. I mean not mine. But the apartment I spent forever finding for me and Mike."

Jesus.

Now I was the one dragging my hand down my face. I didn't need to know more to know what was probably the full story. Mike left Evie for Hillary. Considering how closely they worked, he'd probably been sleeping with her before the breakup. It would explain why he refused to fuck Evie.

"I can't believe this," Evie whispered, furiously wiping at her tears. When I collected her hands in mine and tipped her chin up to face me, she curled her lip and turned away. "Don't make fun of me for crying. I know what you want to say, Drew. That I should never trust anyone. Everyone'll screw you over at some point. You've said it. I get it."

It was definitely the *told you so* moment I lived for, but as much as I loved to prove myself right, I couldn't bring myself to gloat right now. I didn't know Mike or Hillary, but this story didn't surprise me because it was just what I knew of people in general. That said, Evie was blindsided. Again.

I looked at her big wet eyes. That wobbly lip. I thought of how she just curled up in her bed last night and just smiled so peacefully in her sleep. Despite all that, I was still itching to use this time to evangelize her. To bring her into the no-trust club. After all, misery fucking loved company.

But there was a small part of me that didn't want to make her world as dark as mine. It was a sliver, but it refused to fuck her up the way I was fucked.

And for the first time in my life, I listened to the little voice instead of the big one.

"Evie, you made your appearance and you ended on a high note. Let's just go home. I'll pour you a glass of wine, we'll watch a movie on the couch and we'll forget this whole night even happened."

"That sounds nice." Her voice was shaky, pitiful. She continued avoiding my gaze as she wiped her tears. "But I feel like – I feel like I need to know for sure. I need to talk to Hillary. I mean I've known her since college. She used to make me care packages because I didn't have money for groceries. She's been such a friend to me for so long – there has to be an explanation. Right?"

"There isn't, Evie. Please. Don't do this to yourself."

"I feel like I can't trust anyone," she spoke over me.

"Welcome to the club."

Whoops. I slipped. The words just came out. And as they did, I watched her cry again, this time into her hands. Her shoulders shook and she tried to stifle her sobs but I heard them, and as I did, I flipped the switch I did whenever women decided to cry in front of me. It generally worked like a mute button so I could comfortably skip this part of the conversation. But apparently the batteries were finally out.

"Look, we'll stay for a little longer," I said, cupping her elbows and bringing her closer. "But this has nothing to do with Mike. This is just to give Helen the benefit of the doubt."

"*Hillary,*" Evie corrected with a frustrated groan but then she broke into a conflicted laugh. "Drew, God. What is wrong with your memory? Did a baseball hit you in the head once?"

"No, I just save my memory for what actually matters," I said, prompting her to blink at me a few times and give me a funny look. But then she wiped the last of her tears and took in a deep breath.

"You don't mind staying a little longer?" she asked, her voice small.

I minded. I really didn't think she was going to find the answer she wanted and I wasn't a fan of wasting my own time. Still, I shook my head "no" for her.

"Okay. Just a little longer," she said, interlocking her fingers in mine. "And then we'll go home?"

"And then we'll go home," I echoed, returning the squeeze she gave my hand before we pushed through the door and headed back out.

22

EVIE

One thing led to another and by a quarter past midnight, the proud "foodies" of the dwindled group – down to about ten now – were talking about taking the after party to an amazing new gastropub inside some boutique hotel in DUMBO. Mike said we'd never get in even with *his* PR connections, at which point some drunk guy suggested we just drop Drew Maddox's name.

And since it pissed off Mike, we did exactly that.

Besides, I was still trying to get my closure on Hillary. I'd seen Mike whisper to her a few times but other than that, she went nowhere near him. That said she avoided me too, and for every time I went up to her and she scurried away I felt my heart sag.

Because I didn't want Drew to be right.

Since the day we'd met, he'd been proving me wrong and I wanted to change that. I wanted to prove to him that there was hope left. That trust wasn't a guaranteed set-up for failure. I couldn't get behind his morbid outlook on the world, and I was desperate to debunk it.

But as everyone but me got progressively drunker, I began to see things.

I saw Hillary instinctively smile when Mike whispered something in her ear while tickling her waist. But when she caught my eye across the bar, she quickly shoved him away. She looked miserable as she continued to duck both Mike and me all night, and at some point, I saw her rubbing her temples before taking shots of whiskey by herself.

And since she was proudly *not* a party girl who famously hated the taste of hard alcohol, I had a feeling she was trying desperately to relieve herself of something. Nerves, definitely.

And guilt, perhaps.

"The hotel gave me a free room," Drew said as he came up to me and tossed a key card onto the bar. My eyes fluttered from Hillary to him.

"What? Why?"

"Because I'm Drew Maddox."

"What did we say about referring to yourself in third person?"

"Sometimes it makes sense, alright?"

I gave him a look.

"Alright, I'll stop," he relented with amusement before dropping his voice to a murmur. "How you feeling, by the way?" he asked. Placing two hands on either side of me on the bar, he caged me in with those strong arms.

"I was feeling vaguely weird. But I'm better now," I replied honestly as I gazed at his biceps, the deep line of muscle on his forearm, and the sleeve of tattoos that covered his right arm, right down to his wrist. I noted the birds, flames and lion heads hidden in the sea of ink. "Do they all mean something or did you just get them because they look cool?"

"The latter. I'm actually a giant poser. I don't even play baseball. It's all a front."

"Screw you," I snorted.

"Speaking of screwing, I want to check out this suite they gave me and see if the guy at the front desk was bullshitting me or not."

"What'd he say?"

"That there are mirrors in the bedroom," Drew laughed as I rolled my eyes. But I bit my lip as he brushed a wisp of hair from my face and cupped my cheek. "He also said there's a pretty spectacular view of the East River and Manhattan if you're interested in that. I know you have a pretty weird boner for the city skyline."

"You're the worst."

"You love me," he said with a cocky grin, sending heat to my cheeks. He traced my dimple with his thumb as he looked down at me for several seconds, and when he spoke again, his voice came back softer. "At the very least, I do think you like me now."

"You're slightly above tolerable to me now."

"I'll take it," he laughed. "Now are you going to come with me or are you going to stay down here?"

Without hesitating, I chose Drew.

Unfortunately, anytime Drew went somewhere, everyone followed.

By now it was past 1AM and the group had dwindled to six, but everyone followed – including Hillary and Mike. Definitely a bit of a surprise to me, though to be fair, Hillary resisted as much as she could, taking another shot before letting Mike drag her away from the bar.

Yeah, enough of this, I decided when they joined us to wait for the elevators. I saw one descending a floor behind the other and when the first arrived, I let everyone pile in before pulling Hillary back last second.

"Hey!" Mike snapped just as the door closed in his face. Hillary's eyes went wide.

"Evie..."

"Hillary." I pulled her into the next elevator and hit the door shut button before facing her. "How long?"

"How long what?" she practically whimpered.

"You and Mike. How long?" I reiterated my question, feeling suddenly ready to leave this bullshit behind me.

Had anyone told me two or three weeks ago that I'd lose Hillary to the breakup as well, I'd probably fall to my knees and mourn the loss of these people who'd been so important to me. But tonight, despite the initial hiccup, I was ready to take a page from the Drew Maddox playbook and just cut these two out of my life.

Trust existed but not with them, and I was ready to end this chapter and move on.

"About a year ago," Hillary finally whispered, looking up at me with wet eyes. "A little longer. I kept telling him to make it right though, I promise. I kept telling him to just break up with you."

"But he didn't, and you stayed."

"He said he needed time to transition."

Oh my God.

He needed time to wean himself off me before going to Hillary. That was probably the most pathetic and despicable thing I'd ever heard.

"I told him to at least stop sleeping with you to make it somewhat okay," Hillary protested.

Nope. Maybe *that* was the most despicable thing I'd ever heard.

Once the elevator reached the floor of the suite, I stalked out without a word and followed the sound of the group laughing and chatting down the hall. The door of the suite was open, and the group was marveling at everything from the view to the bedroom, which indeed had mirrored walls in front of and behind the king-sized bed.

But the laughter stopped the second I walked in, and the second Mike sneered and said, "I take it she told you," everyone slowly looked at each other then trickled out of the room.

Ignoring Mike, I went straight to Drew and put my hands on his chest.

"Let's go," I murmured, repeating myself when he wouldn't stop glaring at Mike.

His broad shoulders were rigid, and I could feel every muscle in his torso tensed and ready to launch into go mode. I would've been flattered by his fury on my behalf, but I was too ready to get the hell out of this place. By now, it was just Drew, me, Mike and a sniffling Hillary standing by the door.

"Look, I deserve a chance to explain myself," Mike broke the silence.

"If you really believe that, you're a bigger idiot than I thought," I snapped.

"Just let me talk to you alone for a – "

"Watch it," Drew growled the second Mike reached for my arm. I didn't know when it happened, but he was suddenly standing in front of me. "Read the room, asshole. No one here has any interest in hearing you beg, so save your own breath and go the fuck home."

"I've known this girl for way longer than you have," Mike snarled, making me want to roll my eyes out of my head. "And I want to talk to her privately."

"You're not going to get to," I retorted.

"Yeah well, I'm not going fucking anywhere till I get a chance to."

"Suit yourself."

The words came from Drew before he pulled me into the bedroom and slammed the door in Mike's face.

"What are you doing?" I hissed. "Let's just go home. I know he's not going to leave!"

"Good," Drew muttered. "He made you watch him and Hillary all night, so I'm going to make him listen."

"To what?"

"Me fucking you."

My eyes fluttered wide. Tingles of mischief darted across my skin as Drew closed what little gap there was between us.

"But you're not fucking me," I whispered.

"Trust me, I'm aware of that." My breath caught in my throat as he pushed me up against the door. "But I want him to think I am right now. I want him to think I have you pinned here with my hand up your skirt and my cock teasing your pussy," he muttered, thrusting his body against mine and rattling the door behind me. "I want him to know how loud I can make you moan."

"I can't fake moans very well," I breathed as Drew kissed and nipped along my jaw. "So you might have to help me out a little."

His low laugh rumbled against my neck.

"That shouldn't be a problem," he murmured, his warm, rough tongue nuzzling me for several more seconds before he sank to a kneel in front of me.

I swallowed as I watched Drew assess my legs, smoothing a hand up the side of my thigh as he tilted his head to look under my skirt.

"Hold it up for me."

"What?"

"Your skirt. Lift it," Drew said firmly. "Just like that. Now hold it there," he muttered, wetting his lips when I flashed him my mesh and lace panties. They were black but they were sheer and in my heels, my pussy was right at his eye level, making me feel completely naked despite the fact that I wasn't.

Yet.

But I did feel vulnerable as all hell just standing there, especially with Drew tormenting me. He was taking his sweet time, sending a million little tingles over my skin as he rubbed his hands up and down the backs of my thighs, gazing lustily between my bare legs.

"Drew," I exhaled pleadingly. My short, jagged breaths had the door vibrating behind my back, shivering with me in its frame as I simply waited to be touched.

The second he kissed me over my panties, I let out a soft moan.

I knew he liked the sound of it because he glanced up with a smirk in his eyes before he kissed me again, this time closer to my clit.

"More," I begged, hugging my skirt to my chest as I waited for Drew to take my panties off.

But he didn't do that.

Instead he made me gasp as he stretched them off of me, using two hands to rip the crotch right in half before giving my bare pussy a long, wet lick. His wicked tongue pushed between my folds to find my clit and suck on it like candy. He didn't bother to do anything quietly. Everything was loud, smacking, shameless. Unlike last time in my bed, he was going straight for the kill. He was trying to make me come fast and hard, and I swore to God his ruthless pace had me already dizzy.

I felt like I was losing control but the second my knees buckled, Drew's strong hands gripped my thighs, pushing one back up on the door and throwing the other over his shoulder so he could bury his mouth deeper between my legs.

"Drew...fuck!" I had my hand crushed over my mouth at this point, practically screaming into my palm as that unbelievable tongue of his curled and scooped at my pussy, drawing every rush of wetness from the back to the front so he could lap me up like honey.

Oh God. Where am I?

I can't even breathe.

I was out of my mind. I felt like I was on the verge of coming for a full minute before the burst of ecstasy finally rocked through me, forcing me to grip the doorknob to keep from toppling over. My hand pulsed there for several seconds, stars in my vision as I sucked in deep breaths, Drew still gripping my thigh and licking me dry.

Only once I'd caught my breath did I finally open my eyes. They fluttered as I found myself staring at my flushed reflection in the mirror behind the bed. I got one hot glimpse of Drew's muscled back under his shirt before he stood up again and blocked my exquisite view.

But I couldn't complain about this view either – his green eyes sparkling at me as he licked the last of me off his lips.

Without even looking down, I palmed his cock, biting hard on my lip when I confirmed that it was rock fucking solid. I wet my lips as I stroked it, still dazed from my orgasm but already needing another.

"I want you to fuck me," I breathed, a frown twitching my brow as he removed my hand from his erection.

"Not here."

"Why not?"

"Because I don't have a condom," he grumbled in frustration, pausing as if waiting to hear that I might. But I didn't and that made him growl under his breath. "I don't fuck without condoms. We have to go home."

I blinked, surprised by his resolve. I was used to guys being desperate to fuck without condoms, but clearly that wasn't the case with Drew. And it made me curious.

"That's a lot of self-control."

"You keep underestimating me in that department," he muttered, shooting a glare when I blocked his reach for the doorknob. "What are you doing?"

"I want to test it," I said, feeling a devilish flutter in my stomach. "Your self-control."

"Why?"

"Because no one thinks you have any, and I want to tell them you do."

Total bullshit answer – this was just turning me on, and Drew knew it.

"We're going home, Evie."

"I just want to suck on it for a little."

Drew glared at me, his jaw clenching so hard I could practically hear his teeth gnashing together. In that moment, he looked at me like he fucking hated me, but I didn't care because I had him.

As much as it would torture him, he couldn't say no. I knew that so I didn't back down till finally, without breaking his stare or saying a word, Drew reached down for his belt. He kept his steely gaze pinned to me as he gave three harsh jerks to undo his buckle. I watched his lips slightly part, his left shoulder rolling as he reached into his boxers to pull out his hard cock. I exhaled with anticipation when I felt its heat near my belly, and excitement literally watered my mouth.

But I kept my eyes locked on Drew till he gave me a dirty little nod.

"Go on then," he murmured. "Suck it."

Five words and he sent another rush of heat to my exposed pussy. Wetness dripped down my thighs as I lowered myself to my knees and wrapped my hand around the base of his cock. I felt Drew rake his long fingers into my hair and lean back to get a full view as I wrapped my lips around his wide, smooth tip, sucking till I could taste his precum seep onto my tongue.

"That's too good, baby, you need to stop," Drew growled. But in the same breath, he braced himself with two hands on the door and began rocking his hips, gently fucking his cock into my mouth. "Oh fuck, Evie. Fuck." I heard him drop one hand from the door a second before I felt him grab my ponytail at the root.

I let him control the pace for a few seconds because I was already addicted to the feeling of his size stretching my lips, and to the gravelly, unbelievably sexy sound of his groan.

I loved hearing him get lost in his pleasure, muttering under his breath and switching back and forth between filth and affection. One second, I was his "*dirty little girl.*" The other, I was "*so goddamned perfect.*" Whatever it was, I didn't care – I loved it all.

Of course, I loved it most when I sucked him hard for a good twenty seconds, my cheeks hollowing as I squeezed handfuls of his jeans, giving pulls so tight and wet on his cock that he roared like a wild beast when I abruptly stopped.

Returning to my feet, I caught the blazing fire in Drew's eyes as I wiped the corner of my mouth with my finger.

"Okay. We can go home now," I panted, knowing well that I'd just set myself up for the hardest fuck of my life.

But that was kind of the point.

"Turn around," Drew said.

I thought he was ordering me to immediately open the door, but the second I turned, he bent me over his arm. Ripping my skirt up, he brought a brutal spank down on my ass, prompting my jaw to fall open as I slapped my hand to the door.

"Just so you know what you're in for," Drew said as he dropped my skirt back into place and moved my hand around the doorknob. "Now stand up straight, baby. We're going home."

23

DREW

C learly, she didn't realize that I specialized in punishment.
        Then again, no one really gave me credit for that.

They liked to think of me as reckless. Impulsive. Thoroughly lacking in self-control. They saw the fights, the temper. The times I mouthed off to the umps and got my ass fined five figures in one shot. They took one look at the partying, the late nights at clubs, and they decided that was all they needed to sum up Drew Maddox.

It was like I'd become the best pitcher in baseball by pure coincidence. Like it didn't take seventeen years of practicing patience, grit and discipline, to the point that I started to like when I was sore and aching, in physical pain.

Because that meant I'd worked for it.

"I swear I hate you, Drew," Evie panted as she stayed right where I'd left her – bent over the back of the couch in just her strappy little heels.

"You don't."

I took a swig of water as I closed the refrigerator door, soaking in the sight of her gleaming wet pussy and thoroughly spanked ass from the kitchen. There was nothing about this view that wasn't perfect, from her ripped black panties on the floor to her long hair cascading down between her shoulder blades, settling in that sexy curve of her back.

For the past twenty minutes, I'd switched between spanking and finger-fucking her, and now she was waiting there somewhere between helpless and patient as I took a water break. But she gasped the second she heard the tiny scrape of me grabbing the condom off the kitchen counter and crossing back to the living room.

"Yes, yes, Drew, please..."

Even when she was done begging with her words, she begged me with the sexiest, breathiest cross between a moan and a whimper. It made my dick twitch in my hand as I positioned myself behind her again, smirking as she made coy eye contact over her shoulder. She bit her lip as she watched me tear the wrapper with my teeth, tossing it onto the ground and stretching the rubber over my shaft.

"Hurry," she begged.

But I didn't. I took a second to admire how perfectly spread she was for me as I propped her knee up on the couch.

Then with two handfuls of her ass, I drove my cock deep inside her.

"Drew!"

She cried out in shock as I rolled my head back and groaned, immediately lost in how fucking tight her pussy squeezed around me. I growled as I slammed through every clench of her walls around me, filling my hands with her tits and holding nothing back.

"Does that feel good, baby?" I rasped though I already knew the answer since she only stopped moaning to turn and kiss me. "'Cause I'm in fucking heaven right now," I muttered almost to myself. "I swear to God, I am."

Aside from having my cock buried inside her, I had Evie's tight ass pressed up against me, her shaking tits in my hands and my tongue in her mouth.

It was unreal. Gratification like I'd never felt before. There were no words to describe the sensation of finally having every part of her body in my possession. I hadn't known her for even a month, but somehow it felt like I'd waited years to feel exactly this.

I was beyond content already.

I was convinced it couldn't get better, but once her pussy was perfectly stretched around me, she started moving her hips, meeting me halfway on each thrust till I was just goddamned standing there in awe as I watched her ride backwards on my cock.

"Jesus, Evie," I hissed with both hands thrust in my hair. "You gotta be fucking kidding me with that pussy."

I lost track of time watching her. I didn't know how long I stood there hypnotized by her working those hips, bouncing that ass and covering my cock from root to tip with her sopping wetness. All I knew was that I couldn't look away. I didn't know she had this in her and at the same time, I wasn't really surprised. She was innocent and fiery all in one breath. She gasped at my size a second before begging me to fuck her harder, so there was no telling with her. Not that I was trying to figure anything out.

I was too busy enjoying this more than anything in the goddamned world, and I hadn't even heard her come yet.

"Turn around," I growled when I felt myself getting close.

I'd barely slid my dick out of her before slamming back in, wrapping her legs around my hips and squeezing her ass as I carried her to the couch. I didn't slip an inch from her slick grip as I lay her down, hugging her leg to my side and grinding deep inside her till she went completely quiet.

But I saw her trembling lip and I felt her nails in my back. I read the look in her big eyes as she nodded breathlessly, and even if it weren't for the nonstop spasms of her pussy around me, I'd have known she was seconds away from giving me the sexiest sounds I'd ever heard.

"Go on. Come for me, baby," I breathed out, my own body tingling, numb from the pressure of holding out. I knew the second she came, she'd take me with her.

And she did exactly that.

All I needed was the first second of her blissful moan to shoot off like a fucking cannon inside her. My mind went instantly vacant, but as her walls shuddered around me, I drew on every last ounce of energy in my body – thrusting inside her, still fucking her senseless as we soared and fell together.

24

DREW

I wiped the sweat off my brow, laughing between sets as Iain just stood there scrutinizing me, looking like he was trying to read my mind.

We were at the Empires workout facility, so he stuck out like a sore thumb in his crisp white button-down and slacks. Of course, in typical Iain fashion, the authority of his presence made it seem like he was the one who was right, and we were just the animals who were underdressed for this place.

"You're fucking creepy, you know that, right?" I panted before picking up the dumbbell and going back to my laterals.

I acted like I didn't know what the hell he was here for, or why he was looking at me like that, despite the fact that I knew there was no lying to this asshole. He knew his clients too well – me in particular.

"I just think it was very kind of you to volunteer to go to some boring restaurant opening with her when you had a day game in the morning," Iain said.

Read: I think you're sleeping with her or trying to.

Yeah. I knew what he was implying, but if he couldn't prove it, I wasn't going to say shit. For all he knew, I took Evie home, we went to our separate bedrooms and I passed right out to get some good rest in before having to wake up earlier than usual.

There was no way for him to figure out that I'd taken her home and come harder than I ever had in my life inside her, or that we'd passed out together on the couch.

Though by the time I'd woken up this morning, she was already gone.

"Well, you said it yourself, man." I blew out air from between my teeth as I lifted. "It turned into good press."

Apparently, not asking for pictures didn't mean that the people at Merryweather didn't take them, because by this morning, the gossip pages were flooded with candid snippets of Evie and me. They were taken from the Instagram and Snapchat accounts of Hillary's friends. According to the articles, I was "keeping it low-key" by meeting Evie's friends at a "friends and family only event in Brooklyn."

"According to one source, Maddox was overheard discussing the 'e' word with a few of Larsen's friends – engagement!"

That was Iain's doing. His company represented both actors and athletes, and he was so tight with the media that I would've called him a traitor if it weren't for the fact that he was only ever using or manipulating them.

"It was definitely good press," Iain said, his eyes leisurely scanning the room to make sure there was no one in earshot. There wasn't. But even if there were, the room was just a chorus of slamming weights and animal-like grunting, so honestly, I could barely hear Iain myself. That's why I thought I'd heard him wrong on what he said next. "Anyway, you proposed to her last night."

I had to finish my set before I snorted.

"Come again?"

"In our timeline, you popped the question last night."

"Really? How'd I do it?" I laughed.

"Up to you, Romeo. Anyway, I had the clubbie put something in your locker drawer. Give it to Evie tonight and make her wear it before you take her out to dinner. And pick a place you like because you'll be there awhile. You have to drag out this date so she can properly debut her new ring," Iain said before pausing as if waiting for me to say something.

"What? Did you ask me a question?"

"No. I was waiting for you to gripe about the fact that you have to have a long candlelit dinner. You've never been one for hours of conversation at once, but looks like you're more than game for tonight."

"What can I say? I love this team," I smirked. "And if it cools down trade talks, I'll do it."

"Right." Iain held his eye contact for several seconds before eyeing the time. "Well, from what I hear, the front office is pleasantly surprised by all this. You've got Julian Hoult and a bunch of old guys tracking your love life via tabloid, so good job so far. I just hope you can keep things this smooth and steady with Evie till past the trade deadline. Be smart with her. Or it'll all have been for nothing."

"Yeah, I got that, sunshine, but thank you for the reminder."

"Anytime."

"Alright, well I'm here to work out, not talk, so you should probably get going to whatever meeting you're dressed like James Bond for."

He cracked a laugh.

"Fine. Enjoy dinner tonight," he said, turning to go. But then, just to fuck with me, he stopped at the doorway and called back across the room. "And hey – congratulations on the big engagement, Maddox."

Then as soon as all my teammates' big eyes flew to me, he left.

EVIE

I was still catching up from my day when I heard Drew get home. I knew we had a public dinner scheduled tonight and while I was supposed to be getting ready now, I was running late. I was flustered and still all over the place from how my morning had started.

It would've been perfect if phones didn't exist. To start, I'd woken up on Drew's bare chest, and good God, that was a hell of a way to start a day.

I was glad he didn't stir because after lifting my cheek off his pecs, I had needed more than a few seconds to just look at him.

His inked bicep bulged since he had his right arm bent and resting behind his head. His lips were slightly parted and he had his other arm wrapped around me, his hand resting heavily on my back.

I wanted to just stay there in his arms all morning, basking in the leftover glow of what happened last night.

But I couldn't fully enjoy myself knowing that I'd woken multiple times in the night to the sound of my phone buzzing against the kitchen counter. No one ever texted me that persistently that late, so I couldn't help but get up around 6AM and investigate.

I had braced myself for angry, bitter texts from Mike but it wasn't that at all.

It was something much worse that immediately started my day on a frenzied whirlwind, eventually making me late for all my meetings and causing me to be still flustered now at 7PM.

"Evie?"

I had just finished makeup and moisturizing and was blow-drying my hair when Drew called up the stairs.

"I'm in the bathroom!" I called back, drying my hair for another few seconds before he appeared in the doorway. The second he did, I turned off the blow dryer and felt my first real smile of the day spread my lips. "Hey," I breathed out, my heartbeat doing a little skip as he immediately came toward me.

I closed my eyes as he leaned in to kiss me, the stroke of his tongue melting all my stress away. At least for the moment. I was so lost in how deep he kissed me that I was only vaguely aware of him holding my hand and slipping something onto my finger.

When I pulled away, my eyes went wide.

It was a diamond. A hell of a diamond, in fact. It almost blinded me as I blinked at it.

"We're engaged, by the way," Drew smirked. "As of yesterday."

"Really? How'd it happen?" I laughed.

"I don't know. I assume I got down on one knee."

"Nice. Classic. How'd I react?"

"The usual, I think. You laughed, you cried. You said yes and then we fucked all night."

"That's true, we did," I smiled as I touched up my lipstick. "That was a pretty good night, Mr. Fiancé."

"Agreed," he murmured as he came close again. "You have no idea how much I've been thinking about this pussy all day," he said, his hand under my towel. "Are you sore?"

"A little," I lied softly.

I was a lot sore. Drew was bigger, thicker than I'd ever taken and he'd fucked me harder than I'd ever been fucked last night. But I'd been euphoric like I'd never felt before and I didn't regret a second of it.

There was something about last night that nixed my need to worry about Drew, me, or the contract this morning. I didn't know what it was, but it was something I could swear we both felt last night on the couch, after unraveling together then watching each other come down from our highs.

It was intimacy. An unexpected kind. And I felt it again now as Drew kissed along my bare shoulder while stroking gently between my legs.

"Sorry for making you sore."

I laughed.

"You should never apologize for having a huge cock."

"True. Noted."

"So, what time is our reservation tonight?" I grinded softly against his palm.

"We should leave in twenty. You have a little bit of time."

"So do you," I teased, eyeing the obvious hard-on under his sweats. "Are you ever not hard?"

"Around you? It's a fucking miracle if I'm not."

"Well you did just give me the nicest piece of jewelry I've ever had the honor of wearing out, so a proper thank you is probably in store,"

I smirked, reveling in his immediate groan as I cupped his package and squeezed.

"As much as I'd love to fuck you over this sink right now, your pussy is sore and you just redid your lipstick," Drew muttered, gently removing my hand from his cock. Apparently, I'd quickly come to hate that because on instinct, I unlatched my towel and let it drop to the floor, watching his hungry eyes immediately lock on my tits.

God, yes.

Apparently, I also lived for the moments when I could catch him off guard.

"You said we leave in twenty?" I eyed the time on my phone before returning my attention to him. My mouth curved at the mixture of lust and confusion in his green eyes as I reached into his sweats. "Don't worry. That's plenty of time for me to figure something out."

25

DREW

I was still on another planet as I watched Evie order for us at the restaurant.

She was wearing her hair up with a sapphire blue dress that went off her shoulders, showcasing her smooth skin and that elegant neck. All that combined with her sparkling earrings and the glittering ring on her finger and she looked like royalty.

Royalty that had been wearing thick streaks of my cum on her tits about fifteen minutes ago.

There was something oddly satisfying about watching the men in the restaurant stare at Evie, already in awe of her without even knowing what she'd just done to me back at the house.

After dropping her towel in the bathroom, she'd dipped her fingers into a jar of some kind of moisturizing oil. Then she'd let me watch as she slowly rubbed it all over her tits. I thought she was just giving me a visual to jerk off to but then she led me into her room and pulled me onto the bed with her as she laid herself down.

Then she pushed her shiny tits together for me to fuck.

"Are you there?" Evie teased once the waiter left. I blinked as she flashed me a smile.

"I'm here. If I drift off from time to time, it's because I'm thinking about your tits."

"Maybe don't say that so loudly since this is supposed to be our first romantic dinner as an engaged couple," she smirked, touching the back of her neck. "And please don't spend the entire night looking at me like you want to eat me."

"I do. I've already imagined ten different ways I'd spread your pussy on this table."

"Drew!" Evie hissed, nodding at the couple seated a table away from us. "There are other people in this restaurant who don't want to hear about my pussy."

"Judging from the way that guy stared at you as you walked in, I don't think he would mind."

"Drew."

"Fine, we'll change the subject," I complied just as our wine arrived. "So did I pick a good enough restaurant tonight? Or is this menu not suitable to your sophisticated palate?"

"Um, why are we acting like I'm the fancy person at this table? Your watch is worth more than my entire salary last year and I grew up next to a trailer park."

I paused to process the trailer park comment. I wasn't sure why it surprised me considering I already knew she'd grown up in poverty.

"I figured since you make a living designing menus that you'd be critical of dishes you see at other restaurants."

"Oh my God, no," she giggled. "There are many different corners of the food world, and I'm not in one of the classy ones. My specialty is in designing over-indulgent, borderline ridiculous menu items that taste good but are solely to pique the interest of the media," Evie clarified with a laugh. "And I got this good at it because I was dating a guy who worked in restaurant PR, so he knew exactly what trendy buzzwords the food blogs responded to. 'Vodka-poached,' 'truffle-infused' – all that yummy bullshit."

"And this former boyfriend of yours – what's his name again?"

"I don't recall," Evie replied breezily, taking a dainty sip of her wine. I laughed.

"Good. Though in that case I wish I just picked a burger joint because stuffy places like this aren't really my scene."

"If it makes you feel better, I'm still super excited to be here. This is a beautiful restaurant," she said, gazing around at the enormous flower arrangements on every surface, and the view of Madison Avenue out the double height windows. "I feel like I saw this place on TV before when I was younger," Evie mused. "On like, Food Network. Or the Cooking Channel. Or Travel. Or maybe it was something I watched on Netflix."

Now she was just mumbling to herself trying to figure out where she might've seen this restaurant, which I personally knew had opened only last year because I knew the owner. So this was a pointless train of thought for her, and I probably should've said something, but I for some reason enjoyed watching Evie think this hard.

She was unconsciously playing with her bottom lip while squinting into the distance, and it gave me time to just look at her without her either blushing or saying something smart.

"So, you've made fun of me for my need to eat so often," I pointed out when she finally gave up. "Yet you're clearly obsessed with food."

"But see, there's a huge difference. You eat to live, and I live to eat," she said. "You refer to your food as 'calories.' You practically have a business relationship with your meals. It's just sustenance so you have energy to throw like, you know, a sixty mile-per-hour fastball or whatever."

"I throw at a hundred. Sixty would be unimpressive."

"Whatever, I don't know things. I'm learning, okay?" Evie laughed.

"Fine. Let's go back to your love affair with indulgent food. How did it start?"

"Umm. I think it happened in late middle school or high school when that trend of like, *slutty* food happened."

"What the fuck is 'slutty food?'"

"You know. It was like, overstuffed sandwiches or the biggest ice cream sundae in the country topped with gold leaf or like, Bloody Marys garnished with an entire fucking grilled cheese. Stupid stuff."

"That you clearly fell in love with."

"Yes," she said so unapologetically I had to grin. "We didn't have much growing up, so that kind of indulgence was amazing and fascinating to me. I couldn't get enough of watching it on TV."

"I feel like that would've made me bitter," I said truthfully.

"No. Everything was already bitter. If I was bitter too, then I would just get stuck in that town forever."

"What do you mean?"

"I mean I would've just given up before I tried if I believed everyone around me. All they ever said was that the world was unfair. That some people were born rich while other people were just born screwed like us," Evie said. "The people from where I'm from – they're mostly good people, but they don't dare to dream or fantasize because they 'know' it's pointless. To them, everything's already decided. If your parents were junkies, you'll be a junkie. If your mom was a teen mom, you'll be one too."

"How did you manage to get out?" I asked. But just then, her phone audibly buzzed in her purse. It was the third time since we had sat down, but I'd ignored it till now.

"Um..." Evie tried to act like she was thinking of her answer to my question but I knew she was completely distracted.

My eyebrows pulled tight as I watched her try to subtly remove her phone from her purse and read the screen under the table. In just those two seconds her lips pursed and she tried to take a deep breath without me noticing, but I saw the movement in her shoulders.

"Who's texting you?" I asked.

"Nobody."

"Mike?"

"No."

Only now did I remember that Mike still existed – that we hadn't vanquished him last night by forcing him to listen to us. He was probably stewing in a dark corner somewhere, trashing me on every sports forum on the Internet while sending Evie hateful text messages.

"Evie," I repeated myself sternly. "Whatever you read just now clearly upset you, so tell me."

"Drew! It's no one," Evie reiterated, trying to sound playful but firm. But when she looked up and saw the stern look on my face, she heaved a sigh. "Okay, fine, it's... my mom."

A deep frown furrowed my brow.

"I thought you said you didn't talk to her anymore," I said, vividly remembering her speech about cutting her mom and sister out of her life.

"I don't talk to my sister ever. I... *do* talk to my mom sometimes..."

"That seems like a slippery slope," I remarked.

"And you sound judgmental."

"Maybe I am. If I recall correctly, your mother enabled your sister's addiction for years and eventually condoned her throwing you down the stairs and breaking your arm."

"Yes, and I know you like to preach the idea of cutting out every last person in your life and caring about no one at all, but sometimes it's easier said than done," Evie retorted hotly, her cheeks instantly flushing pink.

But as someone came by to refill our waters, I watched her take in several deep breaths, and once he was gone, she spoke again.

"Besides," she said slowly, clearly trying her best to sound calm. "It was just an emergency situation or I wouldn't have replied now. Not that I should have to justify talking to my mom. She *is* my mom. She busted her ass to raise me for most of my adolescence, and I still miss her sometimes," she said, her voice getting quickly small. She dropped her eyes down her wine glass, quiet for several seconds before attempting a casual shrug. "I mean I don't think it matters how old you are, sometimes you just want your mom."

I said nothing in reply, mostly because I was annoyed to find myself instantly thinking about Pattie. I conceded that Evie might've had a point here, but I didn't say it aloud.

"What was the emergency?"

"She's having some... bad dental issues," she said vaguely. "And she doesn't have insurance... or *money* for that matter... so she's in a lot of pain every day."

"If you're helping with bills, pay directly to the dental office."

Her eyes lifted to me.

"You think she'd lie about this?" she asked slowly, her tone icy.

"I've seen it happen."

My first few years in the league, I had a spreadsheet of eight friends and family members who received monthly checks from me to cover bills. From what I could tell, they really needed the help. Layoffs, kids, whatever. Life happened and if I could afford to help, I was more than happy to.

Of course, the more others heard about my spreadsheet, the more emergencies there were. By the time I was twenty-two, that spreadsheet had more than doubled and I rarely received a call from home that didn't eventually become a sob story.

I wasn't sure if there was a more disheartening feeling than laughing and catching up with an old friend for two hours before realizing it was all a lead-up to a request for money. If I made the rare call home to say hi, the call was treated as a lottery ticket. In my darkest time — during the year that Pattie's cancer came back — I made the mistake of calling an old friend to talk. He ended up asking me for a loan to pay off his credit card debt. When I said no, he asked to at least borrow my BMW while I did my four weeks in "rehab."

So now that spreadsheet was empty.

The last time I mailed just a birthday gift home to a cousin, I got ten requests the same day from other family members who had a sudden "emergency." My cousin's fridge was broken and the kids were stuck eating canned food. My uncle was in danger of being fired because he couldn't get to work. His car needed repairs he just couldn't afford. "Might even be cheaper to get a whole new car," he said before sending me links to the ones he had his eye on.

Daycare money, diaper money, field trip money – there was always a story, and if I offered to pay directly to the school, shop or whatever, I'd get a guilt trip about trust that ultimately ended in, "Never mind, forget it, you've changed." Either that or an invoice for a dollar amount way smaller than the original request.

Save for one or two, every relationship I had in La Palma, Florida – friends, family, old teachers and coaches – soured thanks to money.

So when Evie insisted that her mother wasn't lying – that none of the money was going to Kaylie's addiction – I was unapologetically blunt.

"You're being naïve."

"And you're being judgmental. Again," she countered. Her cheeks were pink and there was a fiery look in her eyes, but she was measuring her words, trying to sound unemotional. "Look, I may not know my sister anymore, but I know my mom. She has her flaws, but she doesn't enable Kaylie by giving her money. She enables her by giving too many chances."

"Please don't tell me she's just guilty of loving her daughter too much. You're defending the woman who let you get physically abused."

"She fought Kaylie herself after I got thrown down the stairs!" Evie argued heatedly. "She was furious. She cried for days. She just also tried to make peace between us after because she didn't want to give up on all of us being together. I chose to leave solely because I needed to be safe from my sister, not because I hated my – "

"Um, excuse me?"

We both sat upright when we heard a breathy voice. When I looked over, I saw a woman in her twenties right next to me, bouncing on her heels and wearing a bright, giddy smile.

"Hi. Mr. Maddox, I am so sorry to bother you while you're eating, and I swear I never do this, but can I get a picture, *please?*"

"Here."

Evie quickly offered to take it before I could bark no like I wanted to, and as the girl squealed with excitement, she flashed me a look that I had no trouble reading.

We forgot we're in public. Let's cool it.

I noted that, but as soon as she took the photo and handed the phone back, the girl bombarded me with a barrage of questions about whether I remembered meeting her at whatever signing.

"I don't," I cut her off. "And I'm having dinner with my fiancée so please, I'd appreciate some privacy."

It was at that point that the mortified hostess rushed over and asked the woman to return to her table. I noticed a hint of amusement in Evie's eye as she twirled her earring and watched me sit back down. She looked at me for a second.

"That was convincing," she finally mused. "And kind of hot," she added in a reluctant mutter.

"What was?"

"'My fiancée.'"

"Right," I said, though I barely knew what she was talking about. I didn't even remember what I said to the woman. All I remembered was being irate that she interrupted our dinner. "What were we talking about?"

"Our impending nuptials. You said no to a destination wedding."

"Funny. I think we were talking about you sending money to your mother."

"Wow, look at that memory," Evie marveled dryly. "Aly said you called her Ellie for the first year that you knew her, yet here you are, remembering exactly how to irritate me."

"I don't like to leave conversations unfinished."

"I remember you saying that the first night we met," Evie crossed her arms and arched an eyebrow. "Do you remember what *I* said?"

"Some things are meant to end before you're ready."

Her eyebrows ascended.

"I didn't expect you to get it verbatim, but yes," she said, surprised. "That's what I said, and it applies tonight as well because we can't talk about this now. We're supposed to be conveying diamond ring bliss and I'm pretty sure it looks instead like we're miserable and fighting on our first day of being engaged. So unless you enjoy getting chewed out by Iain, we're going to change the topic to something pleasant. Right now."

I studied her for a few seconds of silence. I refused to let go of this argument.

"Fine. You know what? I'll be a good girlfriend and *compromise* by telling you pleasant things about my mom," Evie eventually decided, barreling on before I could do or say anything to object. "You already know she'd skip out on eating just to feed us, but before Kaylie started using, she also used to throw a girls' night for us every month where we'd all curl our hair, put on her lipstick and drink super diluted Minute Maid concentrate from plastic wine cups while watching Lifetime. Whenever I was sick, I'd nap in her arms on the couch and I'd feel her kiss my forehead in my sleep. She was really good at just hugging me and telling me everything would be alright. She was my first memory of warmth and comfort, and if you say you don't know what that feels like, then you're a liar."

I wouldn't say I didn't know what that felt like. So once again, I said nothing at all.

"You can't possibly tell me that you have never cried to someone before," Evie challenged.

"As a toddler, I'm sure," I offered, though it only earned me an incredulous look. "But my dad made it pretty clear by pre-school that crying wasn't something boys did."

"That's bullshit."

"Probably, but I was too young to know better."

Evie frowned, huffing hard and looking hell-bent on staying mad at me. But her expression slowly transformed from anger to sympathy, and if it weren't for the topic of our conversation, I probably would've smiled.

"You really haven't cried since you were a toddler?" she asked dubiously. "That can't be healthy. I cry over sad news headlines without even reading the article. I'm not saying that's *normal*," she laughed softly at herself. "But sometimes you just gotta let it out."

"I cried once in eighth grade," I said, remembering only in that second.

"Just that once?"

"Yes."

"What happened?"

"I lost a big game," I replied, thumbing my bottom lip as the memories flooded back with a vengeance. I was thirteen and I was on the verge of my first complete game shutout, but instead, I gave up a base-clearing triple in the ninth and got my team knocked out of the playoffs.

After the game, Pattie spotted the start of my tears and since she knew how my dad would react, she quietly gave me the keys to her Nissan. I wound up crying it out in her air-conditioned car while she walked around outside, sweating her ass off in 102-degree weather and just waiting for me to feel better.

"And at thirteen years old, you're telling me that no one cared to comfort you?"

"My best friend's mom let me cry in her car," I said to shut Evie up.

"Well, that was nice of her."

"Yes. It was."

"That counts as something," Evie said quietly before going altogether silent for awhile.

She bit her lip as she frowned down at her nails, looking as if she were contemplating something. When she finally looked back up at me, there was a glimmer of apology in her eyes.

"And the woman who let you cry in her car..." She trailed off for a second. "Was it Pattie Lillard?"

EVIE

My heartbeat picked up at the sound of her name off my lips.

But I couldn't hide what I knew anymore. I felt like I was lying and somehow, I could lie to the world but apparently, I couldn't lie to Drew's face.

Even if it meant him looking at me now with an expression of anger laced with disgust.

"Not sure why I was convinced till this point that you hadn't Googled me. What exactly did you look at?"

"Well... the interview," I started nervously. "The one where you talked about Pattie. And then..."

"The video in the comments. About Tim."

"Yes, but I closed it out before I finished because I didn't necessarily believe it was – "

"True? It was," he said harshly, pausing as if to take some kind of sick pleasure in the look of shock on my face. "Tim's the varsity baseball coach at our old high school. He was leaving his house in the morning for work when I caught him."

"And... you hit him?"

"That would be an understatement."

My stomach turned.

"What did you do?"

"I blacked out, so I don't remember."

"You were drunk?"

"No. I was angry," Drew enunciated. "I don't remember anything but his neighbors pulling me away. And thinking I probably killed him."

I stared at Drew, completely and utterly speechless.

I wasn't sure if I was more horrified by how badly he'd beaten his childhood best friend, or the fact that he spoke now with such a frighteningly cold lack of remorse. It felt almost as if he were challenging me, punishing me now with more details than I wanted because I had forced him to prove that he cried. I'd forced him to admit that he was human, and now he was doing everything in his power to prove me wrong.

"Drew... I don't understand. Why the hell did you do it?" I finally whispered, though I could barely even hear myself above the volume of my own slamming heart. "That was Pattie's son. That was your best friend."

"He betrayed my trust."

God, not Tim too.

"What did he do?"

"I don't talk about that."

"You can't just say that after telling me everything you just did!" I hissed incredulously.

"I can and I will because I never intended on discussing any of that with you. You just had to know. You needed to believe that love conquers all, or some other happy sunshine bullshit," Drew said coldly. "But at the end of the day, I have my views and you have yours, so let's just agree to disagree. In case you don't remember, we don't actually have to compromise about shit. Just because that's a real diamond doesn't mean this is a real engagement."

You asshole.

I wanted to snatch off my stupid fake engagement ring and throw it right then and there. Seriously. Were it not for the fact that people were watching, I probably would have.

But as increasingly angry I was, I told myself to stay cool. I breathed deep despite suddenly realizing that the blurred lines of our contract didn't mean I was anywhere closer to Drew. Just because I'd opened up to him didn't mean he'd open up to me because clearly, a double standard existed between us.

And I shouldn't have been remotely surprised.

Drew Maddox was used to getting his way. What he wanted he got, and what he had right now was both business and pleasure. He got all of me, I got maybe half of him, and that was just the way it worked in his world.

At least until this very moment.

Because as our entrees came – as Drew turned to smile and talk to the manager who dropped by to ask how things were – I decided to quietly take another page from his book and flip a switch. I wasn't one for double standards so as of this moment, I was going to have to change the way I approached this game.

"And how is everything with you, miss?" the manager asked graciously, turning to me. I let Drew catch a second of my vacant stare before putting on a good face and looking up with a smile.

"Everything's perfect."

26

DREW

For more than a week after our engagement announcement, there was a palpable tension at home.

But as far as faking it went, Evie and I had never been better.

In fact, I was pretty convinced we deserved Oscar nods for our performances to combat the media. *SHE'S GOT THE RING – NOW THEY'RE ON THE ROCKS!* That headline and pictures of our heated conversation had been splashed all over the tabloids the morning after our dinner, along with speculation that I was already regretting my decision to leave my "wild bachelor ways."

It was all bullshit on top of bullshit, but I knew how it looked. My reputation combined with those images created a pretty damned believable narrative. And since I had a job to keep – since I refused to waste all the work I'd already put in – I went with every sappy goddamned date Iain suggested.

And to my surprise, considering the way she'd begun acting since the night of the dinner, Evie went along with them too.

Tuesday, she sat with the WAGs, wearing my jersey fitted tight on her body as she cheered me on to my seventh win of the season. At the end of the game, I jogged over to her by the first base line, flipped my cap backwards and let her cup my face with both hands as I gave her a very public kiss.

"Good game, babe," she murmured as the WAGs cooed behind her.

By the time I got home that night, she was asleep with her door closed and locked.

The case was the same for the next four nights.

Not only that, she was always out of the house when I woke up and only met me at the location of our public date – whether it was a stroll at the farmers market in Union Square, a sidewalk cafe lunch with Diaz and his wife, or grocery shopping in a ridiculously crowded Trader Joe's, her favorite store in the world. Whatever we were doing, I found myself with consistently no time or privacy to talk or ask Evie questions – not that I had any by the third night of this pattern.

I knew what was happening.

I wouldn't talk to her about Tim, so she was reverting strictly to business.

My initial reaction was that of amusement. It felt like a direct challenge from her, and I was always up for one of those. So I laughed to myself, albeit slightly bitterly, and I let that sense of game carry me till Sunday morning, when we went shoe shopping at some store with a big, paparazzi-friendly window up front.

Evie lost her mind over strappy heels, I watched her try on a dozen pairs while wearing little denim shorts, and I was pretty sure neither of us was faking our interest there.

But at the register, the act was on.

"Babe, wait. Which color should I get? The white or the tan?" she asked, her arms wrapped around my neck as she gazed down at the shoes.

"Get them both," I shrugged. The salesgirl smiled as Evie beamed up at me, saying something about me being the best before she went on her toes and kissed me on the lips.

But it wasn't a quick peck like I expected – it was a slow, sexy swirl of her tongue as she pressed her tits firmly against my chest, and after a week without contact, my dick reacted immediately. I knew Evie felt it because she let out a sexy little *mm* into my mouth.

Then the second my hand slid from her hips toward her ass, she pulled away, smiling brightly at the salesgirl who handed over her bags.

I was pretty sure the only reason she waited for me at the door was because there were a few paparazzi camped right outside, and she didn't want to walk alone. Considering how aggressive those assholes could get, I couldn't blame her. I was glad she waited.

But after letting me guide her to the car and open the door, Evie slid in and went straight to answering emails on her phone. I could tell the immediate silence was jarring to the driver because he kept peeking at us through the rearview mirror. It was at that point that I wished I'd just called my usual driver Gary instead of using some app, because I was pretty sure this guy was paying far too much attention to us.

"Everything okay, guys?" he dared to ask with a little laugh after about thirty seconds of silence. I gave him an odd look but just as I wondered whether the kid was going to sell a tabloid some tidbit on our failing engagement, I heard Evie purr.

"Babe, I love them so much. I can't stop looking at them," she said, peeking into the shoeboxes inside the bag at her feet.

I grinned, partially over her wariness of the driver, but mostly over the little fuck-me voice she was putting on for me.

"I'm glad you like them. You should put them on."

"Not now. Tonight. When you get home," she said, leaning back on the window and briefly teasing me by rubbing her ankle against my knee.

It lasted all of two seconds but I couldn't erase the image of her near-naked legs on display for me like that, so when she went back to her emails, I took advantage of our nosy driver's eavesdropping and held my arm out.

"Baby, come here."

Her eyes flicked up at me, and she was silent for a few seconds before putting on a light, teasing voice for me.

"I'm doing work stuff, babe."

"Fuck work. Come here," I grinned, holding my arm out to her.

I stifled a laugh as she stole an actual eye roll before putting her phone down, resuming a smile and sidling up to me. As I pulled her sexy legs onto my lap, she wrapped her arms around my neck, twisting her body to face me and away from the driver.

I ignored her cocked eyebrow and the way she impatiently mouthed *what?* Instead, I enjoyed the fake giggle she managed as I stroked the back of her calves and said something about her hair smelling good.

Considering I didn't get to touch this body at home anymore – considering how she used my own body as she wished in public – I was going to take my sweet damned time here. Hell, I was going to get fucking high off the scent of that coconut shampoo. Maybe I already was, considering I was suddenly imagining Evie lounging next to me on a beach, basking in the sun in a little white bikini.

"We need a vacation," I smirked, buying more time with her on my lap.

"Mm-hm. The second your season is over, babe. We'll go."

"Where do you want to go?"

Away from you, was what she conveyed with that big, inaudible sigh that made her shoulders slump. Still hanging onto my neck, she glanced back at her phone on the seat. I couldn't help but break into a huge grin because apparently insolent Evie was also a turn-on. When she turned back to me, she had her game face back.

"Oh, I don't know. Anywhere at all as long as I'm with you," she said with a saccharine sweetness meant to irritate me. It somewhat worked.

"Name a city," I said. "London? Paris? Milan?"

"No. I need a beach. It's already been too long since I've been in the ocean," she said, almost accusingly, as if I'd been keeping her from it myself.

"What, you a water baby like me?" I asked as she avoided my eye, gazing longingly out the back window like she preferred to get out in the middle of traffic than sit on my lap.

"Please. I'm more of a water baby than you," she mumbled.

"Doubt that. I was born and raised in Florida. What do you got, Massachusetts girl?"

Just as I hoped, that set something off. I tried not to laugh as Evie pinned a brief but hot, incredulous stare on me.

"For your information, there are lots of beautiful and famous beaches in New England," she started sharply, clearly about to school me. I was all for it. I'd set her up for it because as much as I enjoyed the sweet, breathy voice she used with me in public, I missed the sound of her real one talking about real things. "Palm trees are not a requirement in order to be considered a beach. Ever heard of Cape Cod? Martha's Vineyard? Good Harbor Beach?"

"I've definitely never heard of the last one. That sounds like someone got tired while naming beaches."

She snorted but caught herself.

"Stop. Don't be rude," she said tartly. "That was my beach growing up, and it's beautiful."

"Probably still only half as good as the worst beach in Florida."

"There was white sand. Lighthouses. Nice people," Evie seethed adorably. "It's even pretty in the winter. I hitchhiked at least once a week to get there."

"Hitchhiked? How old were you?"

"When I first started? Thirteen, fourteen."

I must've looked fucking horrified because she slid her eyes back to me and actually laughed.

"What?"

"Nothing. Must've been a good beach," I remarked.

"It was. It was my one place where I could pretend I was normal," she said, her sentence getting progressively quieter before she suddenly frowned to herself and pulled to get off my lap. "Let me go," she whispered under her breath.

"What do you mean pretend to be normal?" I lowered my voice.

"Nothing," she said, though I already had the answer pictured in my head. At the beach, she didn't have to think about her rocky home life or the lack of money. She had sand, sun and water like everyone else. It was the universal pleasure of beaches. I had the same in Florida.

"Drew, just let me sit back down," Evie repeated quietly but sternly. "Okay?"

I held her tight but said nothing in reply because I didn't have an argument here. If she wanted to get off my lap, I was supposed to let her. But I hated the way my body felt whenever she physically pulled away. It was a sudden loss of this peaceful feeling, like getting a warm blanket ripped off your body while sleeping.

It was actually easier to bear in the four-day stretch this week when I didn't get to touch her at all. But getting to run my hands over her soft skin and then feeling it get taken away felt like shit.

So for a minute or so, we were engaged in a standoff.

But this time, I had a feeling she might win.

"Drew Maddox. I'll make you regret it if you don't let me go right now," Evie whispered. Apparently just the tingle of her breath so close to my lips was enough for me to risk it.

"Make me regret it then."

She succeeded in the first second.

Climbing onto my lap, she squeezed my hands over her tits and kissed me deeply. The groan I let out was instantly greedy, ravenous. Every hard inch of my body was starved and at her fucking mercy. We were three minutes from home and I was already running late to get to the stadium – I knew that, she knew that, and that was why she was comfortable doing this. I couldn't be late for stretch and I wasn't going to fuck her right in this car in front of our creep of a driver.

So she was using this bit of time to torture me, and I was a willing participant.

"Let me taste them," I hissed when she let me yank down her neckline and the cups of her bra.

"Uh-huh," she exhaled breathlessly as I sucked her tits into my mouth, swirling my tongue all over them and relishing every sweet lick before I felt the car slow to a roll. The app dinged to signal the end of the ride just as the car stopped, and before I knew it, Evie was breathlessly covering up and reaching to grab her bags off the floor.

"See you tonight, babe?" she panted, her lips wet and swollen as she moved to get out of the car. She dug her nails into my shoulder as I pulled her hand off the door and grabbed her shirt, pulling till her tits sprang free again. Her pussy grinded against my cock as I sucked her nipples hard, like I'd never get a chance to again.

We stopped abruptly when the car behind honked and just like that, she threw the door open.

"You gonna stay up for me?" I asked.

"Mm-hm," she hummed sweetly before getting out of fast and shutting the door.

Then as I sat there recovering, telling the driver that there'd be another stop, I let myself picture Evie actually staying up for me tonight, her sleepy head popping up from the couch the second she heard me coming in.

I used to love that couch – now I harbored a vague sense of resentment for the way it failed me every night. Seeing it unoccupied was once the post-game norm, but now it was a letdown.

So I envisioned her sprawled out there tonight, in a little tank top and shorts. I knew it wouldn't actually be the case, but I wanted to believe it.

As tired as it had me, I'd gotten pretty damned good at the whole business of pretending.

27

EVIE

I'd gotten up early every day of the past week-and-a-half, mostly to avoid seeing Drew at home. So on Tuesday morning, knowing well that Drew was out early for a day game, I slept in and wound up waking to a series of weird texts from Aly that induced more than a few sleepy giggles.

"What the hell?" I mumbled, propping myself up on my elbow to better read her early morning craziness.

> **ALY:** Hello???
>> **ALY:** Why won't you pick up it's already 7:45
>> **ALY:** CALL ME BACK PLEEEEASE
>> **ALY:** Fine you missed your window I'll be busy for the next 2+ hours and then recovering for who knows how long and then back at it again k bye

I squinted at the text then the time. It was almost 10AM. According to her schedule, which used to be my schedule, she'd been at the restaurant for almost four hours now, so I had no idea what this could be about.

ME: Hellooo. Just called you back and you didn't pick up wanna stop being weird and cryptic?

I lay around for a bit as I waited for her response and after about twenty minutes, it finally came.

In the form of a picture.

Of an enormous rock on her finger.

"Oh my God!" I shrieked, jolting upright in bed and immediately calling her. But she wound up interrupting my ringing with her texts.

ALY: Woman I can't talk. I can barely breathe.

ME: Oh God you've been having sex all morning. That's what you meant by the next 2 plus hours

ALY: Yes. I think I'm already pregnant

ME: I don't think it works like that. Can we talk about that ring? IT'S AMAZING

ALY: I know. I'm dying. Aly Hoult. I'M GONNA BE MRS. EMMETT HOULT

I was giggling my ass off as she continued on with a dozen texts rattling off versions of her name. Alyson Hoult. Aly Stanton-Hoult. It ended when she realized A. Hoult sounded a little too much like "a-hole."

ALY: Well that was fun while it lasted.

ME: Aly Hoult it is. So when are we celebrating and with who

ALY: Tonight 8PM location TBD. Iain and his girl Keira will be there and heads up she does not know about you and Drew so keep the act up. She's a bit of a chatty one.

ME: How does that work when Iain hates extraneous chatter more than anything in the world??

ALY: I think because they're two of the most blunt Type A personalities I've ever met and he gets to dominate where it counts, according to things I wish Emmett never told me

ME: Oh my. Can't say I'm surprised

ALY: Speaking of doms though how's your prick BF handling the ice out? Because if he's pulled any more dick moves since that night he said the real ring/fake engagement shit, I will dom the shit out of Emmett and uninvite him from this dinner.

ME: No!! He's Emmett's best friend and this is Emmett's night too. Plus it's all good. I know I sounded ragey last week but he and I have struck a balance at home

Lie. Total lie.

Drew and I had not struck anything and the only reason I was able to maintain my all-business ground with him was because I wasn't letting myself see him at all.

I wasn't sure how successful I'd be otherwise because the one time I caught him coming down the stairs just as I was leaving the house, he was wearing only blue boxers, and I nearly drooled onto my shoes. That chest and those abs aside, just the way his eyes always found and locked on me caused such a physical reaction in my body. Every time.

That said I was no longer letting people get their way at my expense.

I just wasn't.

For more than a year, I had agonized over fixing a relationship that Mike already knew was over. He was just waiting out our lease so he could leave me in the most comfortable way possible, so I was done. Absolutely done being unwittingly convenient for others.

And that group of others now included Drew.

ALY: Well good! I'm so glad you figured out a way to deal with Drew. You might be the first one

ME: As long as he and I are in public I can handle anything thrown my way. Besides you are ENGAGED woman!!! So don't worry about me!!!

ME: Tonight's going to be perfect :)

28

EVIE

"To be fair, it's really pretty," Aly giggled as we sat at the end of the table together, our seats all rearranged.

At one point, we were seated with all the couples next to each other, but after three courses and more than a few rounds of champagne, it was musical chairs.

And by now, having sat a solid hour next to Aly, I knew exactly how many facets were on her massive rose cut diamond, exactly how the proposal went down — Emmett surprised her while they were spooning in bed this morning — and the fact that I was going to be her maid of honor.

So now, we had moved onto gazing at my big fake rock.

"I mean it looks so insanely real for being fake," she whispered, peering up to make sure Keira was still in the bathroom.

"No, no, it's not really fake, it's a real diamond," I giggled. "I just mean it's sentimentally fake. Iain chose it."

"*Ohhh*. So you chose this ring Iain?" Aly whisper-yelled across the table. The damned near death look we got from him made us burst into giggles. "I apologize. What I meant to say," Aly started at full volume this time, "was that you did a beautiful job, Drew. I mean she's always preferred princess cut, but it's cool. What's done is done."

"Yes. I did my best," Drew said, as unamused as Iain. To his left, Emmett wore a crooked grin while mouthing for Aly to behave, and as Aly and I snorted, I groaned inwardly.

Ugh.

I hated myself for wishing this moment were real. But it was just so hard not to.

It was my best friend's real engagement, and this felt like such an otherwise perfect moment. Aly was dressed to the nines in a glittery champagne colored dress, I was wearing a backless cap-sleeved lace number I was obsessed with, and the guys all looked so absurdly handsome in their sleek suits and ties. They looked like a fucking cologne commercial.

And Drew... *God.*

I'd actually never seen him in a full suit and tie before and it was killing me. He looked like such a perfect gentleman that it somehow turned me on just to know that he was hiding a whole sleeve of tattoos under there.

"Here," Aly said, taking an empty bowl and holding it under my chin.

"What?"

"You and Drew are doing sexy eyes across the table at each other and it looks like you're going to drool onto your dress."

I grabbed the bowl and practically tossed it back on the table.

"Shut it. It's not easy resisting him when he looks like that."

"I bet. I can comfortably say this now that I'm engaged to the love of my life, but Drew looks absurdly good tonight. He looks like a Viking that you tamed and wrapped in a Tom Ford suit."

"Tamed my ass. Also, are you trying to make it worse for me?"

"No, if I was, I'd tell you that he's looking at your back right now like he wants to lick it from your neck to your ass."

"Jesus, Aly."

"I'm sorry. I've had a lot of sex and champagne today. I shouldn't even be in public."

I managed a laugh with her but I was actually relieved when she had to get up and show her ring to someone she and Emmett knew that worked at the restaurant. Of course, the relief was short-lived because the second she was up so was Drew.

"Hey." He pulled the chair next to me even closer and sat down. I had barely looked over before he took my hand and held it in my lap as he kissed me. I wasn't prepared for it, so when he pulled away, I was dizzy. "I can't stop looking at you tonight, Evie. Iain and Emmett are giving me shit because I haven't listened to anything they've said in an hour."

When I peered up across the table, I spotted Iain talking to Emmett, who caught my eye, smirked and made a heart sign over his chest with his hands. I narrowed playful eyes at him, not entirely sure what he was saying but pretty certain I didn't like it.

"You look good too," I finally returned, letting our legs mingle as Drew sat closer. Maybe it was the champagne, but when he touched my cheek, I let myself close my eyes and lean into his palm.

But before I could relax too long, I heard the return of Keira's raspy voice with that permanent tinge of mischief.

"Aww, you two engagement trendsetters." I turned to find her flipping away her side bangs as she sat down across from us. She shook her head at my left hand resting on the table. "That is seriously beautiful. Although I think you could've afforded to go up a carat just for the paparazzi hell you're putting this girl through."

"She's been handling them like a champ so far," Drew said, massaging the back of my neck. *Ugh God. Yes.*

"As long as they stay far back enough and they're not yelling at me, I'm good," I chuckled while trying not to actually melt under Drew's touch.

"Well, you're a good sport. I told Iain I'd end up backhanding anyone who followed me down the street," she said, making Drew snort. "And I'd just like, burn down the offices of every newspaper if they interviewed the idiots from my hometown and made them talk shit about me."

Both Drew and I paused, and I could tell we were both wondering if Keira was making up a hypothetical situation. She muttered to herself for a second before squinting at our quizzical faces.

"Oh Jesus. There was an article today. You didn't see it?" she asked. But the curious part was that she wasn't looking at Drew as she said it. *Oh God*. My heart dropped when I realized the article wasn't about him.

It was about me.

My hand flew to my phone. I wasn't even listening anymore, but I could hear Drew's hot irritation with Keira as they went back and forth for a bit. He asked why the hell she even read that shit, she said something about Iain and then I found the headline.

COLD-BLOODED COUPLE: FUTURE MRS. MADDOX LIVING LAVISH WHILE MOM LIVES ON WELFARE.

"What the fuck," I murmured, my wild eyes scanning the article.

It mentioned my "unemployed sister" Kaylie, and included quotes from former high school classmates that I barely knew, who claimed I had always "looked down" on others and that I "didn't bat an eye" over the fact that my mom and sister "went hungry."

Seriously?

I couldn't believe what I was looking at.

Because of Drew, some scumbag had dug into my life, aired out my dirty laundry and added bullshit details to make me look completely despicable. And unlike Drew, I wasn't a celebrity so when I eventually dropped out of the spotlight, this horrible story would still be out there about me. It wouldn't be pushed aside by years and years of new headlines – it would exist forever to humiliate both me and my family.

I was so livid I was shaking.

"This is disgusting," I whispered, twisting away from Drew when he tried to cover my phone.

"Evie, please stop reading it," he urged in a murmur as Keira flipped her bangs again.

"Look, don't even sweat it. They're just white trash, and you did good leaving them behind."

"Take it easy, alright?" Drew warned her in a low mutter.

"What, D? Anyone on welfare is going to try to use her to get to your money. You know too well how that goes. Protect yourselves."

"This is not the time, and you don't know the full story, so drop it," Drew snarled despite the fact that I knew he didn't believe his own words. He himself knew the full story about my mother, and he'd told me to cut her off too, but tonight I knew he could feel my hand shaking in his.

And though I recognized that he'd just had my back, I still felt a pit of fury inside me grow bigger for him.

"Hold on," I heard Emmett say to Iain before calling down to us. "What's going on? You guys okay?"

"Yes, everything's fine," I replied fast, shoving my phone in my clutch and refusing to ruin his engagement dinner with this.

And when Aly returned giggling about something or another, I forced myself to flash a big smile and act fine for her, because she didn't deserve to spend her big night consoling me, being mad for me and talking me down from my emotions.

So I held it all in until we left, knowing full well that Drew's eyes had barely left me throughout the car ride home.

"Evie."

I was stiff and catatonic the whole way back, but upon getting into the house I made a blind, angry beeline for the kitchen.

"Evie, what are you even doing?" Drew asked, his voice coming closer behind me.

"I'm making myself tea."

I had no idea why. I was just letting my body make the decisions till my brain sorted through the storm of incoherent fury and figured out what I was most upset about. And apparently, the plan in the meantime was to boil water for tea.

"I'm sorry about the story." I heard Drew toss his suit jacket over a chair. I also heard actual regret in his voice but it didn't thin my wrath in the least.

"It's fine." My reply was clipped as I opened the cabinets to find the tea I'd bought myself last week. "It comes with the territory."

The second those words came out I heard Drew's fist hit the table.

"Goddammit, Evie, stop talking to me like that, alright?" he hissed, coming up behind me. "Just talk to me again. Like a real person. Tell me what to do. Tell me how I can fix this for you."

"*You* want to fix this?"

"Yes."

"Why?" I laughed so bitterly Drew spun me around by the waist.

"If this is your way of implying that I don't care about you, I think I'm making it obvious now that you're wrong," he growled, gripping me tight, refusing to let me just shove him away. "You're upset, I know that, and I don't like it. In fact, I fucking hate it. I hate that the media dragged your family into this. I hate that they're making you play the bad guy, because trust me, I know how fucking shitty that feels, and I wish more than anything that you didn't have to know the feeling too."

"Well, I do, and unless you can erase the Internet, it's too late to take any of it back," I hissed, yanking out of his grip. "So you can just let this go and stop pretending to give a shit."

"If I didn't give a shit, I wouldn't be standing here, Evie – I would be gladly ignoring you because honestly, that would work out a whole lot better for me."

"Do you think that feels good for me to hear?"

"I don't know what it feels like, Evie, I'm just trying to be fucking honest with you," Drew muttered hotly as he trailed me down the counter. "You know I need the focus just to do my damned job – just to keep my head in the game. In case you don't realize what it takes to win as much as I do, it takes consistency. It takes doing the same goddamned thing every day, thinking the same goddamned way and not changing a thing. If I loved anything, it was the routine I had before you came along – in fact, if anyone told me you would happen one day and asked if I wanted to avoid that, I'd say yes a thousand times over, because I have a job to do, a team to lead and a fucking ring to win. But now that you're here, now that I've felt you and I know what it's like not to have you, I can't stand for that either because I fucking miss you, alright?" Drew demanded. "I want you to come back to me."

"Well, you can't have everything you want without giving

anything up. You don't get to kiss me in public, fuck me at home and get to know everything about me and force me to answer all of your questions while ignoring every one of mine," I argued as the kettle went from whistling at me to screaming at us. "In case you don't realize, I've put all of myself out there for you. I tell you what you want to know, I let the media completely expose me, and everyone wins except for me." My voice trembled as I faced decidedly away from Drew, letting steam burn my fingers as I poured the boiling water into my mug. "You want from me what you give to no one, Drew. You keep stripping me more and more naked while you keep staying comfortably hidden, and it makes me feel like an idiot. It makes me realize how stupid I was for ever treating this as anything more than what it is, which is a lie."

"You don't have to call it that."

"Real diamond, Drew – not a real engagement. Remember?" I flung his words back before spinning around to go to my room.

But since he was standing right there, I sloshed half the contents of my mug right down his chest. My jaw dropped like a brick as I watched the scalding water soak into his shirt. But inch-by-inch my mouth creaked shut because Drew gave no reaction whatsoever. All he did was clench his jaw, keeping that wolfish gaze unflinchingly pinned to me as he gripped the knot of his tie and jerked it loose.

"You wanted to know something about me that I've told only one person in my life," he muttered, whipping the tie off his neck and unbuttoning his shirt. "And the only reason I told that person was because I needed an agent. No one wanted anything to do with me after what happened with Tim, and I needed someone willing to take a chance on me. The only reason Iain did that was because I explained myself to him. But trust me, I didn't want to."

My tongue stuck to the roof of my mouth as Drew stared at me while taking off his shirt. I was more curious than ever now, but the storm inside me slowed to a rolling thunder as Drew dropped his button-down to the floor.

"So that's it. I'm still right where you left me. You're not going to tell me."

"I'll tell you, Evie," Drew said between his teeth, stunning me silent. "I'll fucking tell you everything because I hate what I've done to you with this story coming out. I hate that you have to feel even a fraction of how shitty I feel every day of my life," he said, making my heart twist in my chest. "Just don't make me say it now. Don't make me do this tonight because I can't do another second without touching you, Evie. I swear to God I can't. I need you back already."

I swallowed the enormous knot in my throat. He had me and I probably should've let him know, but I was speechless because Drew was officially stripped before me and I never thought I'd see him look at me this way. At anyone. He was thoroughly chipped at. Broken down and pleading with me. I could only manage a nod because I didn't actually know how to react to the feeling of bending something so big and strong.

"Tell me I can touch you again," Drew murmured, closing the small gap between us.

His mouth was an inch from mine, and he stood as tight as he possibly could without touching me. I felt every inch of heat from his body, and I saw the need in his eyes as he waited for me to give him permission.

Because once I did, I knew he wouldn't stop. And just because he was begging for me didn't mean he was going to be gentle.

When I nodded again, I felt a rumble build in Drew's chest. He was primed, ready, but he didn't put his hands on me until he heard me speak.

"Touch me again," I whispered.

The words barely escaped my throat before Drew grasped hold of my neck.

Two fingers gripped my jaw as his free hand shot under my skirt, and the second his fingers pushed into my pussy, his eyes closed as if they were rolling back in his head. His hold on me instantly eased and he exhaled as he pumped inside me, breathing harder with each stroke, like my body was returning air to his lungs.

His eyes blazed into mine as he held me there for a full minute, driving relentlessly inside me, focused on nothing but reclaiming my pussy.

"That's my girl," he murmured with satisfaction as I came desperately all over his hand, my body weak but our eyes locked tight as he withdrew his wet fingers from between my legs.

I gazed back at him, dizzy as he slowly released my neck, giving me time to grasp the counter behind me for balance. Then taking a single step back, he slowly undid his belt, button and zipper.

"Take your clothes off. Everything except the shoes." Drew stroked his erection over his boxers as I did as I was told. He mirrored me as I shed my dress and my panties, till we stood completely bare before one another, all our clothes strewn in the same corner of the kitchen floor.

"Now?" I asked, barely able to stand in my heels as I soaked in every inch of Drew's body, including the solid nine that hung between his rock-hard thighs.

"Go to my room." *Easy enough.* "And keep your pussy spread for me as you walk up the stairs."

Goddammit, Drew.

I was needy enough without that carnal demand – and without all the low, sexy murmurs of appreciation he made as I obliged him the whole way up the stairs. The one time I glanced over my shoulder, I saw him four or five steps back, his thumb running across his bottom lip as he held his head tilted just so, enjoying the view. An irresistibly sexy smirk curled his mouth when he caught me looking at him.

"That's right. Keeping showing that pussy. Show me how it belongs to me."

God.

"You better fuck me hard Drew," I said as I reached the second floor.

"It feels like a year since I've fucked you, so hard won't be a problem. Now get on my bed."

"Any other requests?"

"Wait for me on your hands and knees."

My pussy throbbed.

Jesus. If there was any guarantee in the world it was that this man knew how to turn me on like no other. My body was brimming with anticipation by the time I got into his bedroom – a room I'd only peeked into but never stepped foot inside before.

There were books, framed photos and leather boxes on his dresser. Just the dent in his pillow and the rumple in his sheets fascinated me as I climbed onto his bed. It reminded me that this was Drew's bedroom where he slept every night. His home within his home.

"That's fucking perfect, baby."

His pleasured rumble startled me and when I peered over my shoulder, I saw Drew's powerful body striding into the room, a rubber already stretched thin over his cock. He kept his eyes pinned to my naked body on all fours as he moved toward the bathroom, never once breaking eye contact as he twisted the doorknob and pushed.

I bit my grin as the door opened and I saw that his bathroom mirror directly faced the bed.

"Look at how fucking sexy you are," Drew muttered in my ear as he climbed behind me onto the bed, watching me watch our reflection.

I gazed at the dramatic dip of my arched back, at Drew's long body positioned behind me, his muscled arms looking so threatening as he simply cupped my ass. My senses tingled as I watched him palm it gently for several seconds before winding up to spank me.

As soon as I cried out at the impact, Drew rubbed away the pain, his mouth next to my ear as he murmured, "This ass belongs to me too."

"Uh-huh…"

"Everything, Evie. Every inch of you is mine."

I moaned as he nudged inside me, his flared tip throbbing between my wet lips. I closed my eyes as I felt his hand on the back of my neck, the other fondling my breast before gripping my waist.

"Say it."

"I'm all yours," I breathed.

And as soon as I did, he sank the length of his cock inside me. His ragged groan drowned out the gasp that ripped from my throat because like last time, he felt too big, and as wet as I was, I could still hear him grunting – still needing to exert himself to push in and out of my pussy.

But while it hurt, the pleasure overrode any pain. All the sexy, throaty sounds tearing out from Drew's chest made me that much wetter, and on top of that this time, I had the visual of his ripped body in the mirror, his chiseled muscles clenching with every thrust. One glance at the reflection and I saw those deep-cut lats and triceps flexing as he drove steadily inside me, slowly stretching me around his shaft till each push was nothing but pleasure.

"So tight," Drew hissed, circling an arm around my stomach and hugging my back against his chest. His every inch buried inside me as he gave short, hard thrusts that forced me onto my elbows. "You feel so fucking good, Evie," he growled, turning my face and licking my lips as he continued to pummel inside me. "This is all I ever need. Your pussy. These lips." He groaned as I swept my tongue against his. "So fucking sweet."

Our frenzied kiss stayed locked as he lowered his hand down from my belly, reaching between my legs and smiling against my gasping mouth as he played with my clit. With two fingers, he rubbed it at the same harsh pace that he fucked me, rapidly tightening every muscle inside me.

"Oh God, Drew..."

At some point I was on all fours but now my breasts were pressed flat on Drew's bed, my pussy contracting around his girth as I moved my hips to grind against his fingers.

"Damn, baby, look at you," Drew rasped in awe as I grasped handfuls of the sheets for leverage, my muscles burning as I swiveled back against him, controlling the pace under the full weight of his body. "Christ, you make it so hard not to come right away. I just wanna fill you with my cum, Evie. I want to bend you over this fucking bed and watch it drip from your pussy while I spank your ass. All. Fucking.

Night," he muttered, thrusting deeper, harder with every word he muttered.

Holy God.

I never knew that was something I wanted till the image Drew painted had me so hot I was cursing the condom between us.

"Drew, I'm going to come..." I panted as he pulled my hair.

"Do it, baby, come all over my cock."

As I did, he groaned and muttered in my ear, reminding me through every second of my vicious orgasm that I was his.

"Do you hear me, Evie? No one's but mine," he hissed as I moaned and fell limp underneath him, though a sharp gasp choked from my lips when he pulled out, leaving me with a void that I loathed for the two seconds it took for him to turn me onto my back and position himself between my legs.

~

DREW

GRIPPING HER KNEES, I held her thighs apart, no hands needed as I slid my cock back inside her wet heat.

Every thrust gave me a bounce of her tits that tempted my eyes away, but I didn't cave. I refused to break away from the way she gazed at me now, because it was everything I had ached for in the past week-and-a-half. It was all the warmth I missed. It was that look of content and the way she raked that sleepy smile between her teeth in a way I could admit I fucking loved.

Everything about her just felt so damned good.

"Come here, baby," Evie murmured, making my eyebrows pull together for a moment. I realized at a delay that she'd never called me that before, and the second I saw her hold her arms out, reaching for me, I let myself fall into her. I groaned against her lips as I allowed myself to succumb to her sweetness. I let her comb her fingers through my hair as my lips moved from her mouth to her neck to her breasts, kissing every inch of her I could reach till I burst off inside her.

"*Fuck*, Evie," I groaned as she held my face and kissed me, her pussy gently coaxing out every last drop of my cum.

A part of me expected to feel regret for everything I'd promised her the second after I came. It was just the way I was. But to my own surprise, I didn't feel an ounce of that. Still buried in her, all I felt was a sense of calm and ease – like I'd misplaced something before, but now everything was right back where it belonged.

"You feel so fucking incredible," I exhaled as I lay on top of her, our limbs entwined and all my senses drinking her in. Her touch, her scent – all the breathy little sounds she made as I went back to kissing her all over. The way she seeped into my skin and got into my head was everything I never wanted, but at this point I was too lost in her to stop it.

She just felt too damned good.

29

EVIE

I woke up first the next morning and upon opening my eyes, felt myself immediately hit with an emotional hangover from the drama of last night.

The tabloid. My fight with Drew in the kitchen.

The mind-blowing sex that followed.

Biting my lip, I lifted my cheek off Drew's bare chest and looked up at him, soaking in the view. *God, this man.* He was still asleep, and he looked so peaceful and handsome I couldn't bear to wake him up, so slipping out of bed, I hopped into the shower, taking my time to rinse off the stress of last night.

I must've taken awhile because by the time I got out of the bathroom, I noticed the bottom drawer on the dresser was open. Drew was up and sitting shirtless at the edge of his bed, the width of his muscled shoulders on display as he leaned forward on his knees.

There was a letter in his hand, and judging from his rigid body language, it wasn't one he was particularly fond of.

"Hey," I frowned when he looked up at me. "What's that?"

He didn't answer immediately, instead waiting for me to go over to him. Once I was close enough, he pulled me onto his lap, immediately kissing me deeply, as if needing to draw strength or patience or something from my lips.

"Are you okay?" I asked softly when I pulled away.

He ignored the question to answer the one I'd asked before.

"A stranger sent this to me four years ago," he murmured, picking up the letter again. "Right before everything that went down with Tim."

"Oh." Hugging the towel to my chest, I blinked down at it in his hands. "Why are you looking at it?" I asked gently.

"It's been four years since I touched it. But it's what I showed Iain. To explain why I did what I did to Tim."

Oh. Shit.

My eyes widened as I stared at the thing. Suddenly, it went from a normal letter to a map into the mind of Drew Maddox, which was precisely why I expected Drew to just read me bits and pieces.

But to my surprise, he handed the whole thing over.

"If there's anything I'm not good at it's talking about this subject," he said, his voice softer than I'd ever heard it. "So just read that first."

I looked at him – at the pain storming behind his green eyes as he held out the piece of paper. But I noticed that his broad shoulders relaxed as soon as I took it from him – as if I'd just taken an actual burden off his hands.

"Okay," I murmured as his arms circled around my waist, holding me still on his lap. My heart was already beating fast before I started reading.

But once I did, my heartbeat only quickened.

Hello Mr. Maddox,

I am writing to you as both a longtime fan (North Florida native here!) and a mother of a child undergoing cancer treatment. I watched your ESPN interview four years ago, in which you opened up about Pattie Lillard, her extraordinary impact on your childhood, and finally, her cancer diagnosis. I am aware of the significant financial help you have contributed to Ms. Lillard's treatments over the years, and even donated to her GoFundMe when you first publicized her story.

I have long felt connected to both your story and Ms. Lillard's, so it was deeply saddening for me to hear about the return of her cancer. I have followed both your stories for years, so safe to say it was of great surprise for me to spot Ms. Lillard at the same hospital in which my daughter has been receiving treatment.

I want to inform you that every Tuesday for the past month, I have watched her enter the building and appear nowhere near the infusion center. Admittedly, I have on two occasions watched her arrive at the hospital and spend approximately two hours in the cafeteria before exiting the building and being picked up to go home. I am holding out hope that there are explanations for these incidents, but I am writing to simply urge you to keep a closer eye on Ms. Lillard's story.

Wishing all the best for you.

Sincerely,

Jill Marino

My stomach twisted furiously by the last words of the letter, and for some reason, I held out hope that I'd read this wrong – that this didn't mean what I thought.

But when I brought my wide eyes up to Drew, he confirmed my suspicions.

"She didn't have cancer," he said. "The first time or the second time."

My heart dropped into my stomach.

"What... what was she sick with then?"

"Nothing. She wanted money," Drew said, his Adam's apple moving as he swallowed hard.

I shook my head, already having trouble processing.

"But..." I remembered the images they showed during that interview in which Drew talked about how much he loved her. "There were pictures of her in the hospital bed. She didn't have her hair anymore. She looked so sick."

"That was Tim's doing. He did a fucking stellar job keeping up the act," Drew muttered, shaking his head in disgust.

The look of revulsion continued to twist his features as he told me everything – about how he'd gotten the letter and immediately called Tim to make sure it was a lie. But Tim wavered, found an excuse to hang up fast and ignored Drew's texts and calls for the next day.

Five hours before the first pitch of the game he was due to start that night Drew booked a flight from L.A to Florida. On the plane, he tried to remind himself about how Tim had looked out for him as a kid – how he kept him out of fights in school or on the field, and how he tutored Drew on all tests and homework so he wouldn't flunk himself off the team.

He thought about that and then the years of lies Tim fed him as an adult – about how sick his mom was feeling, and how hard she'd vomited all night. He thought about the detailed stories of the pain that came with chemo, and how Pattie was no longer able to eat.

"He made me feel all those years of gut-wrenching pain for something that wasn't even real," Drew said, his brittle voice barely above a whisper. "Fucking hell. I spent so many nights just sitting up in bed and hating the world for how cruel it was to good people. Especially when the cancer came back. I'd been so high off her beating it, and when they told me it was back, I felt fucking broken. I lost my mind a little because I felt like I had personally failed her – that I didn't do enough and I could've paid for even better doctors." His eyes were lost in memory as I held his jaw in my hands. "For Christ's sake, he kept me on this crazy hell of an emotional roller coaster for four years. Just so he could cash checks from me whenever he wanted."

"God, Drew," I whispered, my forehead touching his as I shook my head in stunned shock. "I'm so, so sorry. That is evil what they did to you. I can't even fathom how they could stomach that kind of lie for so many years. I can't even begin to understand how they could betray your trust like that."

"His justification was that they didn't realize till too late," Drew said. "They didn't realize how much they were owed for what they did for me growing up. He said at the time, they did it out of love and the kindness of their hearts. But years later, when they saw what everyone else was getting from me, they realized they deserved some kind of cut. And probably a big one considering they did so much more for me than any of the other assholes from home that I was writing checks to."

"That's horrible. That's not an excuse for what they put you through," I said furiously. "What they lied about is despicable. The world needs to know the truth about them, Drew. Why did you never tell?"

"The same reason you still help your mom out," Drew murmured, looking me in the eye. "Because I couldn't help but care about her still. I thought about all the good memories when the love was real because there was no money in the picture yet. And as much as I hated her, I couldn't sic the media on her either."

"Especially now that she's gone," I said softly, to which Drew nodded. "How... did she pass?" I asked warily.

"I heard a heart attack, but I don't even know for sure, which fucking kills me." Drew closed his eyes, breathing in deep as I gently rubbed the back of his neck. "After I found out the truth about her cancer, I ignored every time she reached out. I tossed all the letters she wrote me without ever opening them. And now that she's gone, I somehow feel like shit about that. About the fact that I'll never know what she wrote in those letters." The breath he exhaled as he opened his eyes was shaky, and a sharp pain twisted in my chest when I noticed his eyes were glassy, wet with tears he still refused to let spill.

"Drew. It's okay to feel regret about that. You're allowed to."

"You sure about that?" he laughed bitterly. "She stole a quarter of a million dollars from me and put me through a living hell, but I still miss her sometimes. It doesn't make any fucking sense."

"Of course it does," I said gently. "She played a huge role in your life. She was genuinely good to you at some point. She did love you. But as much as it hurts to say, good people don't always stay that way. Sometimes something happens and they turn. But we're human, Drew, and some days we'll miss the good times we had with those people. That's just how it is."

Drew nodded, quiet as he looked into my eyes, as if he knew I was thinking of Kaylie. I was remembering when I was nine or ten, and how she taught me to stand up for myself against the bullies at school. I thought of Mike, and how I only ever dared to dream of a better life because of him. Both of them were instrumental in carving out a lot of the good qualities I still had today.

But the people they were when they helped me do that were gone.

"I always thought as a kid that life would get easier as I got older," Drew said with almost a laugh.

"No. It gets harder," I said quietly. "We meet more people, we love more people. Sometimes they leave and disappoint you. Or they pass and we miss them forever."

"So why care about anyone?"

His question surprised me – not in the words he said, but the tone he spoke in. It wasn't cynical – it was honest. Genuinely curious. It made me search hard and fast within myself for a good answer, because I knew Drew needed to hear one.

"We care because love is stronger than hate, and it's worth the risk," I finally said. "Even if it doesn't pan out, it turns you a little closer in the right direction. Every time."

"You believe that?" Drew asked. Like his last question, it was an honest one. I bit my lip as I thought about it.

"I do," I said, feeling a little smile drift slowly onto my lips as Drew simply held me and gazed at me. He was quiet for a bit before finally nodding and returning my faint smile.

"Well, if you believe it, then I guess I can give it a try."

30

DREW

Against Iain's wishes, Evie decided to fly in for the L.A leg of my West Coast road trip.

"She does realize how much L.A hates you, right?" Iain asked, having called me the second I told him of our plans. "She's not going to have fun in the stands by herself. The fans are going to heckle her just for being your girlfriend. You have to realize that."

"I do, but she'll be sitting with the rest of the WAGs, including Diaz's wife so she'll be in good hands," I said as my car crossed the bridge into Brooklyn to get to the stadium. "Trust me, I'd rather her avoid L.A too but she wanted to go. She said she's never been to California before and this is her shot," I lied.

That wasn't the reason. It was more so the fact that Evie now knew why L.A hated me so goddamned much.

I had missed five weeks of games after putting Tim in the hospital. I had been forced to go to anger counseling and when I returned to L.A, I was broken down enough to let a former fling become something more. I needed the emotional support.

But I wound up discovering that she was emailing the team daily updates on me – when I got home, who I spoke to on the phone, and any info she could get out of me regarding Tim. I was an expensive investment for them, and they didn't trust me to stay out of trouble, so they paid someone in my life to spy on me — to monitor my day-to-day behavior.

It was why I demanded a trade from L.A the same year they traded three key players to acquire me. It was why their manager, current roster and front office hated me, and why the fans went out of their way to heckle me when I visited.

It was never a particularly enjoyable city to play in. In fact, I hated being there. Four years later, and I'd yet to touch down in L.A without thinking about all the drama that went down when I was on that team – especially since the fans loved to use the Lillards against me while heckling.

"Would it make your stay a little easier if I came?" Evie had asked yesterday morning, after our long talk in bed.

It took a good minute for me to answer because on instinct, my tongue refused to admit that I needed anyone for anything. Even after I'd proven to myself that I was no good without Evie – that my body physically ached when it wasn't near hers – I refused to just flat-out say that I wanted her to come.

That I would be happier if she did.

But eventually, I fought myself for long enough to utter the words, "I'd like if you did."

"Cool. Then I will," Evie had smiled breezily, completely unaware of the fact that my body had just gone to war with itself to give her that five-word response. It was honestly ridiculous, and I recognized that. For so long, I'd trained myself to function just fine without re-lying on anyone but myself.

But now that I'd had a taste of Evie's brand of warmth and comfort, there was no going back.

"Maddox. You know they're going to go harder than usual, consid-ering this is your first time back since you punched their captain in the face," Iain said, reminding me of that home game a few months ago.

Cody Bryce had said something about how Pattie was rolling in her grave over what a piece of shit I was. I responded by throwing a fastball high and inside, damned near skimming his fat mouth. He stormed the mound, I clocked him in the jaw and a few days later, I was covering my bruised knuckles with Keira's makeup, in a car that would eventually take me to meet Evie.

That night had been only months ago but it felt like well over a year at this point, because I could barely remember what my life was like before this contract – before knowing Evie.

"She's tough as nails. I promise you she can handle whatever the L.A crowd has to say to her," I said.

"You better hope so. After that tabloid story about her family, the last thing you need is for one more drama to explode in her face and chase her away."

"Have a little faith in her, Iain," I said, a grin on my lips as the car pulled up to the stadium. "I promise you she isn't going anywhere."

~

EVIE

AFTER MY FINAL meeting on Wednesday, I caught an afternoon flight into Los Angeles. And pretty shortly after touching down, I realized that Drew hadn't been exaggerating in his warnings to me about L.A.

"Hey! Fuck the Empires!" some guy in the airport yelled at me with a big grin, inspiring someone else to pipe up.

"Fuck Drew Maddox!"

Jesus.

I was pretty sure I was getting recognized more here than I was at home. Thankfully, there was a lot less walking to do in L.A than in New York, which meant that for the rest of the day, I was pretty much hidden in the safety of a car. I was even able to enjoy a little bit of shopping and a solo lunch in relative peace and quiet.

No one called out at me, but I *did* have a pretty bad case of the giggles because Drew would not stop checking in on me.

DREW: Hey. What are you up to?

ME: Pretty much the same as when you checked in on me twenty minutes ago silly

DREW: Hey a lot can change in 20 minutes. We lost the World Series last year in a matter of 20 minutes

ME: Fair enough. Though I should say no one has said anything to me since leaving the airport

DREW: Paparazzi?

ME: Not that I can see

DREW: Good

ME: Shouldn't you be stretching or bagging flies right now or something? Why do you have your phone on you?

DREW: Shagging flies. And I just wanted to check in to make sure you're okay

I smirked to myself, trying to suppress my amusement since I was attracting eyes around the restaurant for laughing to myself so much. But I couldn't help it. Drew Maddox being protective was as adorable as it was sexy to me, and I honestly couldn't believe he was taking time out of his pre-game routine to check in on me so much. I kept imagining him in uniform, jogging back and forth between the field and the clubhouse to sneak texts to me.

ME: Drew as cute as you are to worry about me I'm going to tell you to get back to doing your pre-game thing. Still not sure how baseball works but I do know I need you to win tonight, especially if the crowd is going to be as bad as you say.

DREW: I will win tonight. And they're probably going to be even worse than I said.

And as it turned out, he was right on both counts.

Because as soon as I got to the stadium the heckling started up again, and were it not for the company of the other WAGs, particularly Angie Diaz, I'd be a little intimidated – mostly because the majority of the yelling was directed solely to me.

It was mostly a lot of *"fuck Drew Maddox"* with some *"stupid gold-*

digger" and *"whore"* comments peppered in, but by the time we sat, the hecklers got more creative.

"What's a nice girl like you doing with a psychopath, huh?"

"Is he holding you against your will, sweetheart?"

"Hey, blink twice if you need us to call the cops!"

"Ignore them, girl." Angie squeezed my hand while wearing a big grin and waving down the field to her husband, Alex – or as Drew called him, Diaz.

"I am. Not even looking behind me," I reassured her.

"Good. The boys always worry when we come to L.A games because the fans get rowdy," she said between her brilliant, smiling teeth as she blew Diaz a kiss. "And they were even more worried today, but I told them we're big girls, and we don't scare easy."

"Yes. Totally," I nodded vehemently, but then I frowned. "Wait. Why were they particularly worried today?"

Angie turned to me with a funny smile.

"Well... because you're here today, sweetie," she said as if it were obvious. "Drew can ignore the hecklers easy, but with you here? The fans know he's got a weakness now, and if they can't get under his skin, they're gonna try to get under yours – which is why we're just gonna let that shit roll off our backs, right? Because we don't want to give our boys anything to worry about."

"Oh yeah. Totally," I agreed readily, though I couldn't help but feel a tinge of worry.

And guilt.

For God's sake, I had come here to serve as Drew's emotional support, not his Kryptonite.

"It's okay, honey," Angie said, patting my hand when she read the look of concern in my eyes. "As long as you stay strong for him, he'll be fine. All Drew needs is to know you're okay, and he'll be okay, too. That's just how love goes."

"Of course," I said, blushing like an idiot over the L word.

Still, I did manage to heed the rest of Angie's advice by staying calm and giving the crowd nothing to work off of for the next two-and-a-half hours – even as the abuse started to move away from Drew and more toward my family. Clearly, these people were Googling me between innings because the taunting was starting to get insanely specific.

"Evie! That beer you're drinking could pay your mom's mortgage this month!"

"Hey, Belfield girl, are you really his fiancée? Or are you his drug dealer?"

"Hey, sweetie, I'll buy you a pack of cigs if you suck my dick."

"Fuckin' *trailer traaaash!*"

I could see it getting to even Angie.

"Jesus, these fuckin' *pendejos*, are they serious?" she muttered to herself, in the midst of turning around in her seat before I stopped her.

"Angie. It's okay," I said, forcing a laugh. "It doesn't bother me. I've already started getting used to it."

"Well, good," she huffed, taking a second to calm down. Once she did, she eyed me with a smirk. "See, you look like the nice girl next door, but I should've figured you were a tough cookie. No way you lock down Drew Maddox without being a bad bitch."

I laughed.

"Oh yeah. He can be difficult," I admitted, feeling every bit like a real girlfriend as Angie and I commiserated over the bullheaded tendencies of our men. "But he's worth the fight," I said eventually.

And I meant it, especially as I remembered our last morning in bed together. I had the real Drew Maddox wrapped around me. His real embrace, his raw emotions, his real kiss. It had taken awhile, but I finally had all of Drew.

It felt incredible.

"Looks like he's finally met his match," Angie said as she studied me.

I grinned. "Maybe."

And for the rest of the game, we successfully ignored the yelling and shouting – especially since the seventh inning saw the Empires scoring four runs to up the lead to 8-1, which meant Drew was pulled in the next inning.

"He killed it, honey. They just want to send in some relief pitching to let him rest," Angie explained to me as Drew got a dozen pats on the back from his teammates before hopping off the mound.

I had to laugh at the instant chorus of boos that rained down on him as he jogged from the mound to the dugout because he was completely unfazed and grinning, and my God he looked good.

That uniform fit tighter on his lower body than any of the jeans he wore on a regular basis and Lord, that ass was calling to me. I was pretty sure watching Drew jog across the field was what men felt like when they watched the women running on the beach in *Baywatch*. Even as I looked around, I could see some female fans in L.A gear biting their lips at each other and shrugging as if to say, *yeah, gotta admit, he's hot*.

I was pretty sure it didn't get better but just as Drew passed my section along the first base line, he looked directly at me. Locking eyes on me, he pointed, grinned and blew a kiss.

As he disappeared into the dugout, I promptly melted into my seat.

"Omigod!"

"*Evieee!*"

The WAGs were squealing, pinching me and losing their minds so hard that I could barely hear the hecklers booing even louder around me now. All I could do was laugh my ass off because I couldn't believe this was my life. I had survived the L.A hecklers, my man had gotten the win and we were bound to celebrate tonight with a room service feast at the hotel before passing out together in bed.

"See?" Angie murmured to me after we'd all come down from our giggles. "Isn't it fun being Drew Maddox's fiancée?"

I said nothing, simply nodding because I wasn't sure what it felt like to be Drew's fiancée. But I did have an idea of what it felt like to be his girlfriend.

And that, I had to admit, felt better than I could've ever imagined.

31

EVIE

"She died hating you."

That was the drunken jeer we heard as we approached the taco stand we'd stopped at on the way to the hotel. Drew needed some "hold me over" food and it didn't seem like the worst idea considering there was no one else waiting in line.

Of course, we failed to factor in the sports bar a few doors down – and the fact that it was full of L.A fans watching post-game coverage of Drew's win tonight.

"Hey, sweetie, get away from him while you can!" yelled some guy hanging outside with the bouncer. "Make a run for it! Now!"

I ignored the shouts, my neck tense till I looked up at Drew. His eyes were somewhat covered by his baseball cap but his jaw was relaxed and he looked utterly unfazed. The only giveaway that he'd heard was the fact that he held me tighter to his side.

"You good?" I whispered up at him.

"As long as you are," he whispered back, looking down at me with a crooked grin touching his lip.

After he ordered and paid up with the cashier, he sat me at the colorful metal stool in the window, while he leaned against the counter. It made us sitting ducks for the heckling, but the way Drew smiled at my Maddox jersey and denim skirt had me easily ignoring the occasional jeers from a few doors down.

"Think you might have to come with me on all my road trips now," he said.

"Oh yeah? Why is that?"

"You made it easy tonight. The game just went by fast. I didn't feel the usual shit as much," he confessed.

"What do you mean the usual shit?"

The cotton pulled tight on Drew's T-shirt as he shrugged his big shoulders.

"I don't know. I just didn't feel the stress as much. The shit they said to me – I wasn't just pretending not to care this time. I really didn't," Drew said, his brows pulling tight as if he were realizing all this as he said it.

"And you think that has to do with me?" I laughed gently. He didn't return my amusement.

"Yes," he said, looking me in the eye. He stood closer now, stroking the back of my calves as he gazed down at me. "Helped just knowing I had you to come home to tonight. Kind of made it feel like everything the fans were saying didn't mean shit. Pattie, Tim – the fans use them against me because they think that's as personal as it gets with me. That that's what I care about most."

"But... it's not?" I asked slowly, feeling a dorky smile curl my lips. Drew laughed as he watched me.

"No. It's not," he said.

"What is it then?"

"I think you know the answer to that," he murmured, leaning in to kiss me softly on the lips.

I didn't even care that he didn't say it out loud. *You're what I care about most.* It would've been nice to hear but I knew how hard it was for Drew to say even as much as he had just now. So as I kissed him back, I told myself to give him time.

Eventually, he'd come around.

"Aww, look at these fuckin' lovebirds."

I heard the jeer and immediately pulled away from Drew's kiss, but he caught my jaw with his hand, pressing his lips to mine for another hot second before letting me go. Then he eyed the heckler standing in line to order.

"Don't let them get to you," Drew murmured just as our orders arrived.

"I won't," I said calmly, though I could feel the tension rising as more bar patrons trickled over to the taco stand, all of them hawking us like a damned zoo exhibit.

Fuckin' Drew and his hunger emergencies, I groaned inwardly as the hecklers got closer.

There were two in particular who worried me. They were in their fifties with ruddy faces and beer bellies. They looked like actual pigs to me, especially as they talked loudly about being able to see up my "slutty little skirt."

"Don't," I whispered under my breath to Drew. "Don't give them a reaction."

He had his back facing them and his eyes staring straight ahead into the kitchen, but I could see as he chewed his food that his jaw was tightening. I could tell from the way he stopped blinking that he was focused on these assholes without looking at them, and his sudden concentration scared me. He seemed suddenly locked in the way he was when he was on the mound, and it made all the hairs on the back of my neck stand up at attention.

"Save yourself, sweetie," the one with the ponytail said, waving at me in the corner of my vision. "You don't wanna end up like that poor Lillard bastard."

"Team Lillard!" someone shouted from a few doors down as Ponytail's friend laughed.

"Yeah, you get this guy fired up enough and who knows what he'll do. I'm sure he's hit a woman before."

"Plenty, in fact."

Disgusting assholes. My jaw clenched as I folded my paper plate and tossed my unfinished food in the trash.

"Let's go, Drew," I murmured, exhaling in relief when he simply nodded.

"Oh, no, sweetie, you leaving?" Ponytail asked me as I got off my chair, though his bleary, mischievous eyes were on Drew as he said it. "You sure you wanna go with him? We won't mind taking you in for the night."

"No, we'd love it. In fact, I'll let you sleep in my bed if you take that Maddox jersey off."

"Watch it, motherfucker," Drew barked, making my pulse jump.

"Drew." My heart slammed as I pulled him closer to me, feeling eyes from all directions pinned on me as I looked frantically for where our car had parked. *Dammit, where the hell did it go?*

"Alright, bye, guys. Nice talkin' to ya," Ponytail chuckled as we successfully passed him without saying a word. *Thank God*, I exhaled just as I spotted the car. But then I heard him whisper to his friend about whether or not he was recording.

And before I knew it, I was gasping from the sensation of ice-cold liquid splashed all over my back.

"*Drew!*" I screamed, pulling him back even before I fully processed that someone had thrown a beer at me. "Stop. Stop, Drew! Stop!"

I said it so many times in so many ways that I barely recognized my own voice anymore. All I knew was that my heels were digging into grass, and I was exerting every muscle in my body to get in front of an unhinged Drew. He looked like a raging bull. His jaw was so tight the veins in his neck were protruding, and my heart pounded because it felt like I was hugging the mouth of a cocked and loaded gun.

"Drew, stop. Look at me. Look at me!" I pleaded as the drunks around us hooted and hollered, egging him on with talk of how good I looked all wet. "Look at me." I grasped his face and tilted it down, repeating for him to look at me until he finally did, his green eyes wild on me. "They want this reaction from you. They're recording you now. They've got no stakes but you do, so breathe. Calm down." My calf muscles strained as I dug my heels to push him backward, unblinking as I kept his glinting green eyes locked on mine. "This is what the world expects of you, so prove them wrong. Show them the

Drew I know. Show them that nothing comes before a championship. Do it for me, baby, please," I begged breathlessly, grasping handfuls of his collar. But my grip loosened as I listened to his jagged breaths slow down, and I was convinced I had him pacified.

But then another holler rang out.

"Stay with him long enough, and you'll meet Pattie Lillard real soon!"

"Drew!" I threw my weight against his rock-hard chest, but then I realized he wasn't moving.

He hadn't charged. He hadn't reacted. Standing there, he simply looked down at me, his shirt stretched tight around his heaving chest. There was still fury in his tight shoulders, and fiery wrath in his eyes, but as primed as he looked to knock someone the fuck out, he didn't.

Yes. Perfect. Breathe, baby, I willed him to hear as I stared up at him, in awe of the fact that I had wrangled such a beast. But I knew my job wasn't done till he was safely in the car, so with two hands flat on his chest, I whispered in his ear.

"I know you're pissed, Drew, but if you turn around and start walking now, I promise to blow your fucking mind once we get back to the hotel. You can choose my pussy or my mouth, but either way, I'll make you come harder than you ever have in your life. Okay?"

When I pulled away, his wolfish stare was still hard on me. But he let it linger another second before pulling me tight and cupping the back of my neck as he crushed a furious kiss to my lips.

Then with a gaping crowd behind us, we got back into the car.

32

DREW

My blood was still on fire by the time we were back at the hotel, but my hot focus was no longer on the drunken hecklers.

It was a hundred percent on Evie.

She walked ahead of me, teasing me with every step in those heels, every sway of those hips. The way she sauntered across the marble floor caught the eye of every man in the lobby. From guests to staff, she had them all staring in the way she knew I both loved and hated.

This woman. She knew me well enough to know just how to rein me in. Another thing I both loved and hated. *Little cocktease*, I ground my teeth as I watched her, my pulse rising with the need to just lift that skirt and spank her ass till she couldn't take anymore.

Fuck. She was so damned good at turning me into an animal. I'd already forgotten whatever sequence of events that had led us here. It was all a fog because all I saw was Evie, and the second I trailed her into the elevator, I cornered her, standing tight against her body to hide her from cameras.

"Come here," I muttered, holding her neck with one hand as the other reached under her skirt. Her mouth hung slightly open, her lips curving in a breathless little grin as I reached between her legs and palmed her soaked panties. "Jesus," I muttered, licking her smile.

"Take them off for me."

I grasped a handful of the lace, relishing the sound of her raspy yelp as I ripped it clean off her pussy.

"That hurt," she pouted as I slid her panties into my pocket and rubbed her wet pussy.

"Does that feel better?"

"Yes."

"This?" I slid two fingers inside her. She tightened around me.

"Oh God." Her nails dug into my chest as she whispered, "It feels so good."

My teeth skimmed her sweet lips as she panted against me, moaning softly as I pumped my fingers inside her. I started slow, picking my pace up gradually, till my fingers were fucking her so hard the sound of her wetness was bouncing off the walls. "Drew," she exhaled, her moans growing louder as she grinded her clit against the heel of my palm.

"Are you going to come all over my hand?"

"Yes," she breathed with desperation breaking her voice. But in seconds, she ripped her body away from me because the elevator had stopped on a floor that wasn't ours. "Fuck," she hissed, writhing in torment against the wall opposite me.

I had to stare.

She looked like walking sex. And not just any sex – dirty sex. Her hair was messy and her skirt was twisted askew. Her tits were ready to spill and those pillowy lips were so red and swollen I couldn't be surprised at the reactions of the two guys who walked in. I wasn't easy to miss but they didn't even see me as their wide eyes flew right to Evie pressed up against the wall, staring speechlessly back at them. Secretly dripping from her naked pussy.

One of them muttered "wow" but the second he stepped toward her, I cleared my throat.

"Oh! Fuck."

In one breath, he acknowledged both who I was and the fact that he'd just been looking at my woman. It was all he needed to shut right up and do a one-eighty.

I caught Evie biting her smirk because for the next four floors, both men were wide-eyed and silent. They stood dead center between us, staring straight ahead and so still you'd think I'd turned them to stone.

The second they got out, I had Evie pressed back on the wall, both our hands frantically grasping at one another as we kissed till we got to our floor.

I barely remembered how we got into our room. All I knew was that I was watching her skirt fall around her ankles, exposing her sweet pussy to me as she whipped my jersey up over her head.

"Bounce those perfect tits for me, baby," I murmured as she unclasped her bra and let it fall to the floor.

"Ah, ah," she smirked, cupping her breasts and pushing them gently together. "I told you I was going to make you come harder than you ever have in your life, which means I'm in control tonight. You just tell me whether you want my mouth or my pussy first."

"Let's start with that smart mouth," I muttered as I undid my belt buckle.

"Perfect," Evie grinned, mischief glimmering in her eyes. "Now go lay down in bed. You've had a very long, trying day, and you deserve to be taken care of now."

God, she was so fucking sexy.

I didn't need to be told twice. Peeling off my shirt, I lay down in bed, folding my arms behind my head and just watching as Evie climbed naked on top of me, her tits bouncing softly between her arms as she began to work my sore quads.

"Fuck... " I exhaled, closing my eyes. A post-game massage by a naked Evie was pretty much exactly what I needed to wind down from tonight. I was pretty fucking content as it was, but then I felt her nipples graze my thighs just before I felt the heat of her mouth on my dick, kissing it over my boxers. "Holy shit, baby, what are you doing?" I rasped as she continued moving her mouth up my shaft, wrapping her lips around my tip as her palms applied more pressure to my thighs. "Oh my fucking God, Evie..." I groaned when I realized she was about to suck on my cock *while* working on my sore muscles.

I was delirious by the time she'd stripped my boxers off.

"Are you kidding me, baby?" I hissed, watching in awe because the way she took my cock was out of control.

She had my pulsing head at the back of her throat, and at the same time she was massaging the hell out of my sore muscles, never losing the rhythm of either stroke. It was fucking wild. With every push of her palm up my hamstring, she dropped her mouth down my cock. With every pull back, she sucked slowly back up to the tip, her cheeks hollowing as she spoiled every hard inch of me with her unbelievably skilled tongue.

"Holy shit. Fucking marry me," I groaned, my fist pulsing around my handful of her hair. "That feels so fucking good. You're gonna make me come so fast, baby."

"Come whenever you want. I can do this all night," she murmured against my pulsing tip. She lifted those big eyes and watched me as she stuck that pink tongue out slowly and swirled it around me like she was savoring an ice cream cone. The shuddering sensation was heaven enough but top that with the sexy little look on her face and I almost busted right there.

"You have no idea. I'm trying so hard not to come right now, baby," I rasped. "I swear I'm wearing out every muscle in my body trying not to blow my load right fucking now."

Evie's sweet giggle against my cock sent a little buzz humming down from my tip to my root.

"Wear 'em out then. I'll always be here to massage you if you're sore."

Holy Christ, this woman.

"You're fucking perfect. Do you know that?" It wasn't even a rhetorical question. I needed her to know how incredible she was. How I loved when she proved me wrong. How she made me feel things I never thought were even real. "Oh fuck... baby."

My balls were so tight I knew I couldn't last much longer. She knew it too because she licked around the throbbing head of my cock while asking me, "Where do you want to come?"

God. Every little thing she did. Every fucking word she said was the sexiest thing I'd ever heard in my life.

"I need to come inside you. Get on top of me. Let me see you ride my cock," I muttered fast, both loving and hating the fact that she knew to roll a condom on first. I wanted to feel her skin to skin, with nothing in between. I wanted my cum to fill her pussy but I wasn't about to dwell on those thoughts as I watched her straddle and lower herself onto me. "Yes. Just like that. Just like that, baby... you're such a good fucking girl," I growled, dizzy with lust as I watched her mount me, gripping me and guiding me between her wet folds. A deep groan tore from my throat as she sank that warm pussy down to the base of my cock, her round ass pressed tight against my churning balls.

I swore it couldn't get better but the second that thought crossed my mind, Evie smoothed her palms up from my chest to my shoulders, rubbing my sore muscles and treating me to the incredible view of her full tits bouncing heavily as she rode me.

Once again, I tried holding out. I didn't want this to end. I couldn't let it. Never in my life had I felt this good. This taken care of. For Christ's sake, not only was this the most beautiful girl in the world, I had her in my arms and I could see in the way she looked at me that she was mine. All fucking mine. That she wanted no one and nothing but me.

And it was the best feeling in the world.

I never wanted to let it go.

But the second Evie lowered herself and pressed a sweet kiss to my lips, I exploded inside her, growling like an animal as she bounced on my dick and milked every last drop of cum from my tip.

For what felt like a full hour after, I lay in bed recovering. I could barely open my eyes.

All I could do was bask in the blissful haze she'd put me in, letting a delirious smile drift onto my lips as I heard her giggle and felt her brushing soft kisses along my shoulders, my cheeks, my lips.

It was probably 1AM when she laid on my chest and whispered my name. I opened my eyes to see her looking up at me, and she gazed at me for another few seconds before murmuring, "I love you."

Three words and she rearranged everything inside me.

My brain, my heart – they both knew different truths now. Trust was real and so was love because I loved Evie more than I thought I could love anything. As I held her to my chest, I swore I could feel all the good in her soul. I felt the warmth of it seeping into mine, filling in every chip and crack I'd sustained from every instance of hurt in my past.

She made me whole and as I felt all that, I tried my hardest to return those words she'd gifted me.

But they never made it out of my mouth before we fell asleep.

33

DREW

As soon as Evie and I touched back down in Seattle, we were told we'd gone viral. I shouldn't have been surprised, but there wound up being passerby footage of the L.A fans dousing her in beer and setting me off like a cannon.

I wasn't particularly pleased about that moment being viewed by millions, and played repeatedly on sports talk shows, but of course, Iain was and I knew why.

STRONG MAN, STRONGER WOMAN.

That was one of many headlines that credited Evie for holding me back. Some of the stories insinuated that she had me whipped at this point – probably just to piss me off – but it didn't. I knew well that Evie had saved me from a guaranteed suspension that would've probably pushed my name further into the Empires' trade talks.

So safe to say, I didn't give two shits about what the media was trying to say. For all I knew, she'd just saved my career and I owed her the world for it.

"You do realize that shit was exactly what I was trying to help you avoid, right?" Iain said when he called me after my win in Seattle, after I'd gotten home from a peaceful, heckle-free dinner with Evie.

"Yeah, man. I do," I conceded distractedly as I sat at the end of the bed in the hotel room.

"Jesus. Did I just hear you admit to being wrong?" Iain laughed.

"Sure," I smirked, too tired to come up with a rebuttal. There was also the fact that I was distracted as all hell as I watched Evie wander out of the bathroom, freshly showered and hugging a towel to her tits. I failed to suppress my groan as I watched the towel droop as she let go of it to grab her toothbrush out of her bag on the couch.

"Maddox."

I ignored Iain to grin at Evie as she let the towel just fall the rest of the way to the floor, walking around the room ass naked.

"Drew. Jesus," Iain muttered, sounding both amused and disgusted. "Considering you're openly groaning on the phone with me while undoubtedly watching Evie do something or another, I guess we can take this time to stop pretending that she isn't actually your girlfriend. Right?"

"Yeah, probably," I said as I enjoyed my view of Evie leaning naked in the bathroom doorframe, smiling innocently at me as she brushed her teeth.

"Thought so, prick," Iain said with a snort. "Anyway, I'd give you a lecture on holding onto her for the sake of your career, but judging from how ridiculously lovey dovey you've sounded throughout this phone call, I don't have to worry about that. I'll just leave off on the fact that the Empires saw that L.A debacle as your crazy ass turning a new leaf. As far as I know, they're pretty much sold that you're a changed man," he said. "So long story short, you're lucky as shit you had your girl that night, Maddox."

That night. In general.

"So, am I fully safe now or what?" I asked as Evie came back out in one of my T-shirts and a pair of black lace panties. I grinned when she climbed straight into my lap where she belonged, letting me wrap my arms around her and suck on her bottom lip as Iain answered my question.

"You're as safe as it gets, Drew. From what I've heard, the team's no longer looking to make any moves before the trade deadline. Talks have pretty much slowed to a stop."

"Good to know," I mumbled, barely listening now as Evie pushed me onto my back, rubbing my shoulders as she kissed me gently. "God, I could get used to this," I murmured to her just as Iain cursed under his breath.

"Alright, asshole, I'm not listening to you whisper sweet nothings all night. See you when you get back to New York."

I laughed when Iain hung up, tossing the phone aside and letting Evie massage my left forearm with both hands as she straddled me. I wanted to let my eyes roll back because it felt so damned good, but I didn't want to miss the view. I narrowed my eyes at her as she simply smiled down at me.

"What?" she giggled.

"Nothing. Just wondering what I did to deserve you," I replied. "Pretty sure I've been nothing but an asshole my whole life."

"Stop," she said firmly, looking adorably annoyed. "Stop letting everyone else sum you up with a buzzword or a headline. You know you're not the person they say, and you don't have to bear this burden forever, Drew. I'm not saying you have to tell the world the truth about Tim and Pattie, but I'm just saying you should give yourself a break from being the bad guy." Her eyes were locked on mine as she brought my fingertips to her lips, kissing them gently as she continued massaging my forearm. "You're not that person, Drew. You have such a big heart. You have so much good in you, and I think you've always known that. But now you have one more voice to say it to you, so maybe..." Her eyes floated off as she shrugged. "I don't know. Maybe you'll believe it now."

I looked up in her eyes, my heart aching in a way I'd never felt before, because it was a good ache. For the most part. It was an ache that made me wonder why it took so long for me to find this woman – why I'd been forced to go through so much pain and bullshit before God, or the universe or whoever it was gave me Evie.

But then I thought about what she'd said that morning we had in my bed.

Love is worth the risk. Even if it doesn't pan out, it turns you a little closer in the right direction. Every time.

I wasn't sold the day she told me, but I definitely was now. And as I gazed up into her eyes, I tried to say those three words I'd never uttered to a soul in my adult life.

I felt them. And I wanted to say them.

"I don't know what I'd do without you, Evie," I finally murmured, my heart beating faster at just the look of the smile on her face. It wasn't what I wanted to say, but I still meant it.

Baby steps, I told myself.

At the very least, I was getting a little closer.

EVIE

"Woman. You have to tell me *every*thing," Aly said as soon as I touched down in East Hampton.

Literally the day I got back to New York from my California trip, she insisted I take a damned *helicopter* from the city to the Hamptons, because apparently, that was the lifestyle she was now used to with Emmett. And, apparently, she "required" my company for a variety of reasons.

"One, you must provide detailed reports on everything that went down between you and Drew in L.A because I saw the pictures and the video, and holy shit, woman," she rambled a mile a minute as she drove me from the helipad to her house. "I took a whole day off to hear the juicy gossip so you better spill."

"You took a day off just to hear about stuff I've basically told you via text already?" I giggled.

"Yes. Because I want to hear in detail how you managed to tame the Viking. Also, I need emotional support for a thing I have to do today."

I cocked my head at her curiously.

"What thing?" I asked slowly, somehow already expecting what she was going to say before she said it. "Are you...?"

"Pregnant?" she blurted, restlessly drumming her fingers on the wheel as we stopped at a light. "Maybe. Hopefully." She shoved her Ray Bans up her face as she turned to look at me. "Or not hopefully? Do I want to be pregnant before the wedding? I don't know. I have no idea, and I'm freaking the fuck out."

"Aly, breathe," I laughed, squeezing her shoulder till I heard her breathing normally again. "If your biggest concern is rocking a baby bump at your wedding, you're in good shape. Don't worry. We'll figure this out together, and my L.A stories will keep you nice and distracted while you wait for the results. Okay?"

"Yes. Perfect."

I knew it probably broke some sort of code, but I wound up showing Aly some of Drew's texts to me since I'd gotten home. It was all I could do to get her to calm down as we sat on the floor of her bedroom waiting for the results of the pregnancy tests.

"Holy shit, woman," Aly murmured in awe as she read the last text Drew had sent me, which I had already memorized by heart. *I keep trying to pretend you're in the stands. Tell me you'll wait up for me when I get back on Sunday. I miss you like fucking crazy.* "Evie... do you realize what a big deal it is for Drew to say that to someone?"

I tried not to beam like a giddy idiot, but I could tell from the way Aly burst into giggles that I'd failed.

"No wonder you're not worried about that whole 'I love you' thing," Aly mused as she reread the text.

Right. The whole "I love you" thing.

"I don't know why I said that," I mumbled, thinking back on that unbelievable night. "I just... felt it in that moment."

"Which means you meant it, and you had every right to say it," Aly reasoned gently, with a little shrug. "You're not like him, Evie. You say what you feel without going through a million walls and filters."

"I guess," I murmured, looking down at my hands in my lap. I had meant those three words when I said them, but it was easier for me to pretend they'd just slipped out in the heat of the moment, especially since he didn't say them back.

"I know you hate the idea of needing time, but give Drew a little more of it," Aly said. "Look at those texts he sends you. You know he feels the same way about you. He just has a shit ton of mental blocks because of... whatever reasons. Reasons I'm sure you know by now."

I bit my lip and blushed as I looked up at her.

"Yep. You do. He's told you everything he never even told Emmett, hasn't he?" Aly laughed, shaking her head.

"Maybe."

"And you won't even tell me what his deep dark secrets are because you love him! Oh my God," Aly exclaimed incredulously as I covered my giggling face with my hands. "Evie. You two are so in love it's ridiculous. You realize what this means right?"

"That your test results are ready and you can stop giving me a hard time now?"

"I was going to say that the four of us are about to have double dates like it's our jobs, but sure, yes, let's go see if I'm pregnant." Aly jumped to her feet so fast I had to laugh. It was so clear to me that she desperately wanted this baby – she was just trying to find reasons to be nervous about it because that was just the way we were.

When things were too perfect, we questioned it.

"Oh my God. Oh my God."

"What? What?" I giggled excitedly, running into the bathroom to find Aly standing there holding the pregnancy test on the right – the one I'd taken with her in solidarity.

"Evie..." My heart thumped against my ribs as she turned to me with wide eyes. I shook my head, denying her two words before she could even say them to me. "You're pregnant."

34

Waiting for Drew to come home to New York was a unique kind of torture. It was like an emotional purgatory in which I constantly told myself that maybe Aly was right, and things could turn out just fine. Actually, the mental limbo was a whole lot like the one I'd been steeped in the first night I met Drew – when I was still trying to figure out where I stood with Mike.

God.

That name was like a foreign language to me at this point. Once upon a time, it represented my world. Now, it couldn't be more of an afterthought because not only was I in love with Drew Maddox, I was carrying his child.

It was so unreal to me that I kept bursting into tears without warning.

Because the truth was that as completely unexpected as this was, I wanted this child. With Aly, I'd taken several more tests to confirm it, but by the second one, I had already made up my mind on the matter.

I was going to be a mother in about nine months, and nothing anyone said was going to change that. I wanted my own family. I wanted a son or a daughter whom I could shower with all the love I missed from my own mom.

With the Empires game playing in the living room, I stood against the kitchen counter, cradling my belly in my arms and crying again when I imagined the life this child could have with both of his parents.

In my imagination, it was idyllic and perfect. In my mind, I vividly pictured an emerald-eyed little boy playing catch with a father he worshipped and adored. I imagined us sitting with ice cream on the couch, watching Daddy on TV.

I imagined a lot of things that deep in my heart, I didn't think were going to happen.

Yet at the same time, I held out hope.

It wasn't purgatory, actually – it was hell. And by the time I heard that elevator humming up to the penthouse, I was at the edge of my sanity. As I waited for Drew, I fought my own negativity with all the *mights* and *maybes* that Aly had fed me with.

Maybe he'll be excited to be a father.

He might be craving the stability.

Maybe this will be his push to realize that he loves you.

When the elevator doors finally opened, I was standing in the middle of the kitchen with my breath hitched in my throat.

As usual, Drew's eyes found me immediately, and just like that, those steely eyes I had watched all night on TV warmed over. When he smiled, I felt the emotion well up in my chest.

"Hey, you," he said, sounding that distinct kind of post-game tired that I'd come to love so damned much. I closed my eyes as he floated over to me, pulling me into his arms and holding me tight as he murmured into my neck about how much he missed me.

I closed my eyes as I melted into his embrace, my breaths becoming hiccups as I fantasized that he felt two heartbeats pressed against him instead of just one.

"Baby. What's going on?" Drew pulled away, frowning when he caught the look in my eyes. He brushed back the hair from my face. "Evie. Did something happen?" he asked, his tone hardening as if he was already preparing to take care of something or someone. When I shook my head, he thumbed a tear from my cheek. "Then what is it, Evie? Tell me so I can fix it."

My heart twisted at his words, and I gazed up at him. He was so damned gorgeous as he searched me with those sparkling green eyes. He looked so full of warmth and love and concern, and all these things I'd never have expected to see in his face before.

I told myself it could be fine. I repeated it a thousand times in my head before just blurting it out.

"Drew, I'm pregnant."

My heart promptly broke when his hand dropped from my cheek. I forced myself not to cry as I watched him immediately step back.

"Evie. What are you talking about?" He looked at me like I had lost my mind. "That's not possible. We used protection every time."

"I – I don't know..." I trailed off, realizing I'd never paused to wonder how this could have happened. "I don't know how it happened, Drew. Maybe a condom broke. I don't know. All I know is that I took a pregnancy test *as a joke* with Aly, and before I knew what was happening, she was telling me that I'm the one who's pregnant."

Drew stood a full two steps back now as he stared at me. I felt my pulse rising with every second of silence that passed – with every second that his gaze returned from warm to steely.

"Don't you dare look at me like that," I hissed.

"Like what."

"Like I'm just another person in your life you can't trust. Don't you dare look at me like I somehow planned this, Drew."

"That's not how I'm looking at you."

"It is," I seethed, the knife in my heart twisting as Drew fell silent, not even bothering to deny it any further. I let a tear fall as he turned away from me, palming the top of his head as he stared at the wall. I watched him shake his head, as if he refused to believe this.

This *nightmare*.

"You think this is easy for me, Drew?" I whispered. "I agonized for days about this. A part of me knew you were going to react exactly like this, and it's been eating at me for so long that all I want right now is for you to hold me. I just want you to hug me again and say you can fix this, but you won't. Right?" I demanded, my voice trembling and the tears falling as I watched him stand there coldly.

It was silent for so long, but when he finally spoke, I wished he hadn't.

"This wasn't part of the plan, Evie."

Ouch.

I hadn't thought this could hurt more, but apparently Drew wasn't finished.

"A lot of things haven't been a part of the plan," I replied shakily. "I wasn't supposed to fall for you, and I did. You weren't supposed to care about me, and you do. This baby wasn't supposed to happen, but he's here." Drew shot me a look. "She's here. Whatever it is, it's not going anywhere."

"You want this baby?" Drew asked.

I stared at him.

Four words and I was officially shattered. To pieces. Because it was clear to me at this point that we were done here.

I wanted our child, Drew didn't, and that was that.

"Where are you going?" he asked when I turned to go upstairs. I was numb at this point, and I barely recognized my own voice as I answered.

"I'm going to sleep, Drew."

"Go to my room."

"No," I replied harshly, though a part of me held out hope that he'd stop me – or that he'd sneak into my room, lift me out of my bed, and bring me to his.

I held out hope the entire night.

But in the morning, when I woke up in my own bed in the guest room, I lost that last naïve dash of faith.

And with a glance at my empty bags by the closet, I knew what was left for me to do.

35

EVIE

There were more boarded up buildings than the last time I was here. That much was for sure.

Whether it was houses or storefronts, half the buildings that were once occupied no longer were. At this point, Belfield just felt like a long stretch of marshland with a road, some old billboards and dusty bus stops.

But if any one thing stayed the same, it was bearded Kurt who worked at the gas station where I picked up my mom's lotto tickets. He was in his fifties the last I saw him. Now he was in his sixties and he still wore suspenders and the same Patriots cap that was so faded now it was grey.

"Just so you know, Missy Remsen said her daughter didn't say those things. I think those reporters – they just make up lies," he said as he rang up the Snapple I threw in there for Mom as well.

"They definitely do," I said to keep it simple.

The last thing on my mind was what my high school classmates said to the media or not. But that was all Kurt and I had to talk about when I came here before going to Mom's.

I didn't stay right in Belfield, let alone in Mom's house. I rented a car and booked a motel a few towns over. I told myself that if I wasn't sleeping in that house, I was still being somewhat responsible.

Because the reality was that I knew it wasn't smart to be here.

But I was distraught like I'd never been in my life, and I just needed to be in my mom's arms. I needed to feel her combing her fingers through my hair like she did when I was little, and saying, "Mommy's got you. Everything's going to be alright."

I needed the given of that comfort, even if I knew it would be short-lived. Even if it would blow up in my face in a month, a week or maybe even tomorrow. At some point, the novelty of my being home would fade. The stress would be hard to ignore, and Mom would begin picking fights about my absence all these years.

Kaylie would act out. She was already resenting the fact that I'd shown up, spending a lot of time away with friends while I was around during the day, and screaming at Mom at night once I left.

There was no way in hell things wouldn't blow up between us. She would steal from me or hit me. Maybe pick a fight about the money I was spending on a motel, or perhaps go missing for days. She would hate that my pregnancy took Mom's full attention away from her, and she would do something drastic to get it back.

She'd done it before and I knew she'd do it again.

So I wasn't sure if I was walking on thin ice or in a minefield, but either way, I was bound to be miserable in the near future, and I was bound to be putting this baby through stress it didn't need.

But right now, I needed the comfort. My brain was in shambles, and all I could do was cry and feel scared or guilty – guilty mostly for what I'd done to Aly.

For two days, I'd let myself stay with her and Emmett in their East Hampton home, and as much as Aly took care of me before and after work, or kept me hidden and doted upon in the office of our restaurant, I could see her being constantly worried about me. I could feel myself bringing her down and considering she was supposed to be enjoying real post engagement bliss, I couldn't continue to cry to her about the fact that Drew had clearly made up his mind about us, since he hadn't so much as texted since the morning I left. I could feel myself drowning her, and it made me feel like the most needy, selfish person in the world.

So I came here to Mom.

I had called her to tell her why I was coming home before I did, so the second I walked through the door, all she did was hug me.

"It's a blessing, and everything's going to be alright," she whispered before burying a kiss in my hair.

It was simple yet exactly what I needed and wanted to hear.

So for three days now, I was picking up scratch-offs and OJ or Snapple for her in the morning, chatting a second with Kurt, driving straight to the house, and spending the day with her on the couch. We'd watch daytime talk shows while looking at her boxes of old photos on the couch. Kaylie would pop in and out, say something either neutral or hostile to me, and Mom would whisper, "She's just adjusting," to me and give either a little eye roll or a squeeze of my hand.

Most curiously, she'd pay Kaylie very little mind before turning back to me, trying to get me to look at a picture of when I was baby wearing pink and purple socks she knitted, and talking about how we should perhaps start knitting.

For the first time in a long time, I had her attention back.

And it felt good.

"When did you start showing?" I asked as we settled into the couch today.

"I started showing with you when I was nine weeks, so good luck with that," Mom snorted, patting a gentle hand on my tummy. "Whole town's gonna know soon 'cause of Kaylie's mouth anyway. Did Kurt try to convince you to forgive the Remsens today?"

"Sure did," I managed a smirk as I jammed my thumb on the old remote to turn on the TV. It took about seven tries.

"That ass. Don't let him worry you about that. You got enough on your mind, sweetheart," she said, squeezing my hand. "Tell him you're busy making ten fingers and ten toes, for Chrissake! And they're probably gonna be big ones, considering."

Considering.

She knew well that Drew was the father. I wouldn't confirm it to her, simply because I felt wary – and then guilty about feeling wary – carrying a millionaire's baby into the town of Belfield. My overactive mind pictured people hearing that I was pregnant by Drew Maddox and suddenly showing up to tell me to get him in court, to get that child support.

It was the last thing I wanted to think of right now.

And thankfully, Mom didn't press. Much to my relief, she said, "If Daddy ain't in the picture, we don't need him, honey. When did the Larsen girls ever need a man?"

"Never," I had said, sounding convincing enough for her to beam at me.

But I was lying to myself that day and I was lying to myself now as I thought about what Mom said. Because I couldn't help imagining the incredibly torturous image of Drew Maddox – happy, smiling and sitting next to me at the hospital, helping me count those ten fingers and ten toes.

36

DREW

"Drew, you were already coming off a bad loss in Cleveland on Monday, and tonight's performance was obviously no better. Six innings. Six earned runs. Can you tell us what might be behind the offensive meltdowns in this two-game losing streak? Perhaps the flare-up of an old injury or... distractions in your personal life?"

And there it is.

There was always one reporter that got tired of my well-practiced stoicism during my post-game interviews. Win or lose, I didn't give the press much to work with because no matter what I said, it was twisted and used against me. So I stuck with the usual responses.

My focus tonight wasn't a hundred percent. There are no excuses. Next game.

Since those words weren't easy to twist into some juicy headline, there was always some asshole who started prodding me with scumbag questions, just to see if he could get a fed-up reaction to turn into a good sound bite.

But even tonight – even after the stress of the past five days – I refused to give the little shit the satisfaction of my anger. So without a flicker of expression on my face, I lied straight to his.

"Physically, I'm a hundred percent. My personal life couldn't be better. As far as the seventh inning goes, it was just a loss of focus."

Lie. It was more so Emmett's text about Evie.

"But what was the cause of the loss of focus?" the asshole pressed on.

The fact that he told me there "might be an emergency" and to meet him after the game ASAP, I thought furiously as my lips gave a different answer.

"I think I let myself get hung up on what I thought was a bad call from the umpire. It took me out mentally for just long enough to do offensive damage. I definitely won't let it happen again."

And after that sufficiently bland answer, the interview wrapped. Though of course, that didn't stop one reporter from calling to me, "Might be time to start bringing your lucky charm again."

The prick looked at me for a reaction – perhaps some flinch or grimace to give away the fact that I hadn't seen Evie, my media-dubbed "good luck charm", in almost a week. He was hawking me for something, anything, but I gave him nothing because the reality was, it had only been five days.

Five days since the morning I woke up and she was gone.

I couldn't say I was surprised that morning because I'd expected her to leave. I had driven her away with my reaction, and I knew that. In fact, a part of me knew it would as the words *this wasn't part of the plan* were coming out. It was an undeniable piece of shit thing to say, and I knew it wasn't what she wanted to hear.

But it was my cynical asshole nature coming back to protect me from what she had told me.

Pregnant.

I still couldn't believe it.

It was the word I'd been trained to fear since the day I came into the league. For Christ's sake, there were official league training videos we were required to watch as rookies, just to protect us from women who were after our money.

These women want child support from you. They'll poke holes into condoms. Always bring your own rubbers. Never get a girl pregnant.

In my heart, I knew Evie hadn't poked a fucking hole in a condom. I knew she wasn't swindling me out of some desperate need for money.

But at the same time, I forced myself to question her. She'd reversed a good amount, but she hadn't gotten rid of all my doubt and cynicism – the side of me that believed that every person in the world had a price. There was at least a sliver of that side of me left, and it reminded me of what Iain's girlfriend Keira had said the night of Emmett and Aly's engagement dinner.

Anyone on welfare is going to try to use her to get to your money. You know too well how that goes. Protect yourself. I replayed those words in my head. I thought of Evie's mom. Her drug addict sister. I ran through all my cynical thoughts for the first two days that Evie was gone.

And on day three, I concluded that it was all bullshit.

She wasn't some scheming, conniving con artist – I was just eager to find one. I was eager to believe that over the course of my career, all the walls I kept up, all the suspicions I had for everyone in my life weren't just for nothing. That I was justified in my lack of trust for anyone – that I had always been right.

But the reality was that I wasn't now, and I hadn't always been.

"Asshole. There you are," Emmett greeted me when I finally got out of the clubhouse and found him in his usual suite at the stadium. It was right behind home plate, and since that meant he had a fantastic view of me fucking blowing it tonight, I braced myself for some smartass dig. Rather, I hoped for one. It would mean that whatever he texted me about wasn't actually as grave as it sounded – that everything was already resolved.

But since no dig or joke came, I frowned hard at him.

"What? What's going on?" I asked Emmett. The way he rubbed his jaw and took a deep breath set the blood in my veins on fire. "Emmett, what the fuck happened? Is she okay? You said she was in good hands."

He had. And I'd believed him.

The morning that Evie left, the first person I had called was

Emmett. Not her. Maybe a dick move on my part, but I wasn't ready to talk to her. The first few days were when I was entertaining the dark side of my brain – the part that tried convincing me that Evie had been playing the long con, and that she was in this solely for the money.

So I didn't trust myself to talk to her yet.

But I'd trusted Emmett, who told me she had gone to his and Aly's house in East Hampton.

"Look, she's likely fine right now," he started evenly, but it set me off immediately.

"'Likely'?" The word launched me from zero to sixty fast. "For Christ's sake, Emmett, she's *pregnant* – there's no room for 'likely!'"

"Well, if there's no room for 'likely' then why the fuck haven't you called her or come to see her yourself?" Emmett challenged, making my fists ball tighter. "How long were you planning on relying on the comfort of knowing that she was safe with us? Were you going to ignore her forever as long as she was under our roof?"

"I told you I needed time to get my fucking thoughts straight. Considering the shit that was going through my head, I can guarantee you I would've made things worse by talking to her."

"Well, whether or not that's bullshit, the fact of the matter is she hasn't been at our house for three days now."

"Are you *fucking kidding me*, Emmett?"

I wanted to choke him out, but instead I turned to storm out and find her – before realizing I had no idea where the fuck she was. With my hands thrust in my hair, I faced Emmett again.

"Tell me you know where she is," I said, my voice shaking with fury. I already had a guess as to where she was, but I was praying for him to prove me wrong.

"She gave us a hotel name and we confirmed that she had a reservation there. But Aly went the other day and they told her Evie never checked in."

"Why the hell didn't you tell me, Emmett?" I demanded.

"Because Aly made me swear not to tell you shit," he said, getting in my face. "You already proved to her what a piece of shit you were by not calling Evie the day she left, so she doesn't trust you to do the right thing anymore. She told me she had it covered, but I know she's struggling to find coverage at the restaurant. She wanted to leave to find Evie today, but she still can't get away from work."

"Fuck that. I'm going," I said. I didn't even realize my feet had begun walking already till I found myself in the hallway, Emmett trailing behind.

"Do you even know *where* you're going?"

"Belfield. In Massachusetts."

"That's where she's from?"

"Yes."

"You think she's with her mom?"

"I know she is, and there's no way in hell I'm letting her stay there one more fucking day," I ground out, my heart slamming in my chest as I thought of Evie living alongside an unpredictable addict while pregnant – with my child, no less. It immediately dashed my need to wait things out, to talk to her only when I felt like I knew what I wanted to say. It lit a fire under my ass and reminded me that some things happened before you were ready – and this was a prime example.

Because while I didn't know what I wanted to say, I knew I needed to feel Evie safe in my arms. I knew I loved her – that I loved everything about her, including the man I was around her. I knew I'd never forgive myself if anything were to happen to her.

Or our child.

And suddenly, I needed to tell her that in person. STAT.

37

EVIE

This morning, I ran into people I actually knew at the gas station, which would've been terrifying if it weren't for the fact that it was the Bloom siblings — Carly, Ashlyn and Trevor — who had always cracked me up in high school because they were more preoccupied with arguing and one-upping each other than anything else in the world. At least the twins were, whereas Trevor, the youngest, always stood there kind of stoned before eventually saying something breathtakingly weird and random.

"Evie, don't listen to Kurt, the people in this town are so bored they will absolutely say anything to anyone about anyone. Trust nobody. No-bo-dy," Carly said as Ash argued the opposite point.

"No one said anything about you, Evie! That newspaper emailed a bunch of us and I told everyone we'd agree on 'no comment.'"

"You're full of shit, Ash! No one emailed your ass!"

They went back and forth for awhile until, as usual, Trevor interrupted to say something that sounded super high and unrelated.

"I heard someone's comin' to get you, Evie," he giggled while making eyes with a bag of Fritos. We all paused and turned to look at him funny, but he didn't look up till Carly smacked him hard on the arm.

"Trev. Why do you always have to say such creepy shit when you're high?" she snapped before turning to me and rolling her eyes. "Sorry. We watched scary movies last night."

"It's cool," I laughed as I saw another car pull in outside. As harmless and actually enjoyable as this interaction was, I didn't want to risk any more unexpected run-ins today, so I quickly paid for my things and started backing out. "Guys, I gotta get going but it was nice seeing you again," I said, as all three Blooms stopped yelling at each other to wave and sing bye as I walked out.

I wore a vague smile on my lips as I got in the car and started driving, because I needed that laugh this morning.

Badly.

Last night, I had stayed longer than usual with Mom because we were having a conversation about all the things she'd help me do for the baby. Kaylie came home, heard the baby talk then started slamming drawers in the kitchen, eventually accusing me of eating something in the fridge that she'd been saving for herself.

Mom stormed in there to quiet her down and before I knew it, we were all in there screaming at each other.

The night ended with me in tears, and Mom also in tears, but still putting on her calm, soothing voice as she told me to go to the motel and come back the usual time in the morning.

"Tomorrow will be a fun day, promise. I'm going to have a surprise for you," she said in the driveway, holding my cheeks and kissing my forehead before watching me get into the car.

We ended on a nice note but I felt horrible as I pulled up to the house today because I knew she'd probably been up all night dealing with Kaylie's wrath. It was probably why I got her the usual from the store but also bought out pretty much all the chocolate bars Kurt had in stock. I wanted to make it up to her for last night.

"Mom?" I called when I tapped open the creaky front door of the house. I stepped over something or another and spotted that the closet door in the den had been left open, with a bunch of old boxes and board games spilling out.

"In the kitchen, Evie."

Right away, I felt like her voice sounded strange, like she was reading from a script. I smirked because I had a feeling this meant she had her surprise for me in there, and I was pretty sure it was the box of yarn and all the knitting needles she said she'd dug through the closet to find.

"Mom, I hope it's not just pink and purple yarn you've got, because I have a feeling this kid's gonna be a — "

I shut up the moment I stepped into the kitchen.

Right away, every part of my body froze, my heart stopped like a floating rock in my chest. The blood drained from my cheeks as I simply stood there and stared.

Because sitting with Mom at the tiny kitchen table, on the "good" crown back chair that would actually hold all his weight, was the last man I'd ever expect to see in Belfield, Massachusetts.

"Evie."

I dropped my bags at just the sound of Drew's voice saying my name.

"What are you doing here?" I breathed as he rose to his feet.

From the corner of my vision, I saw Mom cover her mouth the way she did right before she cried, and only then did I realize that I had started it. Tears were already welling in my eyes from barely a second of standing in front of Drew, because I was so immediately overwhelmed.

Looking at him, I was somehow as angry, confused and embarrassed as I was completely relieved. Apparently, it was still my instinct to feel comfort, relief when I saw him because my body was still trained to want to be near him. I still wanted to melt into his chest, and even now, I had to stop myself from running straight into his arms.

I had to remind myself of the way he looked at me last. Like he didn't trust me and never should have — like perhaps this whole time together, I'd had ulterior motives.

"Please tell me what you're doing here, Drew."

My breath rattled in my throat as he came closer to me. It was too bizarre to see him in my childhood home — the place where I'd dreamt and fantasized and wished for a different life. It hurt more to see him here than it did somewhere else, and despite the fact that he'd clearly come all the way to Belfield to find me, I refused to get my hopes up for what he was about to say.

Clearly, he'd passed some of that famous Drew Maddox cynicism to me because a part of me was preparing myself to hear him say that he'd come to write a check to buy my silence on the baby, or maybe he was here to sue me for somehow breaking my NDA.

But when I felt him cup my face, his thumbs stroking my cheeks, I knew I was wrong and I immediately burst into tears.

"You know why I'm here," he murmured, wiping my tears as he kissed me on the forehead.

"Just say it," I whispered.

"I'm sorry. I fucked up that night when you told me, and if you'll forgive me, I'm here to take you home, baby."

The words alone made me cry into his chest for who knows how long. Mom was up at this point, standing a few feet away with her hands pressed together in front of her lips, waiting for the moment when she needed to step in and take care of me. But she didn't, instead standing back and smiling through her sniffling because apparently, I was in good hands. And she could tell.

"Trust me, I let him have it when he first got here," she said the moment our tears wound down enough to make room for talking again. "I didn't make it easy on him."

"She didn't," Drew smirked as I looked up at him in awe. I could've sworn I was dreaming. I still couldn't believe he was here.

"How did you find me? Even Aly doesn't know this address," I asked when Mom went into her room to give us privacy in the kitchen.

My voice was still shaky, and I was still trying to keep at least some of my guard up because Drew was touching me so tenderly, pushing locks of my hair from my eyes, and it made me want to forget everything he'd ever done to make me question him.

But I couldn't do that. Not just yet.

"I Googled you, Evie," Drew answered my question with a laugh.

"Apparently all I needed was your name and hometown. That said even the GPS couldn't find your street when I got here. I had to roll my window down and ask someone. Not that it really helped. He was high off his ass."

"Ohhh..." I wanted to ask if that someone's name was Trevor Bloom but I highly doubted Drew asked for a name, and I had far too many other questions to ask. "Drew..." Of course, despite all the questions, I barely knew how to start. "Drew, the last time we spoke, you were — "

"An asshole," he finished, quietly but firmly. "I was... shocked. And overwhelmed. My instinct was to question. But that's not an excuse, Evie. It was knee-jerk reaction because I still have a lot to fix with the way I think. It's habit for me to question everyone in my life, and I know it's fucked up but I've already started turning some of it around." His Adam's apple moved as he swallowed and brought his gaze from our entwined fingers to my misty eyes. "And it's solely because of you – there's no denying that. Just being around you showed me that people can be good. Hell, I enjoy everything around me more when you're by my side. My world's just better with you in it, and I don't want to go back to how it was before you came, Evie. I love you. I love you too much to let you go."

I was crying again and he had me sitting now — propped up on the shoddy kitchen counter I barely trusted to hold me. But my legs were too weak to stand and if I fell, I knew Drew would catch me.

I hiccupped as I tried to get out my words.

"The baby though, Drew..." I could barely look up at him as I said the words. "I'm going to keep it."

"I want you to," Drew said, sounding urgent now. Emotion tightened his voice as he held my cheeks and forced me to meet his eyes as he spoke. "Look at me. I want this with you."

"If you're just saying that to — "

"I'm not saying just anything to win you back, Evie," Drew interrupted me, fire in both his eyes and his voice. "I'm saying everything I know in my heart because I'm not hiding anything from you anymore. I'm done with that," he said vehemently, his insistence far too strong for me to fight. "Believe me when I tell you that I want this with you. I want every step of this journey with you. I want to see that little bump of yours wearing a Drew Maddox jersey when I win the championship in October. I want to make your life as good as you've made mine."

He was gently squeezing the backs of my calves now, and I was suddenly giggling deliriously through my tears as he cracked a grin.

"I know you're a little better than me in the massage department, but I swear I'll fucking blow you away with my foot rubs. I'm going to make you the most pampered mom in the city," Drew said, making it feel like my heart was swelling too big for my chest. "And the best part," he laughed as he feathered kisses on my lips, "is that our kid's going to be older than Emmett's, which means he's going to be automatically better."

"Drew!" I smacked him though I was cracking up hard now, wiping happy tears from my eyes. I was suddenly thinking of Drew and me raising a child alongside Aly and Emmett, and it made me want to bawl with pure joy and disbelief. I imagined beach days with them in East Hampton, and bringing the kids to the restaurant to try their first lobster roll.

I was so over the moon I had to control myself, sniffling for a few seconds before tilting my head up curiously at Drew.

"You said 'he.' You think he's going to a boy?"

"No, you do. I heard you about to say that when you thought it was just your mom in here," Drew laughed, his thumbs skimming my cheekbones. "Speaking of your mom, she really let me have it when I first got here. She almost didn't let me in."

"She can be pretty tough to her family members, let alone a non-related male. I'm surprised she even allowed you to sit in the kitchen," I mused.

"Yeah, I groveled a bit on your porch," Drew laughed at himself. "But we managed to have a nice talk before you came. And she said she can't wait to be a grandma."

I swallowed. I knew Mom couldn't – she'd said it a million times to me before – but hearing the words from Drew's mouth as he wore that quiet smile made my heart twist a hundred different ways.

"I want her to be in the baby's life, Drew," I said softly. "I just need to say that now. I don't know how to make it work, but I want it."

"If you want it then we'll find a way," he murmured, looking me in the eye. "That's my promise to you. Do you believe me?"

"I believe you," I whispered, letting him kiss me again before hearing my mom's stirring in her room. "We have to stay a little longer to talk to my mom. But after, you'll take me home?"

He had on a smile of contentment as he nodded down at me, brushing the hair from my face.

"Baby, you know I will."

38

DREW

I always woke up when she woke up now, because there was no ignoring the feeling or the sounds of her stirring on my chest, her cheek still pressed to my skin as she yawned and stretched.

It always put a smile on my lips before I so much as opened my eyes.

Usually, after that, she'd get up and giggle at how I groaned over the void she left on my chest. I felt it every damned morning and yet I still hated the feeling. Of course, I made up for it by waiting to hear the water run before following her into the bathroom and making her late to work.

Three weeks later and fucking Evie in the shower was still my preferred way to start the day. I was pretty sure I was growing dependent on starting my morning with kissing her as she washed her hair, and as I leisurely soaped up her tits. I was always rock-hard and jacking it by the time she stood with her eyes closed under the water, rinsing away the shampoo and all the suds from her body.

I could get used to this view, I thought the first morning it happened. And every day since, I'd been doing exactly that.

Though Evie and I changed it up slightly this morning.

"And here I thought you were trying to get me to work on time for once," Evie giggled, setting the blow dryer down as I got out of the shower and started kissing the back of her neck.

There had been no sex in the shower – I really was trying to get her to work on time since I had another surprise queued up for the morning – but all it took was one glimpse at her standing in front of the mirror and my self-control was done for.

"Just blame it on me when you get in," I murmured as I unlatched her towel and let it drop to our feet.

"Trust me – they're huge Empires fans, so I always do," she smirked as she pressed two hands flat on the sink and arched her back for me.

I made sure to watch her in the mirror as I slid my cock into her pussy.

Christ.

The way her lips fell apart got me every single time.

I fucking loved that look on her face, and that raspy morning moan as I thrust deep inside her. I loved every last goddamned thing about Evie Larsen, and on this particular morning, I couldn't stop thinking about that day down the line that I could call her Evie Maddox.

It wasn't going to be quite yet.

But soon.

"So fucking beautiful, baby. Look at you," I murmured as we locked eyes in the mirror, her lips curving in a grin as I let go of her heavy tits to watch them bounce in the reflection. I kept my stare pinned on her perfection as I rocked my hips into her, soaking in her every breath, her every bounce, her every sexy little sound.

I didn't even remember carrying her into our bed. All I remembered were her honey waves spilled like silk all over my sheets as she came, taking me right with her.

"God... so late," Evie giggled, eyeing the clock on my nightstand as we lay together in a hot, breathless fog. "But so... so worth it."

I grinned at her words because they rang truer to me than she even knew.

Worth it were the unlikely words I'd used to close the chapter on my parents, Tim, Pattie, L.A. Everything. Before Evie, they felt like ugly scars I'd bear for the rest of my life, but now I just saw them as my stepping stones toward everything I needed.

I had lost a lot to my career, but it was nothing compared to what I had gained. Without my love of this game I wouldn't have found the love of my life.

Turns out it wasn't a fucking baseball, and I should have known because even during my happiest moments as a player, I'd still think about what the hell life would look like in fifteen years, when my arm had thrown its last pitch and my body could no longer play the game.

So I should've known the game wasn't my everything. In reality, it was the woman who was giving me a family, a new lease on life and a reason to live off the field. For all that, I was prepared to give her the world at whatever cost.

But I needed the perfect moment to tell her that, and it wasn't today.

That said I couldn't hold in a small part of the surprise any longer.

"Drew, you unlocked the guest room?" Evie called as she made her way down the hall.

I had locked it as a joke the first night she came back, after I'd gotten her from her mom's house in Belfield and brought her home to New York. She had instinctively gone to set her things down in the guest room, and I reminded her that that wasn't where she slept anymore.

And since that day, whenever she was home, I kept that door locked.

But since the project had been officially finished late last night, while she'd been fast asleep, I left the door unlocked and open for her to discover on her way down the stairs to breakfast.

Three... two...

"Oh my God – *Drew!*"

I laughed the second I heard her reaction, and by the time I got down the hall, she was standing in the middle of the room, one hand thrust in her hair and the other covering her mouth.

"How..." She trailed off, tears replacing her words as she stood in what was formerly the guest room.

Now it was our nursery.

"Drew, when did you do all this?" she whispered as she floated over to the mobile hanging by the crib. The little moon and star shapes were made of her ticket stubs from all my games she'd gone to during that road trip out west. The moment she realized that, she turned around, flew into my arms around me and kissed me so hard I couldn't answer her question.

But at this point she didn't care.

"I love you," she whispered,

"I love you so fucking much, Evie," I said, knowing well that I meant those words more than any I'd ever spoken in my life.

The certainty made me almost want to laugh as I stood there with the full knowledge that I was holding the woman I was going to marry, in the room where our child would be sleeping within seven months. All the most important things in my world were right in this room, and life had never felt so good. Or simple.

I had to laugh as I thought about the total lack of material the tabloids were about to deal with. *Drew Maddox Rubs Wife's Feet Before Bed, Wakes Up First to Change Diapers.*

"Why are you laughing to yourself right now?" Evie giggled up at me as I kissed her on the forehead.

"No idea. Too many things," I grinned.

And it was the truth. I still didn't have all the answers, but in Evie, I had my definition of love and trust. And if there was anything I knew for sure, it was that if I had her at my side, I had everything I needed.

Now, forever and always.

EPILOGUE
EVIE

Four Months Later

I had been standing for an entire inning now, and I couldn't tell if I was squeezing Aly's hand numb, or if she was squeezing mine numb. I was pretty sure it was even because we were equally nervous – she as a lifelong Empires fan, and I as the one person who knew just how badly Drew Maddox needed this win.

The stakes were high enough that I actually watched every second of the game instead of drifting off here and there to ogle how damned good my boyfriend looked on the mound.

During the regular season, it was definitely a problem.

I usually sat in a suite behind home plate with Aly and Emmett, and despite having the game right in front of me – and seats most people would kill for – I generally just hawked the TV broadcast on the flat screen, waiting for those close-ups of Drew's green eyes framed between the bill of his cap and his glove.

They were just so damned gorgeous and every time I saw them, I touched my belly to ask the little one a silent question.

Do you have his eyes or mine? No pressure at all. I'm just curious. But I kind of hope you have his.

That was usually how it went, but there was no ogling today. Because this was crunch time.

Game seven of the World Series. Bottom of the ninth. Empires up 4-2 with one on, two outs and the count at three and two.

I literally had no idea what any of these numbers meant at the beginning of the summer, and if I had to be completely honest, I still sometimes cheered prematurely and needed to ask Aly why something wasn't considered an out.

But tonight, I knew exactly what was happening – not just because this was the biggest game in Drew's life but because my man had already made history.

It wasn't common for pitchers to go nine innings in even a regular season game, but in the final game of the World Series, nine innings later, Drew was still on the mound – sore, aching, but still locked in beast mode and striking out batters on ninety-five mile-per-hour fastballs.

He was still laboring, and now he was only one out away from winning it all.

"Omigod, omigod, here we go, here we go," Aly whispered as Drew wound up for his next pitch. As he delivered, she gripped my hand so tight her engagement ring crushed my fingers, but I didn't even register the pain till I saw the swing and heard the crack of the bat.

Fuck.

There was a collective gasp in the stadium followed by utter silence as fifty thousand pairs of eyes flew to follow the ball of white that soared high in the sky, eventually landing foul in the seats.

Then came the collective exhale.

"Oh God, thank God," I squeaked as the stadium returned to a buzz in anticipation of the next pitch.

"Come on, come on, I can't take this stress anymore," Aly breathed, squeezing my hand as we both bounced on our toes.

"Me neither, and I'm feeling very left out," Emmett hissed on her right, to which we both went *shh* because Drew was getting into position again, preparing for another wind-up on hopefully the final pitch of the season.

Okay, maybe I was lying about the lack of ogling, because God he looked so damned tall and powerful on that mound. I held my breath as I watched that long body turn to wind up for the next pitch.

But just before its release, I felt a little twitch that I knew wasn't butterflies in my stomach.

It was the first little kick in my belly.

My mouth fell open just as Drew launched an absolute rocket to home plate. I saw the big, healthy swing just as I heard the ball hitting leather.

And for a second, time stood still.

It slowed before me as I stood there, savoring every aspect of this one incredible moment. The roar of the stadium. My hand in Aly's. Drew's pumping fist.

And our baby kicking once more to celebrate the win.

"Oh my God – *yesss!*"

Aly and Emmett's raucous cheers brought me back to Earth, and before I knew it, I was laughing, crying and screaming my face off with them as well as everyone around us.

Because Drew Maddox and the New York Empires were World Champions.

It was absolute chaos, but in the best possible way, and just when I thought I was out of tears, the mob of Empires finally started climbing off of Drew.

And by the time I spotted him in the crowd of white jerseys, he was already headed my way.

The second our frantic, wet eyes locked he mouthed *I love you*, and the next thing I knew, I was in his arms, his cap flipped backwards as he kissed me so deeply my knees went weak.

"I love you," I whispered back between his kisses, too far over the moon to care about all the cameramen and big, crazy-looking cameras surrounding us.

I was so in love with the man holding me in his strong arms, and I was so overjoyed for his joy. I felt it welling inside him as he held me tight, kissing me so sweetly as I brought his palm down to my belly.

"He kicked right before your last pitch," I whispered excitedly once we'd caught our breaths enough to speak.

Well, I certainly had. It took another second for Drew, especially after processing the words that I said. Cupping my face, he gazed down at my belly before looking into my eyes.

"He?" he repeated breathlessly, his eyes crinkling as he smiled wide. "You know something I don't know?"

"I found out today," I grinned, laughing with surprise as Drew scaled the fence into the front row seats and knelt right down before my stomach. With the crowd roaring around us, I couldn't hear the smiling words he spoke to our son, but I didn't need to. I chalked it up as their first father-son pep talk, and I couldn't think of a better time for it.

The cameras flashed like crazy as Drew knelt before my little bump, and I giggled with Aly, especially as Drew bumped fists with Emmett before giving our little one the last word and rising again to his feet.

"Listen, Evie," he murmured close to me, thousands of eyes upon us.

"Yeah?" I giggled.

"There are a lot of people watching us right now."

"Yes. More than ever. Cameras too."

"Yeah. Thought so," Drew smirked close to my lips. "Should probably wait till later to ask this but fuck it," he murmured, taking my left hand in both of his and kissing me softly as he wiggled the ring off my finger.

I wasn't fully sure what was happening, but when I looked down, a stunning new diamond had replaced the one I'd worn since the summer. It was a similar size to the first – just princess cut this time around – but somehow it was so many million times more beautiful, and it snatched my breath straight away.

Because this time, I knew the man I loved had chosen it.

"Will you marry me, Evie?" Drew whispered his question with a wicked little grin on his lips.

Fresh tears sprung to my eyes as I threw my arms around his neck and kissed him again, giving him the answer he'd already known for awhile now.

"Baby, you know I will."

The End

THE IRRESISTIBLE SERIES

Thank you for reading Hothead! If you enjoyed Drew and Evie's story, don't miss out on a preview of Iain and Holland's story, Now or Never, at the end of this book!

And be sure to check out the rest of the Irresistible Series on Amazon and Kindle Unlimited!

SWEET SPOT - Lukas and Lia
BAD BOSS - Julian and Sara
DIRTY DEEDS - Emmett and Aly
HOTHEAD - Drew and Evie
NOW OR NEVER - Iain and Holland
RECKLESS - Adam and AJ

CONTACT STELLA

Facebook: stellarhysbooks
Twitter: @stellarhys
Amazon
Goodreads
Newsletter

Also Available By Stella Rhys
EX GAMES
WRONG
IN TOO DEEP
TOO FAR GONE (IN TOO DEEP #2)
HAVOC
DAMAGE (HAVOC #2)
DARE ME
SWEET SPOT (IRRESISTIBLE BOOK 1)
BAD BOSS (IRRESISTIBLE BOOK 2)
DIRTY DEEDS (IRRESISTIBLE BOOK 3)
HOTHEAD (IRRESISTIBLE BOOK 4)
NOW OR NEVER (IRRESISTIBLE BOOK 5)
RECKLESS (IRRESISTIBLE BOOK 6)

Turn the page for a preview from NOW OR NEVER!

NOW OR NEVER

He's ten years older. My brother's best friend.

And for the next two weeks, he gets to have me in all the ways he's ever wanted.

HOLLAND

The last time I saw him, he still called me kiddo. But fast-forward five years and more than a few things have changed.

He's still Iain Thorn. He's still my brother's best friend and the painfully sexy man I clearly never stopped wanting.

But me?

Apparently, I've grown up in more ways than he can resist.

IAIN

I'm going to hell for looking at her like this.

She's too young for me. Too sweet and naive.

She has no idea what I would do to her.

But since the day she walked back in my life in that tight little dress, I've felt myself caving. I said I'd never in my life get involved with Holland Maxwell.

But since I'm already going to hell, I might as well make it worth it.

CHAPTER ONE
IAIN

Fuck me if that's her.

A single upward glance and just like that my night was screwed.

In an instant, my pulse doubled, and I could feel my jaw ticking tighter and tighter under my palm as I ran my hand over my face, my eyes devouring her body in ways I told myself had strictly to do with the shock.

Because what the hell was she doing here?

And for Christ's sake, what the hell was she wearing?

My shoulders tensed under my suit and my grip tightened around the lowball of Scotch I suddenly wanted to pound like a shot, because now that I'd looked up—now that I'd seen *her*—I had a face to match to all the filthy, vulgar shit my clients had spent the past two minutes groaning about, and it wasn't just any face.

It was one I'd known since she was only thirteen years old.

"Jesus fuck. How do we trade our waitress for that Playboy bunny-lookin' thing?"

My jaw clenched at Watt's description.

It wasn't far off. In fact, it was surprisingly fucking accurate, but still—I was failing to reconcile what I was seeing with what I was remembering, because the last time I saw her she was a sweet, innocent little thing. This shy little girl wearing a powder blue backpack and braided pigtails—who I made it my job to protect because her own brother had no instinct whatsoever.

But now... for Christ's sake, now there was no trace of that shy little girl as she flitted from table to table in a tight little dress, holding a tray of drinks up high and arching her back so taut I wanted to clench my teeth out of my skull.

"Goddamn, when she bends over in that thing..." Ty growled into his fist.

"Do it again, baby. Come on," Watt willed her, licking his grinning lips and forcing me to exhaust every muscle in my body to keep myself from knocking him the fuck out right there. "See the new waitress?" he turned to ask me, shaking his head and sucking in a sharp breath between his teeth—his way of emphasizing just how badly he wanted to fuck her.

It made me picture my forearm digging into his neck as I pinned him to the wall and detailed exactly why he'd never lay a finger on her.

But despite the vivid image, I managed a nod and a smirk to remain outwardly calm, casual. Sitting forward, I adjusted my onyx cufflinks, throwing in a "very nice" that sounded so convincingly disinterested that Watt rolled his eyes and gave a *pfft* before turning his hungry stare back to her—and that tiny little skirt that had her legs so close to naked I had to look away.

Fucking hell.

I white-knuckled my drink, silently wracking my brain for a plan while reminding myself that no agent had ever put his own clients on the injured list, so I shouldn't aim to be the first. Shane Watt was a top reliever in the league and Ty Damon was one of the best sluggers in baseball. They were two of the best players on the New York Empires, two of the highest-earning contracts on my all-star roster of clients, and I really couldn't afford to kill them right now.

So I opted instead to shut their fucking mouths.

"Enough," I cut in sharply, interrupting their debate about whether or not she was wearing a goddamned push-up bra.

I could feel my eyes on fire, and my blood fucking boiling, but by the time my clients turned to face me, all they saw was an easy smirk on my lips that made them grin sheepishly, because they knew this look—the one I wore right before I set their asses straight.

"Gentlemen, we're here tonight to talk about the Under Armour deal, but if you want to waste my time drooling over some waitress, then you're welcome to find a different agent to negotiate your contract for a third of the price," I said, leaning back in my seat. "But in that case, Watt, you'd have to tell your wife that the new beach house is a no-go. Is that something you're interested in?"

"No! No, no, no," Watt laughed in a panic before socking Ty in he arm. "Come on, asshole. Pay attention."

"What! *Me?*"

And just like that, we were back on topic.

But as I returned to discussing business with my clients—even with my eyes fixed directly on them—I had my attention sharply trained on her.

Little Holland Maxwell.

My best friend's kid sister who was clearly all grown up, and about to make my night a living hell.

∼

CHAPTER TWO
HOLLAND

"Did you see him yet?"

Mia grinned as I practically slammed my tray onto service bar, rushing to skewer cherries for all the Manhattans she was stirring for my latest table. I processed her question at a three-second delay because I was desperately trying to remember what my giant party of businessmen had just asked me for.

"Nuts!" I snapped my fingers when I finally remembered. Off the weird look Mia shot me, I giggled. "I'm sorry—did I see who?" I asked breathlessly.

"Mr. Ass."

"Mr. *Ass?*"

"Mr. Angry Sex In A Suit."

I squinted at her. "Shouldn't that be Mr. Asis? Or A...sias?"

"Don't ask me, your fellow waitstaff made it up," Mia laughed, stirring the amber mixture of whiskey and vermouth with a long metal spoon. "I just go with it because he *is* one absurdly fine piece of ass."

"I thought you weren't into the suit-wearing type. In fact, I distinctly remember you saying that men aren't attractive unless they're sweating through a dirty T-shirt while chopping firewood."

"And I stand by that, but Mr. Ass is an exception because he is criminally hot, and he always looks so stern and serious and... *mean*." Mia's stirring slowed as she bit her lip and squinted wistfully into the distance. "I'm into it."

I burst out laughing. "Well, I'm not really into mean guys, so he's all yours."

"Actually, he's nobody's," Mia corrected, snapping right out of her dream state. "He's been coming here for years now, and none of the girls have been able to get him to look at them for more than the second it takes to order his drink," she said, smirking as Lana marched over. "Not even Tits McGee over here."

Lana huffed and stuck her nose in the air.

"Funny you mention that, since it's all changing tonight," she said, pushing me aside to grab some napkins off the bar. "He's different tonight and I'm pouncing, so get ready to pay up, bitches."

As soon as she came, she went, and when I cocked an eyebrow at Mia, she gave a snort.

"There's an ongoing bet about which of the girls is gonna finally get his attention," she explained, pouring my drinks into their cute little glasses. "My money's on Jasmine the hostess. Mostly because she isn't a raging bitch."

"Well, in that case I'm Team Jasmine too," I laughed before taking off with my drinks to my section.

I was pretty much Team Whoever Mia Likes since she was the only reason I landed this killer side gig a couple weeks back. Aside from being my roommate she was the head bartender here, and basically my tall, gorgeous, potty-mouthed guardian angel since I arrived in New York. Five weeks in and I was still thanking my lucky stars that I found her with that extremely sketchy-looking apartment listing she put up on Craigslist. It had just been a two-sentence description with no pictures at all, which gave it "big time serial killer vibes," according to my friend AJ, but I still went for it.

Because for me, it was a risk worth taking to execute The Great Escape—which was what my brother Adam nicknamed my plan to finally move away from home.

I'd started hatching it senior year of high school, since the day I pled—literally on my knees—for Mom to let me dorm at college. To let me have just the *tiniest* taste of independence. She was the town's most notorious helicopter mom and at seventeen, she still dictated what I wore out of the house, what I watched on TV, how I decorated my room.

For the record, it was all pinks and pastels.

Because all my life, I served as nothing but her precious little doll. Her do-over child who was raised to be perfectly quiet, polite, obedient—basically everything Adam wasn't. He was unmanageably wild, I was exceptionally docile, and that was just how it was in our family.

Which was why I wound up commuting daily from our home in Jersey to my classes at Parsons School of Design. Three hours back and forth every day with a *9PM* curfew—just to ensure that I wasn't out drinking or partying like every other kid my age. And if I ever caught anything later than the 8PM bus home from Port Authority, Mom would grill me for hours, search my purse, smell my breath, and if it was an extra special night, change the WiFi password before reminding me in a fit of tears about the torture she went through raising Adam, and how she refused to let "another Adam" happen again.

So... yeah.

I love my mom—I swear I do—but I was more than ready to move by the time I graduated college, which meant I was more than happy to chance it on Mia's super-sketchy listing.

And thank God I did.

Because now, after four years of secretly busting my ass by working two, sometimes three jobs during school to save up and move out, I was finally, *finally* my own woman. An adult who made my own decisions, paid my own bills and had my own rush hour commute to a job at a company I'd wanted to work for since I was fourteen years old. I was—at long last—living the life I'd been dreaming up and plotting out in a little notebook since I was that painfully sheltered, over-protected child constantly holed up in her bedroom.

And it all started with Mia Zamora choosing me to live with her at her bomb-ass apartment in the East Village—which was why I was still, on pretty much a daily basis, thanking God Almighty for her.

"Hey, babe?" she called to get my attention, whistling me back to service bar once I finished dropping off the Manhattans at my table twelve. "These are the IPAs for your table ten but before you drop them, will you drop this check real quick at Mr. Ass's table? Lana was supposed to like twenty minutes ago, but she's too busy trying to seduce him right now."

"Got it," I nodded dutifully, stacking my tray with the beers before grabbing Mr. Ass's check and narrowing playful eyes at Mia. "Is he *really* that hot?"

"Girl." She shot me a very serious look. "My thong melted off my ass the first time I looked at him, but if you don't believe me, you're about to see for yourself," she said, making me snort as she reached over service bar to fluff my hair and yank my neckline down a couple inches. "Just try not to have heat stroke and die, okay? 'Cause I can't afford to pay rent on my own."

"Oh, thanks, but I think I'll survive," I laughed as I made my way to Lana's section, a smirk already curling on my lips.

I had trouble believing anyone was as hot as Mia described Mr. Ass, but considering how much drama and fighting I'd witnessed among the staff in just my first few weeks here, I was excited to see the one thing in the world they could all agree on—this alleged panty-scorcher of a mystery babe.

It was probably about time, anyway, that I start letting myself *look* at men again. I didn't ever during college because it was just a bunch of pointless torture. I'd had some cute guys hit on me before, but there was no sense in talking for long because once it came to being officially asked for my number, I had to explain that I didn't actually have time to meet, because not only did I still live at home with my parents, I had a bus to catch and a very early curfew to make.

Pretty much all it took was one crush-worthy guy laughing in my face and saying "*yikes*" for me to just shut up about my curfew and stop talking to boys altogether.

Besides, I had my fellow freakshow in Brendan.

He was a sweet, soft-spoken family friend whose mom was best friends with mine. Since he grew up similarly smothered, he commuted home with me every day after his classes at NYU, and we wound up dating junior and senior year because, well, we were each other's only options.

We fumbled through our first kisses together, clumsily lost our virginities to one another, and while I held onto hope that it would start to feel good at some point—like that hot, breathless, passionate sex I saw in movies—we never came anywhere close to finding our rhythm. Partly because doing it in his classmate's dorm room during the twenty-minute window that we could afford to meet up wasn't the most romantic thing in the world.

But mostly because he never lasted more than two minutes.

And I'd never been genuinely attracted to him in the first place, so I tried to break it off senior year, but then he cried very loudly on the bus and reminded me that this would upset our moms, which he was absolutely right about, so I stayed with him till exactly five weeks ago —when I pulled off the The Great Escape.

And now you're free, I exhaled with a minty fresh wave of gratitude as my heeled feet weaved through the candlelit tables in Lana's section. *Free to talk to all the boys you want, go on all the dates you want... free to have all the real, non-dorm-room sex you want with hot guys like Mr. Ass.*

I smirked to myself.

Assuming he's really that hot.

I had to suppress my amusement as I closed in on his booth, because our resident flirt, Lana, was being even sultrier than usual while standing in front of the table—one hand holding her tray up high and the other placed on her very dramatically cocked hip.

Come on, lady, way to block my whole view, I snorted inwardly as I came up behind her, though just as the thought crossed my mind she lowered her tray.

And *bam.*

The world's greenest eyes locked on mine, and I nearly dropped all my beer because holy.

Fucking.

Shit.

Now or Never is Available Now on Amazon and Kindle Unlimited!

Made in the USA
Monee, IL
04 March 2024

54378609R00166